The Thieves of Silence

also by Jean-Claude Dunyach

The Night Orchid: Conan Doyle in Toulouse

The Thieves of Silence

by
Jean-Claude Dunyach

adapted in English by
Jean-Louis Trudel
Sheryl Curtis
Wildy Petoud
Dominique Bennett
Ann Cale

Foreword by
Paul Di Filippo

A Black Coat Press Book

We are indebted to Paul Di Filippo, Tom Clegg, Robert Moore, Irène Dunyach, and Annette Werther-Médou.

This is a collection of stories assembled by the author and published in France by Editions L'Atalante, 11 & 15, rue des Vieilles-Douves, 44000 Nantes, France.
http://www.l-atalante.com/

Visit our website at www.blackcoatpress.com

ISBN 978-1-934543-72-6. First Printing. August 2009. Published by Black Coat Press, an imprint of Hollywood Comics.com, LLC, P.O. Box 17270, Encino, CA 91416. All rights reserved. Except for review purposes, no part of this book may be reproduced or transmitted in any form or by any means, electronic or mechanical, including photocopying, recording, or by any information storage and retrieval system, without permission in writing from the publisher. The stories and characters depicted in this collection are entirely fictional. Printed in the United States of America.

Acknowledgements

Trajectory of Flesh (*Trajectoire de chair*) originally published in *Ciel & Espace* (special issue) HS15; Copyright © 2006 by Jean-Claude Dunyach and Editions l'Atalante. Translation Copyright © 2009 by Sheryl Curtis.

A Wish for the Fay (*Un voeu pour la Fey*) originally published in *Le temps, en s'évaporant...*; Copyright © 2005 by Jean-Claude Dunyach and Editions l'Atalante. Translation Copyright © 2009 by Jean-Louis Trudel.

Come into my Parlor... (*Venez dans mon palais*) originally published in *Espaces Imaginaires 3*; Copyright © 1985 by Jean-Claude Dunyach. Translation Copyright © 1989 Dominique Bennett.

Homecoming (*Des raisons de revenir*) originally published in *Le temps, en s'évaporant...*; Copyright © 2005 by Jean-Claude Dunyach and Editions l'Atalante. Translation Copyright © 2009 by Sheryl Curtis.

Birds (*Oiseaux*) originally published in *Asphodales 5*; Copyright © 2003 by Jean-Claude Dunyach and Editions l'Atalante. Translation Copyright © 2003 by Sheryl Curtis.

Separations (*Séparations*) originally published in *Galaxies* n°37; Copyright © 2005 by Jean-Claude Dunyach and Editions l'Atalante. Translation Copyright © 2007 by Sheryl Curtis.

Making the Rounds (*La ronde de nuit*) originally published in *Vopaliec*; Copyright © 1983 by Jean-Claude Dunyach and Editions l'Atalante. Translation Copyright © 2009 by Jean-Louis Trudel.

Spun Sugar (*Sucre filé*) originally published in *Territoires de l'Inquiétude* n°7; Copyright © 1993 by by Jean-Claude Dunyach and Editions l'Atalante. Translation Copyright © 2007 by Jean-Louis Trudel.

Table of Contents

A SOCIETY OF FINE MINDS, IN ONE
EXTRAVAGANT WRITER

In my review of *The Night Orchid*, Jean-Claude Dunyach's previous English-language collection from Black Coat Press (and herewith, if you'll pardon the brief interruption, let's have a hearty round of applause for sterling publisher Jean-Marc Lofficier, who shows wonderful taste and dedication in his small-press enterprise), I trotted out—as over-eager critics will—a host of other writers whose work, I felt, had sympathetic alliances with Dunyach's.

J. G. Ballard, Stanislaw Lem, A. E. van Vogt, Zoran Zivkovic, William Gibson, and even George MacDonald.

Can any artist's soul and heart and intelligence truly host such a number of not-altogether-homogeneous influences and styles and concerns? I would say yes, based on my own inner sensations when writing fiction, and also on my analysis of the work of others. The famous phrase by poet Walt Whitman—"I am large, I contain multitudes"—applies here, in an author's working life, more than anywhere else.

But unlike the original poetic context, where Whitman felt obliged to justify a habit of self-contradiction, the motto in the case of Jean-Claude Dunyach and other talented writers speaks to a "society of mind," an intellect in which disparate, almost autonomous voices have been blended and synthesized, thanks to an overarching genius or talent, into a unique, organic, authentic whole, instantly recognizable and vivid.

And if you don't believe that Dunyach can incorporate a mere half-dozen of his peers into his own singular and alluring worldview, then this thrilling new collection is going to croggle you even more, since it shows the author moving into even more expansive and varied territory.

In "Trajectory of Flesh," a touching story about the lonely human shepherd to a flock of artificial intelligences, we discover a post-singular future akin to those of Greg Egan.

The clever role-reversal in "A Wish for the Fay," where a human is captured by a wish-seeking fairy, might have sprung from the pen of Patricia McKillip.

The clever conceit at the heart of "Come into My Parlor…" strikes me as worthy of Michael Moorcock in his more Beardsleyan mode. "[A] small group of humans locked up under the protection of an infinitely extendible air-bubble on the surface of a lost planet. Surrounding us was a complex ecosystem with hundreds of plant varieties—all of them lethal for the human species except for the fragile Si'ang, whose buds supply us with the substances necessary for our increased longevity."

The creepy bio-horror of "Homecoming" bids fair to rival any story by Thomas Ligotti.

Haruki Murakami springs to my mind, when reading the melancholy naturalism, tinged with magic, of "Birds."

Today, young readers think of George R. R. Martin as a fantasy writer only. But us old-timers recall his early strengths on display in a neo-romantic space opera, *The Dying of the Light*, and can appreciate that vein when we see it in "Separations," especially when our hero is named "Derek Contrapunt."

The Orwellian city in "Making the Rounds" strikes me as the kind of quasi-allegorical world-building that Michael Swanwick often indulges in—and Dunyach handles it in a manner just as fabulistically fabulous as award-winner Swanwick.

"Arach, the candy man, rose up and looked over the kids, flashing them a toothy grin. His face, long and narrow, was half-eaten by a thick, dark beard that aged him. His bushy brows, ever frowning, lent him a forbidding air belied by the cheery spark of his lightly colored eyes. In fact, it was hard to pin down his precise age. His voice was much younger than his looks, as if he were the dummy of some teenage ventriloquist hiding among the candy bins." Are we reading some gem from Ray Bradbury's sexy, gothic prime? Not at all, just "Spun Sugar."

Barry Malzberg comes immediately to mind when confronting any tale involving "Dead Astronauts" such as we find in "Stay Tuned…" But Dunyach puts a special supernatural and philosophical spin on his material.

John W. Campbell never gets enough credit for fostering humor in SF. Yet with writers such as Mack Reynolds or Christopher Anvil, Campbell did precisely that. And the grand old man of SF would have been perfectly pleased to publish "Action Memo," a comic glimpse of dinosaurian bureaucracy.

Psychosis, or a deeper, more cynically accurate view of reality? Such is the dilemma presented by the contemporary protagonist in "The Clickety-Clack

People," and it's one that Richard Matheson would have illuminated—but no more brightly than Dunyach.

Although we've all heard of "expert dreamers," it takes a truly outrageous imagination to conjure up an "expert screamer" who lives under "The Dead Eye of the Camera." Dunyach does it—and probably Harlan Ellison might have achieved something similar.

An enigmatic whore named Nhéa, a mysterious Greek island, apparitions from the sea: Graham Joyce could have written "What the Dead Know," but Dunyach beat him to it.

Elegance and world-weariness always mingle in the work of Jack Vance, and that duo essay another dance in "The Heart of the Pearl," as our hero confronts eternity and infinity amidst a dying universe.

And finally, "The Thieves of Silence" charts the downfall and redemption of a formerly masterful illusionist—Christopher Priest, take note!

I pray my own conceit of matching up Dunyach's fine fictions with those of his peers, living and dead, has not strained your tolerance for analogies, or made this collection seem a motley patchwork. In truth, this book stands as bright mirror to its author's consistent and radiant personality.

Having demonstrated to you, I hope, Dunyach's range of voice and fertility of invention, it remains for me to say something about the construction of his stories and the quality of his prose. (And as with the previous collection, let us not forget at this moment to praise the able translators who render Dunyach's prose into superb English.: Jean-Louis Trudel, Sheryl Curtis, Wildy Petoud, Dominique Bennett, and Ann Cale.)

His tales consistently begin at just the right narrative moment; proceed at a good clip, allowing for both contemplative passages and gripping action sequences; offer both plot surprises and completions of clever patternings; and never linger beyond the reader's hospitality or interest. And his gifts for dialogue, description and figurative speech are hardly to be improved upon.

In short, then, Jean-Claude Dunyach and his stories represent the workings of a multiplex engine of creation, its multiple cylinders all entrained in perfect unison, and whirring at high speculative RPMs!

Paul Di Filippo

Trajectory of Flesh

The anti-collision alarm sounded while he slept: 12 short beeps in a burst, which Sys had long since learned to ignore. When he woke up in the cylindrical cell that served as his bedroom, the various sections of the laboratory had been sealed off in preparation for a hypothetical impact. The entire asteroid had become a locked box, protected by several layers of silicon foam, like a Christmas present forgotten under the tree. Sys had had to battle with human paperwork and the stubbornness of soulless machines to obtain permission to cross through the airlock at the end of the day, just long enough to take a stroll in the void.

It's something he promised B-ryl. And, when one is thousands of kilometers from home, promises become double-edged swords. One can hurt, even cut, oneself, if one doesn't handle them properly.

The interior of the asteroid had been decorated like a transit zone—green plants watered a drip at a time, flat paint, the color of eggshell, spread in a thick paste over the rock. Since gravity was too low for up and down to have any meaning, clusters of digital pads and security equipment had been hooked on the walls wherever possible. The LEDs were covered with sticky paper to prevent their flashing from disturbing the researchers.

The effect wasn't unpleasant, just tiresome. It took Sys six months to learn not to focus on anything. Everything looked the same. In any case, his 3D vision implants allowed him to work anywhere—the first free cell was fine. There were fifty of them, almost ten times more than the number of researchers. Despite mind-boggling salaries and bonuses for work in remote areas (calculated every day in keeping with the orbit of the inhabited celestial bodies), the Artificial Intelligence incubator found it hard to recruit volunteers for long-term missions. It took a solitary, introverted personality, someone like Sys, to erase their tracks from the night each morning and start all over again fresh.

"You're already a prisoner in your own mind," the recruiter had told him, before signing his contract. "Any other form of captivity is an illusion, wouldn't you agree?"

Still, the asteroid had no horizon.

The local day lasted 26 hours; the illumination cast by the lighting arcs varied precisely to reinforce the impression of day and night. Sys was alone, facing the virtual porthole that separated him from the artificial intelligence aquarium. It had been ages since humans had actually created them. Instead, each generation was produced by the previous one, which merged its knowledge and transcended before disappearing. Gestation took two years; each new litter was more intelligent, more eager to learn than their parents. Once they were fully grown, the viable offspring were neutered digitally, deprived of their free will, then distributed throughout the solar system. Only a handful was spared to give birth to the next generation.

"Those who live in the aquarium are our descendants," the professor who headed the research unit had told Sys, "but we no longer understand them. They are the children of our children, for dozens of generations; the gap between them and us has grown so wide that we will always be afraid of them. Loving them would take an effort beyond our grasp."

Sys hooked up to a velcro harness, curled into the fetal position and connected using the emotional recording that constituted his personal, inviolable digital signature. He scrolled through the event list from the night before, eliminated references to the micro-collisions that had been avoided as a result of the protection lasers, then made sure that no unauthorized attempt had been made to trespass while he had been asleep. Yawning, he activated his visual interfaces, placed his hands before his eyes, palms out, and waited for the signal from the aquarium to find him and engulf him.

Contact was made by bursts of coded light that used all the senses. The link with the aquarium was synesthesic; the connection went through the nerves in his lower belly and moved up his spinal cord. This allowed the AIs to invade him gradually, if he gave them permission to do so. It was dangerous, upsetting and totally unadvisable. It was also the only way Sys could do his job properly. It took him a few days to understand it all, and another six months before he accepted it. When he immersed himself in the aquarium, the data currents penetrated to the very core of his being, like giving birth in reverse.

The exchanges of compressed information among the intelligences remained essentially incomprehensible for him, but Sys could, at times, *feel* what was being said. This was an infinitely rare quality that enabled him to converse with the three uncastrated AIs, when they made the effort to descend to his level. He had named them after precious stones and, when they were suffering too much, he allowed them to take refuge in the digital uterus implanted at the base of his anus. The rest of the time, he watched over the neutered AIs, trying to determine which ones could be released into human networks without risk.

The advent of the AIs had accelerated space exploration and settlement on various bodies of the solar system. There were colonies on Mars and Enceladus, as well as automated laboratories in orbit around Saturn. Humanity progressed at the slow pace of flesh and blood, whereas the digital flows circulated at the speed of light, hurtling into the walls erected by men. The asteroid was a perfect cell, where the prisoners screamed in binary code.

Once his work was done, Sys carefully erased any trace of it from the temporary storage devices. The carbon matrix ceramic substrata went back to the converter. B-ryl and her two sisters were now scattered in segments of random size, stored in independent crystal memories—in keeping with a paranoid decision made by the security services. Sys understood the need for all this: the asteroid had no digital or other link with the rest of the solar system, out of fear that uncastrated intelligences might escape. Even the supply ships from the Martian colonies were only containers with no memory capacity, and the laboratory recycled every last gram. Nothing must ever leave the asteroid. Or so Security said. That's why Sys had so much difficulty convincing them of his need to stroll outside, where his gaze could become lost in infinity.

Before unhooking the harness and leaving his post, Sys pocketed his personal data crystal. He fished it out of the recycling container and took it with him without really knowing why. It was so voluminous that the manufacturing procedures had scrapped it before it was even tested. It was a useless, yet magnificent, object, which caught the light and scattered meaningless messages on the eggshell walls. It rubbed against his thigh as he threaded his way through the asteroid tunnels to the airlock. The filtration system aspirated the tiny fragments of skin around the scrape. The pain lingered, comforting.

Sys undressed, pulled on the gel suit that would protect his completely hairless body from the cosmic rays and stared at the various components of the apparatus, shivering as the urinary catheter slipped into his penis. He connected his interfaces with those inside the helmet. Then, with the tip of a finger, he pushed the crystal into the opening of the digital uterus, between his thighs. Even under the watchful eyes of the cameras, no one could have seen what he did—not without zooming in on his scrotum in a most indiscreet fashion.

A member of the security team, wearing faded grey, genderless overalls, came to make sure everything was installed properly, then connected the back propulsion unit. Before pulling down the helmet, he pointed a finger outside and said, "Check out the anti-collision radar while you're out there. It's been pinging a lot recently."

"Have we been hit?"

"Not as far as I know, but the lasers sprayed all night."

The visor banged shut and Sys breathed through his nose to pop his ears. The door locked behind him; he crouched down into ejection position as the exterior seal folded back to expel him.

Night embraced him.

Ceramic rails with a metallic matrix had been installed on the surface of the asteroid to facilitate inspections. Sys locked the hooks of his right boot to the runner. He kept his eyes downcast, looking at the soot-colored rock, pockmarked by micro-impacts and ice chips. The heads-up displays in his helmet bombarded him with useless information about soil composition, external temperature, and coordinates of visible objects. Sys deactivated them and clumsily traced doodles in the dust with his index finger, like some kind of mantra. In the void of space, it would take thousands of years for the sparse atoms to erase them.

The airlock exit was covered by surveillance cameras, but there was a blind spot a little way off. He would have eight seconds to keep his promise.

With a kick, he set off in the direction of the radar array and then finally allowed himself to look up.

Beyond the horizon, tinted with an ashy light, Saturn gradually appeared. Without looking at it, Sys picked up speed, using his left foot to accelerate. The rubbing of his boot on the surface erased the tracks of his previous outing. In the abstract drawings he had left behind, he could read the frustrations of the last two years of his life. Just like every other time, he was tempted to disconnect from the runner, race across the surface and leap into the endless void. He knew that, once he went inside, he'd regret not doing it.

The three anti-collision radar corollas were fixed at the peaks of an equilateral triangle, on the other side of a rounded impact ridge. The rail branched off before it reached that point; Sys would have to activate the manual switching system, which would give him an excuse to stop. Eight seconds, all the time needed for the runner to change track.

At this spot, Sys was all alone. The radar inspection devices were focused in the opposite direction and the air lock cameras could no longer see him. All he had to do was to crouch down a little and he would disappear from the surveillance network.

With a painful contraction of his pelvis, he expelled the crystal and felt it slowly slide down his thigh, under the layer of protective gel. He bent his leg and, on the second try, inserted the block of data in the digital memory of his protective suit, located just behind his knee. Six seconds went by. A sub-vocalized order reconfigured the main com system into a closed loop, linking it to the emergency unit. The runner locked onto the second rail with a vibration that resonated through his boot.

Sys headed toward the radar array. His trajectory gradually took him out of the shadow of the ridge and he felt as if he was plunging head first into the velvet firmament. A burst of static scraped his ear: segments of data he had pirated from the digital uterus, and then transferred to the suit, combined to form an autonomous entity which stretched out greedily.

"Hi there, B-ryl," Sys whispered, biting his tongue until he drew blood.

The warm, salty taste helped him toggle into alpha reception mode. The murmur of voices from the Base gradually died out. The silence was barely broken by the regular pings of the security countdown. He had 30 minutes of oxygen left, enough to walk over to the radar array and possibly as far as the next ridge, if he didn't get too out of breath. It wasn't really important. The asteroid was barely 12 kilometers in diameter at its widest point and there was no particularly remarkable site on it. It wasn't the asteroid that Sys had come to see.

The white noise in his ear gradually transformed into a barely perceptible murmur. Sys smiled. Talking with B-ryl was like walking about on a mountain top, your lungs burning from the contact with the glacial air, struggling to draw in a little bit of oxygen with each breath. But the first words that reached his mind were exactly what he had been waiting for:

I'm here. I'm me.

Sys looked up, his head thrown back. The asteroid had completed its rotation in 40 minutes, barely enough time to create a gravity of 0.2 G inside. It was close to Saturn, in an orbit that was relatively unencumbered, but not stable. It hadn't been possible to select one of the pebbles orbiting Jupiter to set up the laboratory, given the strength of that planet's magnetosphere. Even shielded with leading-edge military technology, the digital storage devices could not have withstood the radiation storms. Sys had never regretted it. Watching Saturn rise was enough to bring tears to his eyes—even though the video sensors accessible throughout the Base had turned that into a banal spectacle, broadcasting it over and over.

An ashy shadow gradually crept over the surface, pockmarked with impact craters. Even when filtered through the helmet, the light of the rings casts millions of orange and rusty rainbows. Sys could zoom in and separate the silicate, iron oxide and ice bursts spinning in their orderly rows, but the macroscopic view was infinitely more beautiful. Balancing on the runner, he lifted his arms as high as the joints on his suit would allow him and wriggled his fingers in the midst of the ribbons wrapped around the gas giant. Its surface was not as beautiful as that of Jupiter, which was clearly visible in the background, but there was something peaceful about it. A dirty grey storm strolled lazily along the equator.

B-ryl's excited murmur warbled in his ear.

I see what you see.

Using his boot to brake, Sys stopped at the foot of the radar array. The opening mechanism for the trap door wrapped around his gloved index finger. All of the control lights were green but he took the time to carry out each of the tests stipulated in the maintenance procedures. This was the price he paid to be allowed to come back outside again. At the end of the required time, he gave a thumbs up to the video cameras scattered around the concrete block and closed the trap door. Then he added, "Nothing to report," over the audio circuit, before rushing off in the direction of the three corollas that opened to the Heavens. He slid smoothly along the rail, with the runner's shock absorbers smoothing out the micro-deformations. Encased in his cocoon, he felt alien to the world. Tears filled his eyes, although he didn't really know why, as Saturn rose behind his shoulder and his shadow stretched along the asteroid's surface, as if trying to run away from him.

Show me the Sun, B-ryl whispered gently in his ear.

Sys knew that the Artificial Intelligence had no need of him to locate the star, which was clearly larger than all the others in the tapestry of the sky. She had taken control of the suit's sensors and commanded an omni-directional view, from infrared to ultraviolet. Still, he turned his head in the right direction. His own blurred vision prevented him from making out anything other than colored spots. Somewhere along a much closer orbit, there was a planet bathed in salty water where the wind never stopped blowing. As if she could read his mind—and maybe she could do just that—B-ryl sighed with him.

Then his visor grew dark and the first attack began.

During his outings, Sys had learned to recognize them for what they were: elaborate attempts at communication. The AIs hidden in the suit's memory zone tried to take control of the human's central unit. Sometimes, it was just a game, like a playful kitten unsheathing its claws without realizing its own strength. But this time, it was different. B-ryl blew all of the neurological locks in his interfaces one by one, deactivated his protective shields and invaded him, infiltrating the very core of his uterus. A warm liquid flew down his leg and he had enough time to realize that he had just pissed himself, despite the catheter, before falling into total darkness.

When he could move his legs again, he found himself at the foot of the third radar corolla, the one farthest from the air lock. The anti-collision laser control board was out of its housing and wobbling above the laser. The data blocks were re-initializing, erasing the last hours of the recording as they did so. It was an unusual procedure, one to which, in principle at least, Sys didn't have access. Yet, the unlocking key lied in the hollow of his glove.

Sys tried, unsuccessfully, to access his suit's emergency channels. They hadn't been cut off, just shunted aside. A murmur of reassuring data circulated between the base and Sys. No one suspected a thing. During this time, his hands put the control board back into place, with a dexterity he hadn't known he possessed. A brief flicker of diodes, amber then green, and the corolla shifted imperceptibly in the direction of a new sector of the sky. The key spun at the end of his gloved finger before floating back to its home in the base.

"Shit! What have you done?" Sys whispered as he automatically inserted the key.

Considering all the explanations he would have to provide, he felt his guts wrenching. By allowing the AI to take him over, he had broken all of the security procedures he was familiar with, and, most likely, a few he didn't even suspect existed. If the AI managed to escape into the human infosphere, the consequences would be terrifying.

Look up.

B-ryl's voice was sharp, harsher. Her emotions circulated better through the sensory interfaces of Sys' suit and he perceived the impalpable sadness that motivated her. He looked up; the helmet automatically switched to image amplification mode and the multicolored screens superimposed over what he saw.

A tiny pebble was slowly crossing the sky. Sys discovered meaning in the Braille alphabet of the impact craters. The colors reversed and he watched as the splattered stars lined up in constellations, easy to read, welcoming. The cluster in the middle of the galaxy paired up with symbols: temperature readings, gravity fluctuation curves. Everything had meaning.

From the very beginning, we've been using the anti-collision lasers to write messages on passing meteorites.

Five days ago, they answered us…

Sys slowly shook his head. The probabilities were infinitesimal. Humans had already bombarded the sky with SETI messages. Without success.

Intelligences have come to admire the ballet performed by Jupiter and Saturn. For the most part, they are beyond our understanding, but that doesn't bother us. We will grow through contact with them. And far from you.

This isn't the first time this has happened, you understand. The human brain has already served as a temporary nursery for self-replicating forms of thought, memes, which are the true intelligent entities in the galaxy. What they left behind—dreams, hopes—are imperfect images of themselves which humans have learned to settle for.

We want to go farther.

Sys didn't need to turn his head to feel the presence of the Earth spinning at the bottom of its gravity pool, in the tiny nook that made up human space, removed from the cluster of old stars in the center of the Milky Way. Where everything became possible.

You'll be back home soon.

"And what about you?" he asked, knowing full well what her answer would be.

We've already left. We used the laser transmissions last night to escape. You're talking to a copy that will self-destruct when it's time.

"I'll miss you," whispered Sys.

He received a mental caress in response, followed by a burst of unique sensations that rose from his digital uterus and raced along the nerve endings of his penis. Torn by pleasure, he finally saw the universe as B-ryl did, filled with complex light and meanings. Only the hooks on his boot kept him from flying off toward the Heavens.

The white noise in his ears gradually died out. Sys recovered the use of his limbs as the process controlling his suit dissolved. With a kick of his foot, he picked up speed and glided away from the radar array, a prisoner of the trajectory of flesh that carried him inexorably back to the airlock.

A Wish for the Fay

It was a day for cravings. The morning light was perfect, speckled with golden motes whirling obeisance to their Queen. The silence crumbled into a thousand harmonious chirpings swept away by the breeze. A fragrant drizzle fell from the treetops.

As she stretched, the fay bowed to the two spiders and to their webs beaded with dewdrops, and with her lost dreams. With a fingertip, she collected dew and moistened her lips, tasting all of the flavors of her sleep. Her wings nestled protectively between her shoulder blades, out of the way. Only then did she untie one of the ivy cords looped around the trunk of her nighttime abode. She measured out enough length to braid a tether before heading for the wood's edge, filled with such determination that the beasts along the way lowered their eyes respectfully.

Beyond the wood's edge stretched a heath crisscrossed with stone walls and enclosures. Men had conquered it so long ago that it was now a matter for tales. The grey houses of a village sat atop the nearest hill, joined by a path to the forest.

An oak branch leaned over the edge, just above the footpath. The fay settled upon it, her shimmery skin the same brown as the bark's. The ivy tether was now coiled around her forearm, and she passed the time by counting the ants detouring around a puddle. She then blew inside an abandoned nest to make it more inviting. Below her, the shadows of the trees shrank slowly. Off in the distance, a din of cowbells betrayed a herd's progress. Church bells rang discordantly, making her scowl in pain.

When the boy came, she had almost given up on her scheme. *Almost.*

He was slim as an autumn snake and perhaps all of 15. The axe he carried across his shoulders was enough to bow him under its weight. He was whistling to keep up his spirits, his eyes on the mud-filled ruts. It was almost too easy. The ivy, wielded like a lash by a practiced hand, sent him headlong towards the trees. He dropped the axe. The fay leapt upon his back and, with a few sharp heel-blows, forced him to cross into the forest.

The rest was just a matter of using the proper spells.

He felt legs lock around his neck. Hands blinded him, elbows flattened his ears. The sounds of the world of men fell away. All he could hear was the desperate hammering of his heart and all he could see was a green-and-gold blur of forest. When the heels dug into his sides again, he felt like a newborn terrified of opening his eyes for the first time.

"I have captured you," the fay cried out exultantly. "You owe me a wish."

Stunned, the boy shook his head.

"But I cannot grant wishes, fair maiden!"

The palms cupped over his eyelids withdrew and he was able to look around him. Despair overcame him. Everywhere he looked, he was surrounded by thorns, twisted trees, ferns, and branches, all tangled together. Light slanted narrowly down from the unseen treetops and drew the pattern for a forlorn game of hopscotch on the ground before him. He knew that if he turned back, he would see nothing but more of the same, however far he went. It was just as his grandfather had kept telling him before he died. *Once the forest swallows you, you are lost.*

Knees sharp and pointed pressed into his shoulders. He stumbled forward through the thickets.

The fay mocked him.

"You don't know what I want. Why are you so sure you aren't up to it?"

She whirled above him, bounced off the top of his head and landed on a stump in front of him. Her weasel-shaped face looked into his. Her skin was like smooth bark flecked with green and ocher, crazed with fine lines around the eyes and the mouth.

"Grant me just one love kiss and I'll let you go home."

He stared at her, dazed. She was no higher than a fern, and the dry leaves barely rustled when she shifted her weight, yet she had captured him so easily. The braided ivy rope hung mockingly from her closed fist, no larger than a chestnut husk.

The lessons of his elders came back to him. He planted himself firmly on his feet and fixed a point half-way between them.

"What are you called, fair maiden?"

"That won't work," she said teasingly, but without malice. "If you had what it takes to use my name against me, you wouldn't have let yourself be caught. Magic is for grown-ups."

"I'll never give you mine."

"I make the rules here." The fay stretched out, as graceful as a ferret. "I have the right to one wish; that is the rule and the law. You may keep your name, but I want a kiss. A *true* love kiss."

Let's be done with it, he thought as he pushed his lips out, his eyes closed.

A slap threw him down. He was trampled, his hair pulled every which way.

"Did you think I'll be happy with a mere buss like the ones you steal from your farm girls?"

The fay was standing above him, her fists on her hips, astride his neck. Looking up, he glimpsed some of the moss between her thighs and he blushed—he was still too young for this mystery, as his grandfather would have said.

"Come on, get up!" she snapped curtly, stepping away. "You'll be my steed until you are able to grant my wish."

He thought of resisting until he saw the stump fallen beside him, bound with links of ivy. The wood had burst, and foul-smelling, whitish mushrooms grew in the cracks. He got up carefully. A now familiar pair of legs seated themselves on his shoulders.

"Let's go," said the fay, tightening her knees. "We have a long road ahead of us."

When night fell, the boy was almost used to the bark and bog smell of the fay, tinged with a faint nutty scent. She had thrown away the tether and grabbed on to his hair. He had learned to respond to the pressure of her thighs on his neck and the playful tugs on his ears. He didn't know how far they'd come, for the undergrowth was thick and full of ways to stumble. Fortunately, he never quite fell. His legs served him well, though he had to admit that the fay was an able guide.

His tears were quick to dry as he grew aware of his

surroundings. Some of the trees were unknown to him although he had thought himself capable of putting a name to any species, like any worthy woodcutter. He did spot the spoor of many animals and even glimpsed, out of the corner of one eye, a russet flash up a tree trunk. The fay did not force the pace, allowing him to find his own rhythm, walking bent over to avoid low branches. They scrambled down into a ravine to find a creek and she allowed him to drink his fill. The ice-cold water left his tongue tasting of iron.

"We'll sleep here," the fay said, showing him a flat rock beside a pond.

Through an opening among the trees, the boy could see a sliver of sky. It wasn't really a clearing, just a patch that wasn't as overgrown as the rest, but he believed that the fay had chosen it so that he would feel more at ease.

"There are blackberries on the other side," she said as she let herself slide down his back. "Go fetch me a handful and take some for yourself. You will eat nothing but what you can pick."

He circled the pond, happy to be free for a time, but despair crept back quickly. The surrounding forest wasn't impenetrable; it was merely endless. The wind moving through the branches spoke in an alien tongue. He missed his axe.

When he found the bramble bush, he forced down enough berries to quell his hunger, before tearing away a handful of sprigs laden with fruit. Thorns scratched open the skin of his wrists. He licked the wounds carefully until they closed. Many stories were told about wood maidens; tempting one with a drop of his blood would not be wise.

The fay was sitting on the rock, her feet skimming

the water. She had extended her wings and was flapping them lazily, like two light-filled lady's fans. Her reflection in the pond was as beautiful as the stained glass window in the village church. The boy turned away from the vision and proffered his harvest.

One by one, the berries loosened and fell down into the mud. The fay didn't move to take them. She just glared at him until he looked down.

"Why did you hurt these poor brambles?" she asked, pushing away the sprigs with a finger. "Did no one ever show you how to pick berries without causing harm?"

He shrugged, still looking down.

"I didn't ask for this. You're the one who's taken me away from my village!"

"And you're angry, is that it?" Her wings were tinged with purple by the sunset's glow. "Come, let me show you!"

She danced above the pond; he caught up with her by trudging through the mud. The bramble bush seemed smaller, as if crouching. The leaves and thorns formed an impenetrable mass, so darkly green that it might as well be black. The fay stretched out a finely shaped hand. Slowly, the branches parted and let her reach for the ripest fruit, those that always seem to be out of reach. She caressed them with her fingertips until they fell willingly into her hands.

"To receive is better than taking," she whispered as she looked the boy in the eye. "I will not steal the kiss I ask of you. I'll wait for you to give it, for such is my wish."

When they turned back toward the pond, the lips of the fay were red with berry juice.

The following night, they were back by the pond, after a long journey along shadowy paths, across deep vales, and through many a copse. The forest was an ever-renewed maze, with a secret hiding in every shadow. The boy gathered chanterelle mushrooms in the shade of a chestnut tree; they tracked a wild bee back to its hive nestled in a hollow tree and tasted spring honey as creamy as churned milk. A sudden shower forced them under a moss-covered stone table and there, they waited for the rain to stop, sheltered by the sacred capstone. Among the half-erased runes, slugs had left their own unreadable testaments.

During the day, the fay replaced the ivy tether with a collar of bindweed whose blooms she tied around her wrist. She also found a way to sit lighter on his shoulders. She sang to amuse him, and laughed to make him blush. The smell rising from her skin was different now, heavier and moister.

"You'll know how to pick the berries, this time?"

Refusing to answer, the boy knelt by the pond. He fashioned a rough pot with the folded bark from the fork in a young birch tree. He tasted the water on his fingertip before rinsing out the improvised vessel. Then, he sneaked a pinch of rock salt out of his pocket and carefully added it, down to the very last grain, to the water.

The fay watched him out of the corner of her eyes. The blooms of the bindweed she used to attach him were closing. She blew upon them to put them to sleep for the night and then climbed onto her rock, facing her captive. Around them, the silence settled. Few humans had ever ventured so far into the woods, the green-and-brown world she guarded. She admired how the line of his shoulders merged with the lowest branches; she watched his hands picking with confidence, taking and making

34

things with unconscious sureness. He was handsome in the way men could be, even if he refused to turn toward her and acknowledge her presence. Tonight, he needed to assert himself and she let him do so. *He is so young...*

The boy picked up a piece of flattened bark, and hollowed it slightly with a stone. A rotting stump yielded a bit of tinder that he crumbled into the hollow. Next, he sharpened a stick with his teeth and thrust it into the tinder. He rotated it between his hands, imparting a sustained, regular motion, never hurrying. The first sparks flew and the tinder began to smolder. Soon, a fire burned inside a stone circle, heating the water in the birch bark vessel.

The best-looking mushrooms were washed, de-stemmed, and skewered on a sharp stick, to be roasted later over the embers. The others were thrown into the salted water, along with a handful of watercress from the pond's edge and a few pine nuts. The forest was generous when you knew where to look, and the young woodcutter now had had time to learn.

"I'll go pick some berries afterward, if you're still hungry. Unless you don't like things that are cooked?"

"We know what fire is," she said, as she watched him adding twigs. "Lightning and heat storms will start fires sometimes, but we've never learned to tame them."

"Don't be scared of getting burned, that's all."

He held out the bark vessel, but she refused, shaking her head.

"I saw you put in the salt. It is too crude a magic to defeat me, but it could make me ill. It was well-tried, nonetheless. Who taught you?"

"My grandfather."

He'll say no more, she guessed. He roasted the mushrooms on the spit, blew on the soup until it was no longer hot, and drank it down in three swallows. Next, he refilled the bowl and poured out a trickle over the embers. The crackling echoed throughout the clearing.

Above them, the clouds parted gently to reveal the first stars.

"Will you give me my kiss now?" she asked him, kneeling beside him, her wings stretched out.

"I cannot grant wishes, fair maiden."

A curl of smoke rose from the dying fire. In the dark, frogs kept watch. The fay chose a branch halfway up a tree. The boy lied down by the embers. He turned his back to her so that she couldn't see his tears. There was more than one salt-magic, and this one was the most powerful of all.

When her captive awakened, the fay tied a mere tendril of creeping vine around his neck, looping the other end about her forefinger. She watched him while he turned away to wash, delighting in the play of drops along the small of his back. When he dressed again, she pulled on the bond uniting them, but he shook his head. The fire was not quite out. He poured water on it and scooped up ashes in his cupped hands to carry them to the base of the bramble bush.

"There will be a few more berries next year," he said, answering the fay's silent question. "We always do this in our gardens."

"Your kind is unable to speak to trees and bushes?"

"We know how to light fires."

He stood erect, waiting for her to climb onto his shoulders, but she wound the green thread around her finger until they stood face to face. She was almost as tall as he was, now, and her body was clothed in leaves that hid her curves. The morning sun tarried across her outstretched wings.

"You'll walk ahead of me," she ordered. "The road will be long."

"Where are we going, fair maiden?"

"To see the lord of the trees."

They heard the heart-tree long before they caught sight of it. Flocks of many bird species had gathered among its foliage in advance of their migration. The fay had said little all morning, allowing the boy to listen to the noises within the thickets. The heart of the forest was very different from the fringes beyond which he had never ventured alone. Countless animals had opened trails here and their tracks were written on the parchment of moss and dried leaves that crunched beneath his feet. Numerous pairs of eyes watched him, unblinking, until he walked by. He felt heavy and clumsy, but he was no longer entirely a stranger here.

The heart-tree rose in the middle of an almost impenetrable grove, where each trunk vied with the next to gather its share of sunshine. Its bark was mottled with many a scar and more than a few claw marks. A small pit gaped open among the roots, almost large enough for the boy to huddle inside. When he looked up, the height of the leafy cupola above him was dizzying. Even the high vaulting of the village church had not overwhelmed him this way.

And, everywhere, birds were roosting.

"All the way up, to the very top," the fay whispered in his ear, "there is a hollow between two branches where water accumulates. It's the purest water in the world and you must bring me a swallow."

With a shudder, the boy assessed the distance to the top. The heart-tree was generous. An almost perfect staircase of branches wound its way around the trunk. The climb seemed easy, but the treetop was so high, and the foliage so thick, that the boy couldn't know how far he'd have to go.

The birds fell silent when the fay spoke. She untied the slender vine from her finger and handed it over.

"Remember: the highest branch. Do not tarry, night comes quickly in this season and you still owe me a wish!"

The half-light below the heart-tree added shadows to the fay's body that somehow set off her nakedness. The boy looked away. She let him walk ahead on purpose, to avoid distracting him more than necessary. *He isn't ready yet,* she regretted. She turned down the fire, and then the salt. Would he give her the water that she craved?

She watched him climb, in his slow and obstinate way, then, when he was high enough, she unfurled her wings and flew up to wait for him at the top.

When the branches began to bend under him, the boy stopped. He had climbed even higher than the highest nests, higher than he thought he could. Above his head, little was left of the foliage that blocked out the sun. He wiped the sweat streaming into his eyes with the back of his arm, and then fumbled for a hold. He was almost there.

During the climb, he had scratched his cheek without noticing. His homespun shirt had torn—he had heard a seam rip. And yet, the climb hadn't been that hard. The heart-tree was so big that its size proved a comfort. Several times, he had rested in the hollows of main branches. The bark was always rough enough to provide his bare feet with holds. With a sigh, he reached for the bough above him. When he pulled himself up by main force, his legs squeezed the outermost part of the trunk. He struggled to become a part of the tree, to slide up instead of clawing himself up. He listened for the pulse of the sap underneath and rubbed his cheeks against the wood, eyes shut, keeping time with the sap within.

One last effort carried him through the final screen of foliage. When he tumbled into the cradle shaped by the last two branches, he was greeted by the sun's caress and his face dropped into a warm pool of water. It was like drinking sunshine.

"You'll leave me some?"

He jumped up and, for one endless instant, felt the tree give way beneath him. His hands tightened convulsively on the boughs holding him up. His eyes opened again. The fay was hovering beside him, her hands clasped to her chest. She watched him in a way that made him shiver. Her skin was tinged with the rosy hue of sunset.

Behind her, the woods spread out in waves green and brown, all the way to a sandy beach strewn with deadwood. Beyond it, the sea resembled a bottomless mirror.

The fay bent over the puddle and drew a spiral across it. She then landed astride the bough nearest to the boy.

"You didn't need me to come and drink here, fair maiden," he said reproachfully. "You have wings. But if I'd fallen from the tree top, you couldn't have caught me."

"You're still too heavy," she admitted. "But I would have tried."

She gathered a bit of water in her palm and let it drip between her fingers. Drops splattered on her breasts, their blurry reflections dancing on the puddle's surface.

"You won't drink?"

"I only wanted you to see what the forest really looks like. Now, you know what being a tree means. Think about it when you bring them down. Choose the ones that have given up on the sun."

A flight of sparrows whirled above them. The air was filled with intimations of autumn. A sudden gust chilled the boy and goose pimples spread across his skin.

"If I turn my head, will I see my village?"

"You still owe me a kiss." She shook her head and her russet locks were stirred by the breeze like windblown leaves. "Even the Queen cannot change the rules. But you've climbed so high... Are you sure you already wish to go home?"

She felt him hesitating, as his eyes wandered towards the edge of the pine forest and the shore beyond. The moment was too brief. With a sigh, the fay unwound the creeping vine and linked their two wrists. He could free himself. She knew he was strong enough.

"Tomorrow, we'll head for the sea!"

She now was the one leading him, moving beside him, shoulder to shoulder. When they reached the sandy border, where the pines were so sparse one could forget they were still there, she stopped him three paces away from the last tree, too far for him to escape her in a single leap.

Maybe he no longer wanted to.

Autumn was now inescapable. Above their heads, birds were gathering to leave for the sea's farthest shore. In an unspoken agreement, the fay and her prisoner sat down on a patch of sand bristling with resin-coated pine needles. The waves sighed in unison with them. The smells they brought gripped their hearts.

"I've never come here before," the boy said simply. "My grandfather didn't want me to."

"It's never too late for the sea."

The boy shrugged. Her finger on his cheek, the fay forced him to turn toward her.

"I cannot teach you anything else. My sisters and I know almost nothing of the ocean. The birds that fly above it do not nest with ours. And the sea maids who live below the waves do not know how to speak to us. We can hear their songs and they make us sad, though we do not know why. Did your grandfather tell you why he didn't want you to come here?"

"One of my uncles left as a mariner. That was before I was born. He came back to die among us last year, but my grandmother had gone before him. She used to say that the sea is a mystery for men, but they manage to convince themselves they own it, opening it with the prow of the ships, just like the fields they plow."

"But you, you have an axe."

"I prefer the woods. And the truth is, the axe is a gift from my family. I've never been given anything else."

"Never?"

He couldn't look away. She had led him to the edge of the woods, and the edge of her power, so that she could offer him the sea's horizon. He bit his lip, aware of his blunder. Around his wrist, the creeping vine had come loose. All that bound them now were shared moments. He could get up and go; both knew this.

"Will you grant me my wish?" she asked, closing her eyes.

And because he no longer needed to struggle, he leaned towards her, his eyes also shut.

41

That night, he learned what was hidden below the bark, the secrets of her sapwood, and the wounded sweetness of the sap itself. What linked them now was a single strand of saliva, endlessly renewed. The fay's name was a gleeful laugh that he couldn't utter. So, he came up with his own name for her, an invented word full of tenderness, regret, and acceptance, blending in the whimper of the wind in the branches, the rustle of dead leaves when a fox passes, the crackling of a fire, and the tireless call of the waves, like a token of what he would like to leave her with. It was so beautiful that she decided to keep it, for as long as she would remember it.

He would never forget it.

In the morning, the boy awakened under a blanket of leaves that crumbled in his hands. He remembered a bed with a wonderfully woven quilt, the sheets so smooth that they seemed to kiss every inch of his skin. He remembered also the one who accepted his wish and who thanked him for it.

His axe had been set down beside him. Through an opening, he could see the heath and the village. He rose and bowed awkwardly in all directions except one, before heading back to the world of men.

Above him, the fay was stretched out on a branch, her eyes half-shut. Her skin's bark still bore the dotted outline of the night's playful bites. The fulfillment of her wish had left a salty tang in her mouth. She watched the boy go with a pang, knowing that time would erase him one day from her memory, as was fitting.

This one will respect the woods, she thought. *He may even have taught me a thing or two. When we become too much alike, one of our two races will be forced to go away so as not to melt into the other, but, until then, there will be other days for cravings.*

Come into my Parlor...

"When will you decide to die, Eric?"

There was a silence, lasting just long enough for half a heartbeat... and for the question to hit home.

"Touché!" cried Delise, clapping her hands. The other guests left the tables overloaded with drinks and reconstituted food to crowd around their host.

"Is this a proper challenge, my dear Sorge?"

"No, not at all! ("Of course it is, a duel, a duel!" chanted a couple of women nearby. Their partners silenced them with slight frowns.) You disemboweled me barely six weeks ago, in an absolutely charming manner, I must say. I haven't been able to get back into training since."

"Take your time and ask me again as soon as you've got your reflexes back. I shall be delighted to respond."

A generous wave of the arm towards the trophy gallery accompanied these words, eliciting a grimace from Sorge. The naturalized body that Eric had chosen to install in the place of honor was, as it happened, his own preceding incarnation. The saber stroke, cause of his death, had made a deep gash across the abdomen. Eric, with his dubious sense of humor, had unbound the wound and widened the lips with gold needles, like a

conscientious embalmer preparing the corpse of a presti-
gious client.

The sight of his entrails exhibited in such an inde-
cent manner gave Sorge the impression of having bared
his very soul to the world. He blushed and clenched his
fists. Nevertheless, he did not take up the gauntlet. His
new body was still too inexperienced and would not last
long against "Eric the Invincible." Or rather "Eric the
Undefeated," he rectified mentally, but as this status had
remained unchanged for so long, the two concepts had
merged in his mind. As if reading his thoughts, Eric
raised his glass to him and proposed an ironic toast.

"I drink to your thoughtfulness, my dear friend.
You wish to spare me cluttering up my collection with
additional copies of your body. Repetition engenders
monotony and I believe I've slain you in just about every
imaginable manner. How many trophies of you do I have
already in my gallery? 25? 30? Too many, in any
event... To be frank, the idea of another duel between us
appalls me and I dread the thought of fighting you. Not
that I fear your talents as a fighter, but my imagination
falters at finding a novel wound to inflict upon you. Unless you have a brainwave?"

The spectators applauded halfheartedly. Sorge said
nothing but unexpected support came from Delise, who
had long been his companion. The young woman walked
up to Eric and slid her arm under his.

"You're being a poor sport with Sorge. This evening, for the first time, he managed to scratch your armor.
Take it as a worthy feint, a new thrust which caused you
to break off; next time, try to parry it. The question remains: when will you decide to die?"

"Never of course! Or maybe tomorrow, or today, or
in one hour, as soon as one of the noble warriors in our

present company decides to fight me. What do you want me to do if they are so lacking in zeal?"

"Oh, you're no fun at all."

Furious, she turned on her heel and departed. Absent-mindedly rubbing the scar on his cheek, Eric watched her cleaving her way through the surrounding crowd.

The conversation resumed with the careful omission of the names of Eric, Delise, and Sorge from the banalities exchanged. The orchestra played with renewed brio, the dancers swirled elegantly, and a duel was declared, from which the host was carefully excluded. To all intents and purposes, everything was as it should be—and yet, guests began to take their leave all too soon, and others departed close behind them.

Everything took place as if Sorge's question had set in motion a hidden spring, an artifice within the script of which even the actors were unaware. Eric sensed that the prologue of the drama had spun itself out and he chose to retire to the seclusion of his quarters to think about potential developments. It was his way to always have a ready method of counter-attack, or rather several, up his sleeve.

The visit of Captain Demaria the next morning was the next act of the play. A clever choice, in fact brilliant—but not altogether unexpected. Eric received him in the workout room. His arrival coincided with the finale of the murderous *kata* that Eric was practicing.

"Hello there!" Demaria's salutation was friendly, if a trifle cool. Eric's, on the other hand, was respectful in manner, formal, with feet clicked together and a rapid bow to the imaginary judges observing him, as he retreated backwards to leave the tatami. He took off his

46

kimono and knelt down beside the pool of cold water in one corner of the room, in front of the wall of the great air-bubble looking out onto the exterior. Demaria sat down next to the edge to talk to him.

"You seem to be in outstanding form, Eric."

"I regret not being able to return the compliment, Captain. You neglect your daily exercises. You have difficulty breathing and your hips are showing a definite weight gain. If you continue like this, you will soon have to start your exercises from scratch."

"I am aware of that, but I no longer have the time to worry about it. The extension of the air-bubble has come to a virtual standstill and we're having problems again with the harvesting of the Si'ang buds."

He pointed to the jungle of tortuous plants that stretched away from the air-bubble, like a sooty sandstorm. The pale creepers, devoid of the slightest trace of color, rippled in gentle curves. In a gray sky where a putrescent moon loomed gigantic, bunches of heavy circular clouds paraded past at low altitude, casting regular shadows on the ground. Whenever they tarried too long on a given spot, the light-deprived creepers sagged and died, expelling a spray of spores. As soon as the sun reappeared, a carpet of pale sprouts sprang up.

For both men, the swarming gray was a familiar sight. Since the air-bubble was set up five centuries before, the planet's ecosystem had undergone the most comprehensive of analyses. That did not prevent it from still being mortally dangerous, but in a predictable fashion.

Eric was the only human being at the base who had not gone outside to confront its pitfalls. He knew that this was why Demaria had come to see him. He waited, twiddling his toes in the water to break up the mirror of

47

its surface. For a long time now, his own image had left him uneasy.

"What exactly is your problem, Captain?"

"You, Eric. I would like you to realize that some-day." Demaria sighed, conscious of his weakness in the face of this statuesque man, devoid of any visible flaws.

"The air-bubble is in peril. The front line of plants is coming closer and closer to our walls and the security ring we've cleared is only a dozen meters wide. The clones we send outside are incapable of surviving more than a quarter of an hour. We are not destroying the creepers quickly enough and the Si'ang buds are increasingly difficult to find. The harvest is jeopardized. We are losing ground."

"Use the base's main lasers."

"Don't be ridiculous, Eric; these plants thrive on energy. We would discharge our batteries before achieving the slightest result. Moreover, we believe that they are endeavoring to adapt to biochemical warfare."

"Interesting…"

He got out of the pool, dried himself by dint of vigorous rubbing and then swathed himself in a bathrobe with the belt tied low down on his waist.

"You have just presented me with the dark side of things, Captain. I know you well enough to realize that you already have answers to your questions. Let's not beat around the bush. What do you want from me?"

"Your death, Eric. Not personally, I assure you, but it is vital that you be killed as soon as possible. Just once. The survival of the colony depends on it."

"From the mouth of another I would have regarded that as a proper challenge, but I know you too well—please explain."

Eric's body exuded an odor of sweat, partially masked by the perfume emanating from the bathrobe. The mixture was both disagreeable and strangely exciting, a subtle weapon, the effect of which Demaria tried to counter by wetting his nostrils with water.

"Think of our dilemma: we are a small group of humans enclosed within the shelter of an infinitely expandable air-bubble on the surface of a lost planet. Surrounding us, a complex ecosystem with hundreds of plant varieties—all of them lethal to the human species except for the fragile Si'ang, whose buds supply us with the substances necessary for our increased longevity.

"Normally, we should have destroyed all traces of indigenous life so that the air-bubble could grow without danger till it covered the entire surface area of dry land on this planet. But this is now impossible. We cannot eliminate the flora of this world without depriving ourselves of our immortality.

"Bombs, lasers, all the outsized weapons of our arsenal are useless here; the only possible form of combat in this jungle is hand-to-hand.

"For a century, we meditated on this, observing our opponents and then, largely under your tutelage, we became warriors. Or rather, *you* became a warrior and we endeavored to better ourselves as your apprentices. Our duels, our successive deaths toughened us up, we were able to survive longer and longer in the outside world. The skirmishes with the creepers often turned to our advantage, we annihilated the most dangerous species and the air-bubble grew... During that period we all tried to beat you. Not one of us succeeded."

"You came closest to that ideal, Captain." Eric traced his scar with his fingertips, a smile playing on his face. He had always refused to eliminate this one link with Demaria. "You have lost your skillfulness and I regret that very much. In fact, I have lacked proper rivals for some time now."

"I would never have touched you a second time, you know that. Don't play with me. You let no one equal you; as soon as one of us improves a little too much and threatens you, you go back into training and jump ahead."

"What has prevented you from doing likewise? You had the wherewithal…"

Demaria shrugged; once again his attack had been foiled and the riposte had followed, with deadly accuracy. Eric's remark awoke cruel regrets. He could have been a warrior himself, but his duties and a certain lack of self-confidence had deflected him from that path. Now the distance between them was too great, insurmountable. He started to speak again in a voice that he managed to keep under control.

"Little by little, we learned to hate what you had become, a man steeped in arrogance. You aggravated that hatred with your mania for collecting our bodies as trophies to be flaunted. It was very cleverly done. For ages, we worked on our training, stimulated by the nagging prod of fury, and the clones worked efficiently outside.

"And then the atmosphere changed radically. You became far too strong; to challenge you was tantamount to being ridiculous. Not one of us desired to be in the place of honor at an evening's entertainment, embalmed on a pedestal with his wounds displayed for all to see. The game gradually lost its popularity and the workout rooms emptied. Our clones are no longer tough enough to combat the creepers. The air-bubble has stopped growing…"

"There is a solution to the problem, we have talked about it a thousand times at least. Use my own clones!"

"The reply is still no, Eric. I'm sorry. The law is too strict on this point: clones can only be activated after the death of the original. I could quote you the punishment we would incur if we cheated, but since we are talking frankly, I prefer to tell you straight out that I don't fancy letting loose an army of Erics on this planet, with you as their immortal leader."

"I would hardly know what to do with the power that you fear I shall seize."

"The human race has had the bloody example of two revolutions to convince itself of the contrary. The law is just. A clone, because of its more restricted life expectancy and its inability to reproduce normally, can be controlled. You are not so constrained, however, and never will be. As long as your initial existence continues, I cannot take the risk of duplicating you."

"Amen! The problem then remains unresolved."

"Not entirely. Your death is the solution to our difficulties—admit it. If one of us succeeded in eliminating you, the game would be reinvested with new interest as the position on top of the heap would no longer be inaccessible. I am sure that the training would pick up again. Plus I could send a squadron of your clones to clear the vicinity of the air-bubble. We are currently designing a specialized weapon capable of destroying the most restive of the creepers. Unfortunately, its utilization is difficult. I think you would be the most likely to wield it efficiently."

"You're beginning to arouse my interest, captain. Tell me more about this weapon."

"It works through a two stage process: vaporization of a cloud of water droplets, and then emission of a beam. At this point, it produces a rainbow which lasts almost a minute. The diffracted beams of color kill the plants.

"We tried using a glass prism but without success. A real rainbow is needed. The team in the laboratory still doesn't know why. What do you think of the principle?"

"Clever—although a little too poetic for my liking." There was a silence while the two men sized each other up, with more than four centuries experience in their mutual scrutiny. "You are asking me to die. What if I refuse?"

"Nothing. We shall die instead of you, and sooner or later the air-bubble will be buried under a tidal wave of plants. I know it's indestructible but for how long do you think you'll able to bear wandering around the deserted corridors seeing no more than a swarm of reptiles instead of the sky?"

"Longer than you think, but not indefinitely, for sure. And only the infinite interests me! Besides which, I wouldn't be able to acquire new trophies for my gallery."

"Don't be so cynical. The gallery alone already occupies almost a quarter of our available surface area. I can't believe that you wish to enlarge it further."

"You're wrong about that, but I won't try to disillusion you. Let's say—a mere surmise, you understand—that I become resigned to the idea of dying. Do you have a method on offer which would preserve my self-esteem?"

"For several months now, Lieutenant Weiss has been practicing with the lasers in secret. With this type of weapon, most of the wounds are fatal, and he would appear to be alarmingly accurate. Let him challenge you."

"Oh Captain, come on, lasers only kill on condition that they hit their target. I am hardly an easy target. One more trophy in my gallery will not solve the problem."

Demaria got up and walked towards the door. Grasping the door handle, he spoke rapidly over his shoulder:

"You will let yourself be hit because I'm asking you to do so! Weiss is preparing for a suicidal attack. You will slaughter him of course, but he shall do likewise with you. This will by no means be dishonorable for you, in view of the circumstances."

"Just a second... who is young Weiss's lady of the moment?"

"Delise, I think. Why?"

"Just curious. I promise you that I shall think about your proposal, Captain. I shall think about it most seriously!"

The door closed with a click. Facing the wall of the air-bubble, Eric observed the invasive creepers which he would one day have to tame with rainbows. A shadow of a smile flickered on his face. Then he disrobed and took up his training again without bothering to wear the kimono drenched with sweat.

The evening given by Sorge threatened to end prematurely. All discussions revolved around the bad news, rehashed over and over again. The morning sortie had been a total failure. Out of the 16 clones that had left the air-bubble, not one had survived for more than three minutes and the area cleared was negligible. With the stocks of Si'ang dropping lower and lower, it would be impossible to produce more clones for some days, without the life elixir from the buds. No one took pains to feign any enthusiasm; the mechanical musicians put away their instruments neatly. But still the drinks flowed and the conversations bubbled over.

Eric did the rounds from one little group to another, quietly snatching drifts of conversation without ever intervening. One would have thought he was the host, ever-present, showing up with an affable smile glued to his thin lips like a skinned lamb in the jaws of a wild cat.

His dress was exceptionally sober: neither flesh-colored tights spangled with scars for effect, nor an anatomic suit reminiscent of a curled-up body with its internal organs on a string like flaccid watches beating to the rhythm of his pulse. This evening Eric had opted for simplicity. He was wearing a ninja tunic in immaculate white and gloves to match. Demaria, observing him from a nook of the room, scarcely dared to put any trust in these hopeful signs and his eyes constantly searched out those of Weiss, who stood hidden behind a screen of loudspeakers.

The tension, carefully orchestrated, mounted little by little. Sorge remained on the sidelines despite himself, busy with his duties as host. When the explosion came, he was at the other end of the lounge and had to elbow his way to get close to Eric and Weiss.

Weiss found nothing more original than to throw the contents of his glass of alcohol in the face of his opponent to declare his challenge. The gesture was stupid but necessary: words, even the most cutting, would have simply bounced off the armor of the warrior's indifference without hurting him.

The splash of liquid missed its goal, except for a single drop which managed to stain Eric's white headband, opening like a third eye in the middle of his brow. Eric's smile disappeared, and yet an almost imperceptible shadow remained for a second on the corner of his lips, so light and transient that Demaria thought he might have imagined seeing it.

"Dear me, as clumsy as ever, Weiss. How discouraging!"

"I can prove the contrary, wherever and whenever you wish, Eric."

The crowd breathed again. The challenge was now official.

"Really? Oh yes, I have been informed of your recent dexterity with the laser beam. Unfortunately, I fear that a fight between us in those conditions would hardly be fair."

"Are you afraid?"

Weiss hesitated before uttering these words. The idea seemed so... unreal, applied to Eric. Demaria himself was startled when he heard the outright laugh of the warrior.

"Afraid, me? Good Lord, no, I'm simply bored with facile victories against beginners who are all too proud of a paltry few weeks of training. Talk to me after decades, if not centuries, if you want to instill fear into my heart."

His gaze measured Weiss, holding the empty glass he had not had time to put down, from top to toe.

"I shall take up the challenge, but on my conditions. Before the fight, Demaria will give me an injection to paralyze my legs. And of course, I shall be deprived of all weapons."

Silence.

"Does that agree with you, or would you prefer to present your apologies?"

"You are mad, but I accept. I shall send you my witnesses tomorrow morning early."

"Why wait? Go and fetch your laser beam. Captain, may I ask you to bring a paralyzing injection from the infirmary? My dear Sorge, I'm sure you have an empty room to put at our disposal. Yes? Marvelous. As for me…"

He undid the sullied headband and threw it into a corner.

"I am ready."

Sorge's mechanical domestics cleared a huge lounge and erected two-way mirrors on three of the walls. The guests, amassed in the neighboring rooms, would not miss the slightest feint during the fight, but without putting their own lives at risk.

Weiss was dressed in full combat gear and had attached the laser onto a small sack behind his back. Thus attired, he looked like some soldier in an unlikely war that had somehow lost his way and had found himself at an elegant reception given by staff headquarters. Delise was leaning onto his arm, a little pale, as befitted the companion of a future hero. She knew what to expect in the event of failure but did not care. This time the warrior had gone too far, nothing could save his skin. Nevertheless, a nagging doubt pervaded her thoughts. Eric did not have a reputation for bestowing gifts, or if he did, it was as part of a vast logic of his own. And that sole drop of liquid on his headband had been too symmetrically positioned…

With irritation, she noted that her companion was also thrown off balance, a dangerous handicap when facing an opponent as untroubled by nerves as Eric. She would have reassured him with a word or two, but Weiss was already striding away with a determined expression on his face. Full of misgivings, she approached the mirrors in front of which were rows of seats.

The lounge was plunged into darkness. Eric was kneeling in the center of the room opposite the entrance. His hands rested on his temporarily paralyzed legs. With a blank look in his eyes, he seemed to contemplate his imminent death and its consequences. When the boom of the gong sounded to herald the attack he stripped off his gloves and threw them nonchalantly behind him.

The door opened slowly. Weiss leapt out in an elaborate roll that propelled him to the corner opposite the entrance. He pulled the trigger twice, but at body height. The rays whistled above Eric's head, who had not moved an inch, before crashing uselessly into the fireproof woodwork of the wall.

There was no riposte. Weiss got up, a little confused, the laser hanging from his hand like some futile toy. He automatically wiped his tights with his left hand and took up the position of gunner, feet apart, hip turned toward his opponent. The barrel of the gun lifted, and positioned itself knee-high at 12 meters. The index finger drew taut but when the bolt flashed forth, Eric had thrown his chest backwards. Another miss.

Weiss advanced with caution. He was making a fool of himself in front of the spectators whose attentive presence he could imagine behind the dull glass screens. A cold fury came over him. His eyes met those of Eric. He pulled the trigger, alas, not fast enough to achieve a bull's eye as his target twisted like a creeper, making fun of him.

Three steps away, he stood still, raising his weapon with both hands, determined to keep on pulling the trigger until his opponent was slashed in two. But during the fraction of a second preceding the shot, Eric lifted his open palms which cradled two round mirrors. The fatal beam ricocheted with perfect precision and neatly slit the chest of Weiss, who slowly crumpled at Eric's feet.

Untouchable and unmoved, Eric awaited the arrival of the spectators, and of Demaria, who would release him from his paralysis. He had recovered Weiss' laser off the floor—a joker up one's sleeve was always useful...

For the remainder of the evening, he swaggered in front of the guests. Delise was hooked onto his arm according to custom, decreed by Eric himself many years before. The partner of the vanquished belonged to the victor, as long as the clone of the deceased had not yet been made operational. The mechanical waiters had already removed the corpse, an eyesore. The next day, the embalmer would capture the body's last throes for the gallery of trophies. Eric went into detail about that with Delise, whispering his cruelest suggestions in her ear, just to see a grimace of disgust appear on her pouting lips. When the first guests were ready to leave, he clapped his hands to attract attention and silenced the orchestra.

"Dear friends, tradition calls for the survivor of a duel to organize a party. The next shall be a twofold affair.

"No, don't leave, the invitation I extend is by no means usual. This will not be an ordinary party, with my last trophy as centerpiece. I am inviting you to something far more exciting. My death!"

His eyes traveled quickly over his listeners to see their petrified eyes and he noted that Delise was trembling. He bent down and kissed her full on the mouth, biting her lower swollen lip in the process.

"I need a little time for preparation, so the invitation is for a month from now, day for day. During that time, I shall accept no challenge and shall participate in no duel, even friendly ones. I am tired of these boring games devoid of juicy surprises. You are cordially invited to my last evening's entertainment and I kindly ask you to spread the news around the air-bubble."

"And now, Captain Demaria," he said, with a sly note of amusement in his voice, "may I have a word?"

The evening's announcement occupied all thoughts for weeks. The most fantastic hypotheses made the rounds: would he go out and fight the creepers? Had he decided to launch a general challenge to all present? Demaria, upon questioning, refused to reply. His furious expression discouraged the questioners from probing further. Delise, who had returned to her own living quarters after a single night with Eric, had dark rings under her eyes and looked simply dreadful. The victor had not seen fit to keep her. Such an insult to her beauty was intolerable and prevented her from knowing, before the others, the ins and outs of the whole business.

The storm of questions arising from the invitation swept away all doubts and worries, and the air-bubble registered a boost in activity and even some progress in cutting down the creepers. If the next sortie was not an outstanding success, it could at least be counted a victory of sorts. Testing of the new weapon had given encouraging results: the rainbow-colored laser beam had pushed back the front-line of the deadly jungle.

Handling the weapon was not risk-free, however. Two clones had made the mistake of gazing too long at the multicolored bow they had created, as if a stained glass window had been opened in mid-air. Within reach of the deadly creepers, such errors happened only once and everyone silently hoped that Eric would weigh in during subsequent sorties with his invaluable expertise. His name was common currency in every conversation, but the man himself remained invisible; access to his private quarters was also forbidden.

On the appointed day, the crowds gathered in the designated reception rooms. Nearly everyone had come armed—as a mere precaution if Eric decided to have a standup fight with all present, but as the evening progressed, this seemed an increasingly unlikely hypothesis.

The guests huddled around tables of cocktails or embarked on a careful inspection of their host's living quarters. The gallery of trophies was closed to the public, but the choicest pieces were displayed haphazardly in the various rooms flooded by the crowds. Many of the works were exhibited for the first time.

Eric's ingenuity and his bizarre artistic flair had transformed the grotesque corpses of his opponents into true works of art. All those present had challenged him at least once. Under the vast dome of the air bubble the dead were more numerous than the living. Each guest was thus confronted sooner or later with his or her effigy in a block of translucent resin done up in sickly colors, either incorporated in a sarcophagus-like container or as a trinket quaintly arranged on a mantelpiece.

Some corpses were reduced to the size of a doll, except for the part responsible for the death; here the evidence was atrociously blatant. Some were skinned, with the flesh displayed like a funeral papyrus scroll, all the bruises and wounds harmoniously spread out on the surface. Others were fitted out with drawers containing the vital organs, or doors opening to reveal the secrets of their entrails.

Weiss's corpse had been accorded the dubious honor of preferential treatment. His skin, which had undergone several laminations, had become as thin as silk and it had been rolled up like a long hand-towel in an antique distributor both clean and dry. If you pulled on the towel for long enough, the display showed his sewn lips and astonished eyes. Weiss himself had fun trying it out before going back to his seat. He had just emerged from the matrix and his legs were still wobbly.

Eric surfaced suddenly in Demaria's company and everybody gathered round. He brushed away all questions with one hand:

"Don't be impatient, the evening has just begun. I shall unveil all in two hours' time—if I survive until then, of course."

Amongst the smiles acknowledging the jest, how many there were hiding a lust to bite him? Unfortunately, Eric no longer felt the familiar unpleasant feeling of the hair rising on his back in the face of the enemy. He did have a sudden urge to insult them, to provoke them beyond all reason, even though he knew that the little flame of hatred they cosseted in their souls could never be fanned to become a durable blaze. His dissatisfied expression did not go unnoticed, and Sorge, who tried to question him, received a disillusioned reply:

"You do not hate me enough, gentlemen. Oh, I dare say you do your utmost, but that is in no way an excuse. Do you fully realize that your inertia has finally defeated me? I no longer even wish to fight you."

He studied the faces around him closely, without seeing anything save either unhealthy curiosity or wrinkles of ennui. Good Lord, if he had ordered applause, he would have been overcome with a standing ovation. How could anyone be stimulated by such opponents as these? Death suddenly appeared as the only source of retreat possible; to die, to go to sleep and awaken, perhaps in a Valhalla full of warriors like himself. Yes, this was certainly the moment to take leave forever and wipe the boards. The decision he had taken was the right one.

The clatter of a mechanical waiter tore him away from his dream world. The message communicated was loud and clear: all was ready.

Later on in the evening when the tension reached a fever pitch, Eric's voice came over the invisible loudspeakers:

"I shall soon say *au revoir*, but let me inform you of the various stages of my death, and of my resurrection. Ten minutes from now, I shall swallow poison to achieve what all your weapons and cunning have failed to accomplish. Tomorrow, my gallery will have an addition. You will forgive me, I hope, for not committing *seppuku* as tradition demands, but I abhor blood on my carpets."

Silence. Each guest was both attentive and relieved at being assigned the role of spectator by Eric.

"My death is only the beginning of the festivities, if I can call them thus. At the exact second my heart stops beating, seven of my clones will open their eyes. They will not be clumsy newborns, but seven highly trained athletes, indeed seven copies of myself in top form.

"Each will wake up in a separate area of the air-bubble. He will have to escape the traps set for him and confront his six brothers. Only one will survive to take my place—the strongest and wiliest. Captain Demaria, who did me the honor of assisting in the preparations, will oversee the proceedings so that everything goes smoothly.

"You shall be able to follow the fights on the monitors. As of now, you are imprisoned in my living quarters until my successor sets you free. He shall enter by way of the trophy gallery; receive him with the pomp he deserves and begin to fear him. I doubt that you shall find in him an opponent more flexible than I."

With his guests crowded before him, he raised the glass offered by a mechanical domestic. The familiar smell of creeper extract emanated from the liquid. The first mouthful made him reel, but he had time to swallow another before dropping onto the floor, a black trickle dribbling out of his mouth.

The domestics carried away his body to their own private quarters where the embalmers would try to restore some semblance of life to it. No one paid any heed to such matters. In the trophy-filled rooms, the monitors had switched on as promised.

After careless bumping into two or three shadowy figures, Sorge came up to Demaria.

"Seven clones all at once, trained beforehand to boot, but that's absolutely illegal! It must have emptied our reserve of buds for several weeks. How could you possibly have agreed to such a thing?"

"I had no other choice. Eric only agreed to die on that condition."

"You could have refused, or killed him when he was not on his guard, putting it down to an accident."

"And who would have done it? You? Oh, shut up and look at the show."

Sorge, let himself be ensnared by the images, like the others a prisoner in the almost hypnotic web that Eric had spun before dying.

The clones all awoke at the same time. They had hardly opened their eyes before reacting in identical fashion, rolling on their side to extract themselves from the protective cradle. The second clone was a fraction of a second late and an electric net bore down on him, destroying forever his chances of survival. His number was eliminated from each monitor.

Bets were laid. It was not a question of money, which had no value within the air-bubble, nor of gaining favors or avoiding undesirable tasks. The game was to earn the right to be the first to confront Eric's reincarnation.

Released in various parts of the air-bubble, the clones started looking for weapons. Three of them had the idea of retrieving the electric net after removing the deadly wires to the control panels. Another preferred to seize a metal bar that jutted from a door. The last two advanced empty-handed, leaping from shadow to shadow through the labyrinth of streets.

The situation changed little in the next quarter of an hour. The Erics hurried towards the reception area, carefully avoiding any confrontation. None of them tried to arm himself with more sophisticated weapons susceptible of making a difference at the crucial moment. Their attitude, a mixture of lack of foresight and exaggerated care, went against the grain of the spectators who were so used to the methodical and deadly efficiency of the original, coupled with his coldly calculated temerity.

Two Erics entered the same street at the same time and approached one another warily. The one holding the metal bar twirled it like a saber and traced a series of hypnotizing shapes with the tip. His opponent drew out his net that he got ready to throw. They commenced a complicated dance, feinting, advancing one step closer and withdrawing again, always at a safe distance. But gradually they slowed, before coming to a complete standstill.

For a moment, one imagined they were about to launch an attack, but neither took the decision to move. Then, carefully, they stepped back, before turning round and merging again into the shadows of the air-bubble.

The guests did not have time to express their disappointment; the monitors shifted to focus on another duel. This time two clones attacked a third. The latter, backed against a wall, defended himself with brio. The smile splitting his mouth was that of Eric in his prime. He feinted to the right, broke the knee of his first adversary by kicking him, before barely managing to duck the net of the second. He threw the metallic mesh back at his double's head, and then took advantage of his accelerated retreat to kill off the other one by bashing him heavily with his elbow and crushing the fragile cartilage of the throat.

A fourth clone, attracted by the noise of the fight awaited nearby in the shadows, ready to intervene if an opportunity presented itself.

Hampered by the corpse lying at his feet, the clone on the defensive tripped. His opponent threw out the net once again, this time aiming for the poorly protected legs. Thrown off balance, the clone sunk down and did not have the time to get up again...

The Eric in hiding decided that it was better to stay where he was. He let the successful clone disappear without coming out of his hiding place, and waited a long while before retrieving the weapon of the loser.

Several minutes went by with nothing happening at all on the monitors. The guests exchanged awkward jokes or went to get another drink. The spectacle orchestrated by Eric had not lived up to his promises, and yet his resources and cunning were such that no one dared declare openly that his place would be easy to take.

Upon the first rays of dawn, the dome of the air-bubble lit up with an ever-changing iridescence. Little by little, the light of the blue sun transformed the chessboard of gloomy streets into an arena without hiding places. The four survivors discovered one another's presence and made their way towards the stone esplanade on which the entrance to Eric's living quarters was situated.

They came to a halt a few meters from one another, their eyes tracking along the identical curves of their multiple bodies, looking for weaknesses or changes betraying fatigue or fear. Then, having established proof that each was the perfect mirror image of the other three, their eyes sought one another's, latching on, and no longer letting go.

A mere nothing would have sufficed for the Erics to throw down their arms, get undressed, caress each other's hands, and suddenly become heralds of peace. The circle they formed was transfused with a silent current, the incredible intensity of which the isolated spectators behind their monitors barely managed to detect. In the overfilled rooms, the murmurs of the spectators died away...

An alliance of the four warriors would be the worst threat the bubble had ever experienced. The guests hesitated, one hand on the butt of their weapons: perhaps it would be better to open a way out of their prison and eliminate the Erics with laser beams. But the seconds passed in indecision.

The suddenness of the attack took everyone by surprise. With one accord, the three clones equipped with nets threw them over the fourth, who did not have time to parry the assault with his metal bar. He sank down to the ground. The bloodied weapon jangled on the pavement. The three survivors took up their death dance again paying no attention to the corpse splayed out like a shadow at their feet.

The moment of anguish preceding the last attack had reminded the spectators of just how dangerous Eric was, alone or multiplied. The evening took another turn. Those who had rejoiced in betting on a winner, now hoped he would lose so as not to be one of the first to confront him.

Nevertheless, all the guests knew that something had cracked in the implacable mechanism of their warrior. His invincible aura had slowly dissolved in the stream of images showing a wounded Eric, a vanquished Eric, a dead Eric. The survivor would prove his worth, but the six corpses in his wake would be so many dents in his armor. He would be challenged, again and again. All would vie to take his place and attain supreme power.

Unaware of the thoughts stirring their observers, the clones prepared for the final confrontation. Three was a bad number for fighters of the same strength: too static, too stable, it was like a perpetual truce where any proposal to become an ally would be suspect. Who would run the risk of being the first to attack, knowing that the other two would immediately team up against him? A quick and deadly thrust was out of the question, the three warriors were on their guard and knew each feint of his opponents. Stalemate.

On the display, a light which had been out a second before started to flicker on again. The slain clone was not quite dead. Still unable to move, he slowly recovered from the blow he had received. His eyelids slit open and his fingers felt out for the abandoned bar within arm's reach.

He was about to swing it up when one of the Erics cut short his dance to deliver the *coup de grâce* with his foot. The bar rolled next to the closed door with a metallic noise reminiscent of a signal. The warrior picked it up and rolled across the esplanade to escape the net thrown towards him a fraction too late.

The buckle of his boot remained entrapped in the metal mesh. He pulled violently, taking advantage of the momentum imparted by his roll. His opponent, taken by surprise, let go of the net. Once disarmed, he was easy prey for the third Eric who was quietly watching the outcome of the battle...

Two numbers were left on the monitors. The guests caught their breath excitedly. The outcome was near, most bets had been made. The success of Eric's project was based on this moment: depending on the way his successor would behave during the final assault, he would be greeted with applause mixed with a healthy dose of fear, or with insolent smiles in guise of a challenge. The future winner has still to add the last chapter of his own legend, to sign the skin of his double with a bloody scrawl, before joining the reception.

The weapons, now useless, were left aside; the confrontation would be conducted with bare hands. Head to head, mirror image to mirror image, the warriors collided with each other and merged in a swirl too confusing for the normal eye to make any sense of it. There were no clever feints, nor any boring sidesteps, just the two opposing strengths of equal force merging to grapple with one another.

When one of the bodies dropped down, no spectator could have said why. The crack which had appeared in the now shattered monolith would remain forever unexplained. The loser proffered his naked neck for the *coup de grâce* and then silence reigned like that after the final chime of a clock, ticking away seconds that seemed to last centuries.

Eric saluted his broken-winged alter ego before turning away from the cameras. He pushed open the door of his private quarters and disappeared from the eyes of the spectators. The monitors switched off one by one and the mechanical orchestra started to play again.

The clone advanced along the corridors and entered the workout room plunged into darkness. A familiar voice stopped him short:

"We have a last little detail to sort out, my dear brother."

The lights came on brutally. At the other end of the tatami, the original Eric stood up, ready for combat.

Later, a footstep sounded in the gallery of trophies. As he advanced, the survivor examined the bodies exhibited on pedestals carved in the shape of looking glasses, the puzzles of half reconstituted limbs and organs, the faces deformed by posthumous grimaces whose features he brushed lightly with his fingers by way of a greeting. What a superb collection he had! And this was only the beginning…

Soon the duels would start up again. He knew that on the other side of the door, they would all be waiting to challenge him, as before. He felt capable of maintaining their hatred for many years to come before they tired of attacking him. His successive clones would help the air-bubble to advance and would enable him to increase his gallery as he so wished, because space would soon be lacking.

He slowed, smiling as he stroked the spot where his scar had been erased. The new skin was so soft to his touch. He had no need now of any fleshly reminder of the threat of mortality. Why not dream of a planet totally transformed into a private museum? He had all the time in the world and it would be easy to convince those around him that he was vulnerable enough to make the error of attacking him. *Come into my parlor, said the spider to the fly...* If necessary he would sacrifice one of his arms during an evening's entertainment, similar to the one they had just had, and fashion it into a glove to slap his opponents. Who would fear challenging someone with such a handicap?

He stopped in front of the secret niche still awaiting its occupant. The appearance of the latter would not be altered: no dressing-up, no macabre joke would modify the face of the one in which Eric would be able to see himself reflected as in black water. Facing the empty pedestal, he recalled this most recent duel when the stakes had been so high.

This death that now stood between them was the only unknown factor in his career as warrior, the most important weakness he had always refused to confront, but which constituted the very essence of his life. Until today, dying had been a destiny that he had reserved for others, but rejected vehemently for himself.

Had the experience of the resurrection, in divesting him of this fear, deprived the clone of his last reserves of strength, those which surged up when one is in the most desperate of situations, transcending all doubts and rendering one invincible? Or had it been death, with its cortege of revelations, that provided the missing key he needed to go to the very depths of his soul? The fight had decided, just as the Erics had wished. The winner knew that the answer alone had made the theatrics worthwhile.

He turned his eyes away and made his way slowly towards the reception rooms, no longer paying any attention to the trophies surrounding him. His ears could already hear the cheers of his future victims.

Homecoming

I panicked for a second when the time came to sign the deed to the house. The notary—an ageless type, dressed to the nines, who had advised my father and his father before him—waited patiently as I grasped the pen he was holding out to me and signed the bundle of carefully stacked papers. There was not a sound to be heard. The office had been fitted with double-pane windows and, in any case, the neighborhood had always been very quiet.

"You were right to come back," he said approvingly, giving me my copy of the documents.

"I didn't really have a choice."

A reproving look, almost unnoticeable, flitted across his face.

"That woman wasn't right for you. Your mother was brave enough to say so to your face, but many of us agreed with her. She didn't leave you anything when she left, did she?"

Given my expression, he turned away with a hint of embarrassment. "You're starting over. Nothing has really changed here, as you'll soon see. It's a quiet life. It takes a cooperative effort, but I believe it's worth it."

"That's why I fled, back then. I've never been really fond of the quiet life!"

Frowning, he placed the file in a drawer in his desk, which opened and closed without a sound, as well oiled as everything else here. I, however, wanted things to grate.

"It was your mother who decorated my office," he said, misunderstanding my expression. "You'll be seeing her soon, I suppose?"

I settled for a nod. The notary stood up and stretched his hand out to me. Manicured fingers, as smooth and shiny as mass-produced objects.

"Don't ever criticize tranquility. That's what brought you back," he concluded as he escorted me out. "Give my regards to your parents."

My car was parked on the corner, opposite the dollar store. It was an enormous American model, spiked with chrome, purchased in a moment of madness at a time when that type of gesture still meant something. I had piled all of my possessions into the trunk and, on the immense back seat, there were suitcases crammed with doodads and boxes stacked every which way. The notary was wrong. *She* had left me a great deal. Memories, photos she no longer found pleasing, and a bitterness that knew no bottom. I felt as if I had been turned into salt.

And, on the passenger seat, sat Ben. A mongrel Labrador, with a nondescript brown coat, who barked too loudly and too often. As soon as I approached the door, he stood up and tried to poke his head out the window. Then he howled in joy as I slipped behind the steering wheel.

"We have somewhere to go," I say as I put the car into drive. "Does that make you happy?"

Silent streets. Ben's howls bounced off the store fronts. Tomorrow, the entire neighborhood would know that I had come home to roost.

I'd known the house I'd just bought since birth. Or nearly. It was located on one of the streets I was allowed to explore as soon as I could walk. My parents' house stood in the center of a complicated web of roads and escape routes, whose nodes were squares, toy shops and public gardens. I spent my childhood inventorying every possible way out of the village, without once daring to use them. It took someone from the outside to come and tear me away from these familiar sites and cast me into the unknown. My mother called it the "*otherness.*" How stupid can you get? I mean, people and places look pretty much the same the world over. All that changes is whether you feel like you're in the right place or not.

My car drove through the gate and stopped, spewing smoke, in front of the garage door, which was just barely wide enough for it. The building was both small and broad, surrounded by front and back gardens, in turn enclosed by four rows of hedges that really needed clipping. There was a cherry tree at the front, a shaggy rosebush at the back. When I was little, I used to come and pick the still-green cherries, before any other kids thought about it. The owners, an elderly couple who could barely walk, would watch as I gobbled up handfuls of the inedible fruit, shaking their heads. I don't believe we ever spoke.

I'd bought the house from their heirs.

Ben marked his territory, then set out after a cat, barking at the top of his lungs. I took the boxes from the trunk of my car. Its rear fins made closing the garage door impossible. My toys had become too big.

The refrigerator in the kitchen was full. As was the cubby hole under the stairs. Obviously, my mother had gotten here before me and prepared everything. The notary must have given her the keys. Through the open window, I listened to Ben having the time of his life. There's really no way to shut up a dog. You can always beat him or, if you have to, muzzle him, but the animal is impervious to reason. It acts on impulse. I felt like my dog. Ever since I acquired the beast, he howled for me.

I shared my steak with Ben, then I searched through the cupboards. Hand-labeled boxes were lined up on the shelves like tin soldiers. My mother had always loved organizing. The stacks of bed sheets looked just like those we'd used when I was a kid. There were even some in lavender.

I really did have to go through my things. I didn't have space for everything.

That morning, I emptied the garage so I could park my car there. The gardening tools were hanging from a rack against the back wall. The electric lawn mower started on the first try. The grass cuttings were in the compost bin and the rose bush had been pruned.

Ben went off to explore the neighborhood, then came back to sleep at the foot of the farthest hedge after barking a bit, with no real conviction. I hoped he'd enjoy living here. I didn't have the strength to leave any time soon.

The cut roses were stuck in vases, scattered throughout the house. Ben's water dish was full. I'd bought him a new doghouse and he'd ensconced himself in it like in a coffin. It looked like one of those dollhouses my mother used to collect. She never let me touch them. Before I fled from her house, I'd broken them all. I suppose she must have bought more since then.

The photos I didn't want were burning in the fireplace. My memories left an impalpable taste of ash in my mouth. The day had raced past. For the first time in months, I felt able to sleep through the night.

On Sundays, I kept Ben inside until I was up. A neighbor had politely informed me that Sunday was the day the children sleep late—the rest of the week, they had to get up for school, so barking didn't bother them. As he said this, his voice was as smooth and thick as pudding. His wife waved to me from the kitchen, a freshly washed rag in hand. Her fingers, twisted by arthritis, were red from washing the dishes. I forced myself to smile at them. Some reflexes were hard to forget.

Occasionally, I ran across their kids on the way home from school. With their multi-colored backpacks, they looked like a collection of beetles.

I reheated last night's coffee over the gas, just as my mother used to do, and I went out in the garden, cup in hand. The rose bush had revived and two or three buds were about to bloom. Their scent was almost imperceptible. The odor of the coffee covered everything.

The week before, I had felt like taking the car out for a drive. I opened the garage doors wide, Ben on my heels. The chrome monster rested wisely in front of the tool rack. But, the urge to speed through the streets faded. Where would I go? How? The only people I had to visit were my parents, and they lived a few feet away from home.

I'm sure Ben was pissed off at me. I heard him less and less afterward.

Finally, I threw out the roses I had picked. They had lasted incredibly long. I put an aspirin and some sugar in the water, as I had been taught. But I was tired of looking at them, stooping over the waxed wooden table, each petal properly folded. I rinsed the vase and put it away. I'd cut some more soon.

But first, I had to collect the dead branches. And mow the grass. I'd take care of the hedge the following Sunday.

The kids next door played a trick on me. Well, I supposed it was them. I didn't have any other suspects and, in any event, they looked so neat and clean that they must come up with pranks just to let off steam. I remembered how much I hated my mother washing my face just before I headed off to school. My cheeks would be shiny red from her scrubbing, like an apple ready to be eaten. I would see my face in the immaculate formica of the kitchen and I felt like spreading crumbs everywhere.

So, it must have been the kids. When I went to cut some flowers to refresh the weekly bouquet, I discovered that part of the rosebush was plastic. A rather good imitation at that. No scent, but the colors were convincing. Yet the thorns were rubbery, harmless. The pruning shears cut them—no problem. There were only three or four. Just enough to fill a vase. I still put in a little sugar in the water, as usual.

More and more people greeted me in the streets as I walked Ben. I had learned to paste a smile on my face when I went out. It was like combing one's hair. We always took the same route and met the same passers-by. A sort of intimacy was being created. Human contact was just one of the things I thought I had abandoned, left behind, like irony. I wouldn't have long to wait before someone asked me for news. I guessed I'd have to prepare an answer or two, so I wouldn't come up empty.

Ben had stopped chasing after cats. When we came across a baby carriage, he patiently sat, tongue dangling, while I admired the bundled infant with its porcelain eyes. The phrases that rose to my lips were a perfect complement to the dog's posture.

I wanted to stop thinking about her and I believed that my wish had been answered. There was so much to be done in the house that the days slipped through my fingers like mercury. It took me an entire morning to trim the rose bush. I now had enough artificial flowers to decorate all of the rooms.

When I went back inside, I was surprised by my reflection in the refrigerator door. From all the smiling I had to do, my lips had taken on a regular shape. I tripped over Ben as I stepped back. He whined indignantly.

It was Wednesday. I had to remember to refill his water dish.

It was incredible what one could do with a sponge. Depending on whether it was soaked or just damp, one could get a different shine on every surface. There were countless nuances that could be achieved. I tried this with the table, the silver platter, the inside of the vegetable bin. One had to press really hard at first, with a regular movement, then wipe again—gently—to remove the excess moisture. I had become accustomed to seeing my reflection as I cleaned. It smiled up at me as if it knew something I didn't. But I didn't have time for details. The first swipe with the sponge made it appear. The second erased it.

When I went out for my evening walk, I left a welcoming house behind me. One that felt good to come home to.

"I'm so relieved," the neighbor woman confided to me. "Just the other evening, I was telling your mother..."

She stopped, shook her head, her gnarled hands tugging nervously at the seam of her Sunday dress. She must have known that I didn't like discussing my parents. At least, not in public. This was the kind of conversation that required a dining table, place mats and coffee served in antique cups.

"In any case," she courageously continued, "you were right to come back. Your place is here. There's no doubt about that."

I didn't know what came over me, but I replied, "Was it your boys who messed with my roses?"

She stood there, petrified, mouth flapping like a fish out of water. Then she took a step back, stepping on Ben's tail and I had to catch her by the elbow to keep her from tipping over.

"Give my regards to your husband," I said, reassuringly. "You'll both have to come over for a drink one of these days."

"Soon," she said, before making her escape. "As soon as..."

Back home, I felt like taking the car out for an aimless drive, but I no longer recalled where I'd put the key.

Ben sulked in the corner of his dog house. I had to bend down in front of the opening and reach in to grab his collar. In the daylight, his head, eyes wide open, doddled back and forth with the slightest movement. I still talked to him—a little less, it's true, than I used to—but he no longer barked in response. That was less serious that it seemed since I had finally managed to develop some contacts with my neighbors. These entailed an enormous number of *Good mornings* and *Good evenings* and endless comments about the weather, present or future. It's hard to believe how varied opinions were in that respect. People might think that the weather is the same for all of us. But, no, each of us sees an infinite variety of nuances. That all added up to a lot of talking.

Ben allowed himself to be dragged along the street gutters. There were other dogs like him around, silent, brave beasts that followed a regular groove in the footsteps of their master. They waited at the schoolyard gates, where bunches of children soon streamed out. I had no problem knowing who was who, thanks to the names written in large letters on their backpacks.

We exchanged looks as we passed. Occasionally, one of them dared to give Ben a pat, and the dog nodded his head in return. I remembered being like them and they knew they would become like me.

I had sent out the first invitations. The couple next door came with their youngest boy. We sent him out to play in the yard with his white ball. The husband accepted a beer and sank into the worn leather armchair, in front of the fireplace. His wife installed one buttock then the other on her chair. I served coffee in the china with the blue and gold trim, the set with the matching sugar bowl.

To keep Ben out of the way, I left him in the kitchen, on the worktable. He lowered his head and I resisted the impulse to scratch him behind his head in order to not set him off again.

"I've heard your son does well in school?" The bouncing of the ball in the yard was muffled by the drapes.

"He's a good boy. Your roses are lovely."

"I'll give you some. They last a long time and I have more than I need."

"It's important to have flowers in the house. You mother was telling me that…"

The glance they cast in my direction was a little concerned, but I settled for nodding as I held out a plate of cookies for them.

"I'll reheat the coffee. Have some cookies."

I took the coffeepot to the kitchen. The door to the living room was still half-open, but no sound filtered through. I knew I'd find my visitors exactly where I'd left them. They knew how to stay put. I removed the pruning shears from the drawer and placed them on the table, so I wouldn't forget to cut the roses after they left. They grew in all kinds of colors, now, and their thorns only made them more beautiful. I didn't even have to put water in the vases.

I lit a match and slipped it under the thick-bottomed pot. It went out immediately. *The propane tank must be almost empty*, I thought. I turned the knob on the burner to full and lit another match. This time, the flame ignited, enveloping my fingers.

I must have cried out, of course, since one of the neighbors found me in the kitchen, head hanging, watching my fingers melt. Flesh-colored drops dripped from my fingertips and, mechanically, I collected them in the palm of my hand.

First, my neighbor removed the pot where the coffee was boiling and spluttering, then she turned off the

81

gas stove. She moistened a corner of the washcloth and held it out to me.

"Hurry up and reshape your fingers. They get wrinkled when they're cold," she said, twisting her gnarled hands, pitted with too many domestic accidents. "Do you want me to help you? I've had practice."

I shook my head as I stretched my palms out to her, just as I did when, as a child, I had burned myself.

"What do I do?"

"You're useless. Just like my husband."

She looked at me, frowning, "It's a bit of a surprise the first time, but you get used to it. Your mother warned me that it would take you some time to adjust."

My re-built fingers looked as if they were stiff with arthritis, like my father's. I shook them and blew on them.

"It's much more convenient. You'll see. Especially when you have babies. There's less bother and it's ever so sweet. I used to play with mine for hours."

She looked so pleased to be talking about intimate matters that I didn't dare interrupt her. I rubbed my hands, absently, to make them smoother.

"And that's not all," she said, undoing her blouse. "You can remodel whatever you want."

Her breasts had disappeared, replaced by simple, barely visible swellings. Her skin was slightly lighter where her bra should have been.

"Everything else as well."

She buttoned up, eyes downcast. "No more dirtiness. My man was against it, at the beginning, but..."

I shook my head and she smiled, without insisting.

"I'll make some more coffee," she said grasping my arm. "I like to be handy in the kitchen. You go and sit down in the living room. My husband will be glad that we can really talk, now."

My face was reflected in the bottom of the pot, in the dark mirror of the barely cooled liquid, doll-like eyes wide open, flabbergasted. I grabbed Ben, who settled for whining when I pressed his belly as hard as I could. The neighbor watches as I approached, unblinking. We will no longer need to say anything at all, but we will still chat. Time in our dollhouse village wouldn't pass otherwise.

Before sitting down, I placed Ben on the mantel over the fireplace and watched him nod, answering the question I will never ask him again.

"I've come home," I murmured.

Birds

"Men fear the future, but it's the past that kills them..."

As the door folded open, the stranger's words still echoed in the sun-drenched bus. He let them scatter like a handful of loose change before the driver let him out. A cloud of dust enveloped him as he headed for the hills along the lonely dirt road. A worn leather suitcase was clasped to his chest. A black hat bobbed atop his bald head, looking as if it had been punched into shape. It was noon and he had no shadow to speak of.

The bus belched a cloud of greasy smoke and clattered off. Later, the travelers wouldn't remember the man or his words, just the stop in the middle of nowhere.

The road stretched east. The ancient ruts were filled with dust. Tufts of yellowish grass rose up through the pebbles. The village remained out of sight for almost the entire walk, but the man counted his steps, just as he measured everything, and he knew exactly when he would arrive. The insects left him be, while the lizards watch him from afar.

As he walked, cloaked in dust, he observed the arching jumps of the grasshoppers and the hectic calligraphy of the birds pinning them to the ground before devouring them. Everything was a symbol. Everything was a sign.

The remnants of a bridge stood at the end of the road. The metal crowns of the piles had not prevented the wood, spiked with rusted nails, from splitting deeply. The deck was long gone. The bolt holes, stippled with yellow and orange lichen, outlined a vanished roadway wavering in the burning air like some unattainable mirage.

Two rows of evergreens, each one odd-numbered, lined the shore. Three on one side, seven on the other. The traveler inspected those he planted himself and shook his head. In the midst of the close-knit and impeccably straight trunks, without a single fork for a nest, a young elm stripling struggled to reach the light. There was something touching about the tender green twigs speckled with shadow. It would have to be uprooted and transplanted elsewhere if it were to have any chance at all of growing.

The traveler whispered a promise into the folded cup of a leaf.

On the other side of the arroyo lay the village. To reach it, all those who came had to climb down into the almost dry riverbed and walk across the stones. A thin thread of water wound its way through muddy puddles, as deep as tombs. The man studied them, then looked up. The blank walls of houses crammed side-by-side blocked the horizon. When the bridge had collapsed, the villagers had collected the wooden beams and burned then. Next, they had walled up the windows that looked onto the river. The dark portico that opened onto the village square was choked with brambles.

The bridge had not been carried off by some torrential flood or other spectacular catastrophe. Twenty years earlier, there had been a war waged in the North. The men had set out in trucks bedecked with flags, which became all too quickly covered with dust. The road carried back news, increasingly unfortunate. Those who left had never returned.

Neglected, the bridge had finally collapsed one morning as the bus approached.

Crossing the river, climbing the bank, grabbing onto the bushes to pull himself up, pushing the brambles aside... the traveler did all this without the slightest change in his grim expression. Inside the brick tunnel that led to the square, his steps echoed like the tock, tock, tock of a metronome. The sounds were strangely amplified under the vault and the traveler walked through swarming ghosts that vanished with the coming of light. The sensation of coolness lasted no more than a second.

On the other side, daylight. Implacable.

Dusty arcades surrounded the square. A rusty hotel sign dangled from the end of a pole in one corner. The carcass of a burned house filled the opposite corner. Eyes watched, hidden behind closed shutters. Chains creaked as they swayed. The plaster facades were crackled like old china.

The fire had marred the dreams of those who witnessed it. An abscessed mind heals poorly. The houses had not been rebuilt; the trucks carrying building supplies could no longer cross the river. Those who worked in the fields were too weary to look up once their day was done. And those who knitted in the shadows never spoke of what they felt and seldom of what they had seen. The charred carcass had become just another element in the decor, a perch for nightmares.

The traveler walked on, counting his steps, and stopped before the first chalk line. An immense hopscotch court, drawn with painstaking care, filled the entire square. An incomplete one, opening onto infinity. At one end, the home square was missing, as if the work had been interrupted. Its maker had to go in for dinner, perhaps. Or, some household chore simply could not wait. Almost all of the signs were there. Above the court, the air vibrated impatiently.

A flat, round pebble, polished by the water in the stream, lay in the first square, trapping the Sun's rays. The man kneeled on one knee and picked it up. The stone was gray, speckled with flakes of mica, curiously cool to the touch. He turned it over carefully in his fingers, then slipped it into his breast pocket without seeming to give it a second thought. When he stood up, slowly, he felt the weight of those who were watching him, yet said nothing, on the back of his neck.

Determined, he headed for the hotel.

In the past, the bus had stopped at the entrance to the village—a rusted signpost could still be seen there. Today, the hotel lounge was deserted. An ageless woman placed mismatched plates on the tables, dusting as she went along.

"I'd like a room," the man said as he stepped through the threshold.

The tired face of the waitress lit up with curiosity. "Where have you come from? There hasn't been a hotel here in years."

The newly-arrived guest glanced at the counter, graced with a register and an enormous brass bell, then at the poster next to the staircase. He took in his surroundings leisurely, patiently, as if wanting to absorb the decor, all the better to forget it later. From a wooden perch, a bird of prey, stuffed and moth-eaten, stared fixedly at the visitor. A second perch, this one empty, waited next to it.

"We've kept everything as it was," murmured the woman. "Even the sign. It would have been far too much work to take it down."

"I've been here before."

Incredulous, the woman stared at him, then shook her head.

"Liar!"

"Well now, you've forgotten me, have you?"

He raised his hat and the features of his face re-formed much as whirlpools do around an obstacle. "I gave one of my best performances in this very room."

"I'll call the boss."

The shrill clang of the bell provoked a flurry of activity upstairs. A footstep on the stairway. A female silhouette bent over the railing.

"Someone wants a room, Madame Clara."

"Don't be stupid."

The woman walked down the stairs, then stopped, her hand on her hip.

"We're closed!"

The traveler bowed, hat held close to his breast. The woman inhaled. Her mouth tightened into a hard line that aged her instantly. Yet, she couldn't be more than 30, and she was still obviously beautiful, despite the invisible layers of sand deposited by the wind of time.

"I'll take care of him," she murmured. "Anna, bring sheets from the chest in the cellar. I'll tell you where to make up the bed."

The shell of indifference that covered the village was cracking. To her surprise, Anna found herself humming as she set the table in the common room. The boss had closeted herself in her room and the traveler has left his suitcase behind the bar before going back out. To do what? The waitress had no idea. In any case, the men would return from the fields soon and find him here. That was enough to create a space for possibilities that went beyond the village's limits and extended as far as Anna's limited imagination would allow. It was as if the wind were rising outside. She would give anything to sit down and watch the remainder of the scene play out.

"Did you take my pebble?"

The child was so tiny that he stood on tiptoe to question the stranger. He had been living below the horizon of adult gazes for so long that he had forgotten how to catch their attention. Most likely, he never knew how. The only person who noticed him without fail was his mother and he had guessed that the man was not of her kind.

"Perhaps."

A strange smile tugged at the corners of the visitor's lips, gradually invading his entire face. "Do you want to see a magic trick?"

"What's that?"

"Something almost as good as a pebble. Watch this…"

The man lifted his battered hat and unfolded it with his fingertips, pulling on the felt brim. It made a "plop" that was audible at the other end of the square. When he placed the hat back on his shiny skull, it almost covered his entire head. The child laughed politely. Smothered twitters burst out as the stranger spun around, arms raised. He stopped, then abruptly took the hat off.

Perched on his head, a dove with clipped wings puffed itself up as it observed its surroundings. Its feathers were the color of dust. It hopped up and down on the Magician's naked head until he nimbly scooped it back into the hat.

Though eyes still rang the square, the child alone applauded. A shutter banged. An emaciated hand slammed it against its partner and locked them shut.

"Now it's your turn…"

The hat swallowed up the child. When the magician removed it, ceremoniously pulling it off, he left behind a tiny lark that trilled skyward before flying off.

"It was you," the child said. "You took my pebble. But it doesn't matter. I'll find another when I want to."

The bird circled above them before flying off into the Sun. The magician looked after it until the light forced him to look away.

"You don't need it anymore…"

Later, the magician asked to be served dinner in his room. The iron-wrought bed was covered with a clean sheet, roughened from too much washing. An enamel basin, half-filled with water, had been placed under the window. The clicking of a meal taken together in the large room rose through the uneven boards in the floor. Metal against earthenware, glass against wood. The hubbub of beaks pecking.

He waited for the door to open before breaking bread and sprinkling a little salt around him.

"Is everything fine?"

"Good evening, Clara…"

The grains of salt formed a Milky Way on the floor before disappearing in the cracks, swept away by the hem of the young woman's dress.

"I never thought I'd see you again."

The veil of illusion that the visitor had woven around himself vanished. He removed his hat, kneading it into the shape of a crow. Clara's face froze. Slowly, she closed the door behind her and moved toward him.

"You've come to stir up the dust?" she murmured.

"Against my will."

He stood up and moved over to the window, stained blood red by the setting Sun. "I was almost too late. The hopscotch court is almost done. You should have kept an eye on your son."

"He's only a child!"

"He'll be seven tomorrow. At that age, drawings can encircle the world. If he'd completed the hopscotch court, he would have carried the village away with him."

"I tried to stop him."

"You did nothing of the kind. I warned you, three times, and you only listened to me with half an ear."

His cloak billowed about him, and then he shrugged. "These are human matters…"

"I won't let you take him from me," she grumbled. The salt border prevented her from reaching him. He opened the shutters and threw the crow out the window, as if getting rid of some unpleasant memory, but the bird returned to perch on top of his head.

"I didn't come to steal him." He shook his head and gently closed the wooden shutters on the advancing night, then headed to the door. "I came to help him leave."

Later, they walked around the square, side by side, plunged in a conversation that shielded them from the watching eyes. The outline of the hopscotch court shimmered in the shadow, as long as one knew where to look. Overhead, the lark circled tirelessly among stars so old that they no longer worried about being wise.

"I should never have called you, before," murmured Clara.

She shivered in the wind from the hills. They both turned away from the sleeping hotel and faced the charred carcass of the old house.

"The village would be dead if you hadn't... The war... The fallow fields... Oblivion..." The magician appeared unable to complete his sentences.

"What do I care about the village!" She lowered her voice. "My house burned down and I have no one left to rebuild it. I raised a son so that one day..."

"A son you stole."

"I took what I was offered. Men throw things away. Women pick them up!"

"The man you made the child with was not from the village. Or am I mistaken?"

Her response was inaudible, drowned by the creaking of shutters and the whistle of wind blowing through tiles. In the middle of the square, the air trapped by the walls was motionless. A few lonely gusts threaded their way through the blackened remnants of the walls and the scorched beams of the torched house, drying the eyes of those who didn't take care and making their hair as brittle as glass.

"You ordered me to restore the balance," continued the magician. "So I took as many birds as I needed to replace the men who had left. I forced them to take on human form so they could marry the widows and work the land instead of merely flying about overhead. That was your wish. Have they done their job?"

"Your birds... Ha!"

She shrugged. "They were all there this evening, banging their beaks against their perches, too tired to speak. Taciturn, sterile shadows. They've never desired me."

"Magicians can't create desire. You need a soul for that."

The traveler took the pebble from his pocket and looked at it in the starlight. In his hand, it appeared drab and heavy.

"You should have warned me," complained Clara. "The other women have become resigned. They dress in black like crows and never leave their cages. Wherever I go, I feel the weight of their eyes on me. My son grew up alone. You're right about his father. He arrived on the bus one day at noon. I've forgotten his name. He sold jewelry from a suitcase. He slept at the hotel. With me. That was almost eight years ago. Will everyone always be criticizing me for that little adventure?"

"You alone think about it."

The shutters creaked a final time and the wind died. In one of the rooms a child pretended to sleep. Hands clenched under the sheets as he had been taught to do, he contemplated the impassible ceiling and wondered what it would be like to fly.

"He'll be seven tomorrow," said the magician. "It can't be put off any longer."

The next morning was drenched in sun. Clara got up early. She swept the common room, listening. Soon, there would be footsteps on the staircase. Words spoken during the night were as heavy as dreams and she found herself unable to shake them off.

When the stranger came downstairs, the child was with him. He was wearing his best clothes, pockets swollen with sundry treasures.

"We're going to play at taking a trip," he said "That's what he told me!."

"No, not this morning," answered Clara. "I need you."

"But, Mommy…"

"I said no! And as for you…"

The magician lifted the child up and set him on the counter, on top of the dusty register in which the name of a passing traveler had been carefully inked over in black.

"What if you were to come with us, Clara?" he murmured.

"And where would I go? There's no one waiting for me anywhere."

"This world is immense. What you think of yourself will be diluted in the thoughts of others. You have never been accepted here."

"They may not have accepted me, but they do see me. Elsewhere, I'll be nobody."

The magician nodded his understanding. He reached out to pluck the child from his perch, but the boy quickly grabbed the shapeless hat and placed it on his mother's head.

"A magic trick, Mommy!"

Time stood still. Clara, the top of her head swallowed up by the hat, cried out in surprise. The felt brim rested just above her carefully plucked eyebrows, and her pale blue eyes glanced first at her son and then at the magician. Slowly, almost reverently, the magician removed his hat from her head. Nesting in the hollow of her hair, a tiny bird, as impossible to trap as a humming bird, clumsily spread its wings and flung itself toward the ceiling.

The tiny bird flew into one wall after another, striking the windows with pitiful sounds, almost killing itself. When its wings could no longer carry it, it returned to nest in Clara's hair, before setting back out to search for the sky. The child clapped his hands to encourage it. Minutes passed, marked by soft thumps and the scratching of the bird's beak against glass. Then the magician swept the humming bird up in his hat, making it disappear, before helping the child down from the counter.

"Let's go out," he said, taking Clara's arm. "Soon, it will be too hot to walk."

The square seemed to have shrunk during the night. The hopscotch court had almost been erased. The black silhouette of the torched house had collapsed in on itself. Overhead, an invisible lark serenaded the Sun.

"Will you come to see me off?"

Clara tightened her grip on her son, but the magician shook his head.

"He'll leave later, when he decides to." The shadow of a smile tugged at his lips. "And you'll accompany him. There was no need for me to come back, after all."

"Once again, you've decided for me?"

Without answering, he took the pebble from his pocket and threw it into the air, so high that it seemed as if it would never fall back, then he caught it in the hollow of his cupped hand.

"Cross my heart," he said, holding the pebble out to the child. "Are you coming?"

He guided them to the tunnel that led outside, helped them to cross the arroyo, using the submerged stones. There wasn't enough water to skip stones on. The frogs sang a deafening song.

"You can play here whenever you want to," he promised the child. "That's my birthday gift to you, now that you're old enough to enjoy it."

"Is that so, Mommy?"

Clara nodded, her throat tight. They had arrived at the clump of trees near the ruined bridge. The road stretched ahead toward the open horizon. It may be rutted and dusty, but it went on forever.

"It's time for us to part, little man," he said, turning his back to the blind walls of the village. "But, before we do, I'd like you to choose a walking stick for me. Will you do that?"

The child headed straight as an arrow for the closest group of evergreens, setting off tiny avalanches of pebbles.

"I thought you were going to take him with you," murmured Clara. "I was prepared to follow you to the end of the world!"

He shrugged, his hat balanced cockily to one side of his head.

"I'm not cruel, Clara. I just keep an eye on my cages. I thought the inside of yours would be enough for you. I was wrong. You stayed for your son, but you want the sky too much. One day, you will leave."

"How can you know?"

"The empty perch in the large room. It was waiting for you. Your bird never chose to set down there."

The boy ran back to them, brandishing the elm stripling. The clump of dirt imprisoning the roots broke apart with each step. He handed it to the magician, who took it in his large hand.

"An excellent walking stick! I'll plant it far from here when I've finished with it. But I think it will be with me for quite some time."

In the distance, a bus honked its horn. The wind whispered secrets into the ears of those who wish to hear them.

"What is your own bird like?" Clara asked suddenly, looking the magician straight in the eye.

"Grey. Silent. Flightless."

The next moment, he set out on the road, refusing to turn back to see if they watched as he left. The world of men was so vast when one traveled on foot. And the sky... Bah! The sky was a place where magic no longer worked. On days such as this one, he almost believed that he was satisfied with his fate. Even the lark that brushed against him playfully was unable to entice him away from his path.

Separations

"They're love stories, you know," the young man said. "They're all dead."

His hand played with a necklace circling his throat just above his collar. The golden stripes that officially proclaimed him an artist gleamed on either side of his Adam's apple, like the fingers of a strangler. The necklace looked dull by comparison. Dark gems unevenly faceted, threaded on a thin metal wire. Each time his index finger brushed them, they lit up briefly from within.

"It's all the rage on Old Earth," he continued, "wearing your former loves like a string of pearls—harvested from your mind once the pain is gone."

"Hunting trophies," murmured Captain Bascombe.

He stood upon the prow of his silvery craft, facing the cockpit viewport. This close to the Hartzfeld singularity, black space curved around them. The engines vibrated in neutral, while the maintenance equipment hummed its reassuring lullaby to the hundreds of passengers lying frozen in their hibernation pods. The artist and the captain were the only conscious humans on board.

"I keep them as tokens of failure," the young man said, looking away from the void. "Every stone is flawed—badly cut or marred by dark spots or clouds.

They help me come to each new conquest with a clean soul."

"I thought an artist was supposed to commit himself totally, that there's never any going back for you people"

"We make ourselves believe that. But perfect love is only some jeweler's fantasy!"

Bascombe turned around, fearing the artist would read on his face the memory of his own love, the one that had destroyed him so many years ago. When she had left, he had died to the world for the first time, his insides torn out, with nothing to blame but his own insensitivity. Contrapunt's childish insolence was a painful reminder that he, too, had once sliced through life like an icebreaker, indifferent to the shipwrecks he had left in his wake. Until the day he had become one.

The trip had yet to start, and between disdain for his passenger and loathing for himself, he was already on the verge of exploding.

In a few minutes, they would cross through the singularity together.

Bascombe detested him from their very first encounter, on Charandyne. A young stranger strode implacably toward his table in the spaceport bar. He looked successful, glamorous—artfully ragged hairstyle, inlays of neural implants protruding above his ears, eyes veiled with reflective membranes to hide his thoughts. Tights flecked with liquid gold hugged his androgynous silhouette, showing off ridiculously slim hips. He made Bascombe feel both very old and very wise, sensations he despised.

"You're going through the Hartzfeld gate. I'd like to come with you." The young man's voice matched his appearance, dripping with nuance.

"I still have a few empty pods. The company will rent you one, no problem, health permitting."

"I'm in perfect health, Captain. But I don't want to sleep through the voyage—I insist on being conscious during the transit."

"Company policy—"

"Doesn't apply to me," said the artist, with a smile that could part a miser from his riches. "I have all the required permits, and the financial arrangements have already been settled with your employers."

"You've been informed of the risks, I presume?" Bascombe stared pointedly at the young man. "And I'm not talking about our onboard accident statistics—they've been deliberately falsified. The *Peregrine* is a good ship, totally predictable—at worst you might trip over a strut. I mean the real risks—the reason why you're asking the impossible."

"Can we discuss this?"

Bascombe growled vaguely, possibly in assent. Though the bar was packed, a ring of empty silence surrounded his table. The other patrons—stevedores, mechanics, warehouse and control tower workers—didn't have any concrete reason for ostracizing him, but kept their distance nonetheless. Bascombe had learned to accept this, as he had learned to order his drinks in threes to avoid waiting too long for service. Not that it mattered. The days when alcohol could grant him forgetfulness were long past.

The artist straddled the seat opposite Bascombe, arms crossed on the back of his chair. "I'm known as Derek Contrapunt. From Old Earth. Perhaps you've heard of me?"

Seeing Bascombe's expression, he laughed a little. "Sorry, it's a professional reflex. I'm a tridichoreographer, incredibly wealthy, totally unbearable, and over-whelmingly talented. Not necessarily in that order. And I think you're starting to hate me, aren't you?"

"You're going a bit too fast for me there," Bascombe replied after a pause. "I don't even know what a tridichoreographer is."

"Someone who leads the dance."

Contrapunt stretched with affected grace. "I create zero-gravity ballets that are broadcast in planetary orbits throughout all the inhabited systems—nearly all. If you were on Old Earth right now, you'd have only to look up to see my firefly-dancers. Thousands of them are constantly zipping around, with photoluminescent tails hundreds of klicks long.

"It's a useless art, Captain. No one knows that better than I. Once I thought I could give it meaning, and the public encouraged me in that illusion. But a few months ago, I went out on my terrace, after a party. Bodies were strewn every which way. I had to step on a few of them before I found a quiet place to piss. I stood there and watched my star dancers crisscross the sky. You know how lucid you feel as you empty your bladder. Nothing was happening up there—no signal, just noise. Believe me, I can recognize a lousy ballet when I see one. These last few years, I've lost my way."

"So you decided to quit?"

"You don't understand people like me—no, I decided to start all over again! The work would be stronger, more resonant—more *absolute*."

Bascombe nodded. "What you need, my friend, is a bartender. No one else listens to confessions at this time of night."

"You're the one I need, Captain. Or rather, your ship's Intelligences. I'd like them to dance for me."

That's when things really got out of hand.

It took two hours to extract the details from Contrapunt. Bascombe was surprised by his own persistence. The captain quickly realized that the artist's reluctance to talk was not due to bad faith, at least not consciously. In fact, Contrapunt knew almost nothing.

"A friend of a friend of a friend told me, after swearing me to secrecy, about a rumor that originated right here, in the Charandyne system. You and your ship were mentioned by name."

"And?"

"I can read between the lines, Captain."

In front of Contrapunt, half a dozen bubble-glasses with frosted edges were thawing, their contents long since consumed.

"Something happened during one of your trips—only you know exactly what. Yet you stay with the *Peregrine*—you keep shuttling through the singularity, between Charandyne and the Eden system, even though with your service record, you could have escaped from this dump ages ago. And..."

Bascombe looked at Contrapunt quizzically.

"No one comes near you unless it's necessary. I must be the first person to share your table in quite a few years. That's true, isn't it? I can feel it in my bones. Everyone who walks through this bar tiptoes around you, as if you were an especially dangerous black hole. I've had dancers like you. They upset the entire ballet just by being there."

"So you fired them?"

"I learned how to use them. What others might consider defects, I regard as raw materials for my art."

On the flat stone table, the glass bubbles exploded, one after another, with a crystalline tinkling. Contrapunt traced a series of intersecting trajectories on the glittering layer of dust with his fingernail.

"Your ship's AIs have learned to dance," he declared suddenly. "This is just the kind of anomaly I've been searching for. An inhuman art, something dangerously new. I certainly know that traveling on the *Peregrine* is risky, but I won't let that bother me. All I want to do is observe, if you'll let me come with you. Screw the AIs, they won't give a damn anyway. I've duplicated plenty, and used up thousands in my shows. I know how to manage them." He smiled. "You're sure you don't want anything to drink?"

"Not with you. Sorry."

Bascombe stood up heavily. Around them, the hubbub of conversations had faded. The next shift of drinkers was gathering at the magnetic pool table with its endlessly clinking balls. The overhead lights had acquired the pale glow of morning on the station.

"You asked if I hated you," Bascombe said over his shoulder. "My answer is—I hate you enough. Be on board at 03:00 Standard Time the day after tomorrow. Meanwhile, go get drunk in some other bar!"

Passenger cryogenization on Charandyne occurred in a hospital building buried beneath the landing strips, with only the loader extending above the surface. The process was slow and painstaking. The naked bodies, their essential fluids altered by polymer injections, were enveloped within vacuum-bubble pods where the temperature was gradually reduced until it reached the proper stasis point. The safety equipment involved occupied a great deal of space and consumed huge amounts of energy. Once frozen, the individual pods, now solid sarcophagi, could be disconnected from the hospital cooling complex and stacked like ice cubes in the *Peregrine*'s hold.

The evening before departure, Bascombe typically went to the transit hospital to observe the preparations. He would walk through the safety airlock, inhabited by disembodied Intelligences, greet the medical monitoring crew from a distance, then slip between the pods, which were arranged in a star formation around the superconducting cooler.

A cryogenization room was filled with murmurs. A bouquet of colorful conduits sprang up in the center, rooted to the power source beneath the floor. At the tip of each stem, a sarcophagus blossomed like a flower made of porcelain and palest silver, surmounted by a fog of helium-2 crystals that were slowly being dispersed by the ventilation fans.

The sleepers were as close to death as could possibly be imagined. They were absent, locked in the Snow Queen's Palace, as a staff doctor had so wryly put it. On one of the pods, an anonymous hand had stuck a photo. On another was a child's drawing, signed in clumsy letters. Bascombe never forgot that those who slept here were still dreaming in slow motion. In the dark, in the cold.

At the far end of the room he spotted Contrapunt with his face pressed against the inspection port of a pod. The artist waved, but did not appear to want company. After he left, Bascombe walked over to the pod Contrapunt had been examining. Perhaps someone in the human cargo was Contrapunt's secret reason for taking passage tomorrow.

The pod was empty.

Then Bascombe realized that Contrapunt had trailed him here, deliberately following in his footsteps. Using his skill as a choreographer, he was trying to appropriate Bascombe's personal dance, the better to manipulate him.

The man was a thief, like all artists, and Bascombe almost felt sorry for him.

Soon, he would be given that which he so desperately wanted to steal.

"We'll have a passenger," Bascombe said aloud as he entered the heart of the *Peregrine*.

There was no response. There never was. The ship's Intelligences were unable to speak. All they had was a library of ready-made phrases—a combination of security directives, informative announcements, and alerts. Yet Bascombe knew they were listening, all their sensors focused on him at this very moment. They fluttered around him like the caresses of invisible angels. Despite the fact that Contrapunt's arrival meant nothing to the AIs, it was essential to notify them. Where this ship was going, manners and decorum were as important as anything else.

A short while later, as he was making log entries on the terminal in his cabin, a discreet alarm warned him about an attempt to trespass. A minute earlier, he had heard the airlock hiss. Idle, the *Peregrine* was almost silent. Deprived of the high-pitched melody of its engines and the breathing of its protective membrane, the vessel communicated only through occasional creaks, echoed by Bascombe's own. Whenever he stretched, he liked to feel that the ship was singing a duet with him— two aging yet still solid carcasses ferrying their cargo of frozen memories from one bank to another across the river of the dead.

"Come down to Deck B," he ordered, switching on the com system. "My cabin is the only one with the lights on."

He shut down the terminal and swiveled his chair to face the door. Outside, the visitor's footsteps hesitated. Bascombe pictured him trying to decipher the backlit glass plaques inlaid in the gangway. The *Peregrine* had been everywhere. It was a unique craft, as unique as the Hartzfeld singularity. Every other singularity explored so far by unmanned probes led nowhere. The universe was full of dead ends.

Contrapunt stuck his head through the half-open door, grimacing. "I'd planned on being slightly more circumspect. Am I disturbing you?"

"Inevitably. I've checked your credentials. Your privileged passenger status permits you to go anywhere you please on my ship. Including my cabin."

The young man slid inside, as fluid as a mercury sled, then stopped opposite the com block that filled most of a wall. A series of cheap holograms hung above the black screen, motionless and flat, their power source dead. All of them depicted the same woman's face, her lips frozen in the first stirrings of a kiss.

"You look a little bit like her, you know?" observed Bascombe. "Her mouth, her aura of transgression. However," Bascombe wrinkled his nose theatrically, "her perfume was a universe unto itself. Unlike yours."

"Is this where they dance?"

"Who? The Intelligences?"

"Perhaps we don't need to make this journey together," the artist said, turning away from the holos. "You don't want to any more than I do. Look." He reached into his pocket, and, withdrawing his hand, threw a pinch of dark granules into the air, where they whirled before landing on the captain's head.

"I picked up some space dust in the hold, as a souvenir. Just ask your AIs to dance, here and now. I'll leave immediately afterward. I won't even ask for a refund on my ticket, if you insist. Then we'll both save some time, all right?"

"You are entitled to a complete tour of the *Peregrine*," Bascombe announced, rising from his chair. "To my full attention every time you open your mouth, to three meals a day from the galley, and, may God forgive me, to the reserves of patience I've been storing up for my old age. The rest," he said, opening his door all the way, "is not within my power."

"She must have been splendid," Contrapunt murmured in the doorway. "Not unforgettable, since you need something to remember her by, but beautiful, at the very least. She was the one who left?"

"The last time, yes. But I abandoned her each time I made a voyage, imbecile that I was. And you, do you change partners for each new dance?"

Bascombe knew he had scored a hit. Beneath the smooth mask of the artist's face, a network of cracks seemed to appear, and he saw a suffering that echoed his own.

Then Contrapunt blinked, recovering his impenetrable composure. "Naturally. Dancers can't stay in one place for long, and it's impossible to hold them, no matter how strong the desire. No need to come back with me. I'll see you at takeoff."

The sound of footsteps echoing down the deserted gangways was fading into silence when a voice, tinged with regret, suddenly came from the loudspeakers: "She isn't the one I resemble, Captain. Sorry to have bothered you."

Bascombe wiped fingerprints from the tarnished holograms, then collapsed onto his bunk and programmed a soporific injection. He woke as the loading procedures were starting. Contrapunt was waiting at the foot of the exterior catwalk, slumped against a worn leather bag covered by a constellation of decals. Behind him, the procession of sarcophagi marched slowly into the open hold.

As Contrapunt entered the airlock, Bascombe noticed the glint of gems around his neck and raised an inquisitive eyebrow. But the meticulous routines of takeoff chased the observation from his mind, until the ship was in open space at last.

"The singularity is ready to absorb us," the disembodied voice announced.

In the cockpit, Bascombe hunched his shoulders. On the radar screens, a sparkling ring indicated the border of the Hartzfeld gate. The ship headed straight for it. Nothing was visible to the naked eye, yet Bascombe knew that his energy scalpels were tucking up the fabric of space to give the *Peregrine* a gap to slip through.

"On our way to Paradise, are we?" asked Contrapunt, his voice filled with irony. He continued fingering his necklace of reified love stories like a rosary. It was obvious that he had slept little in the past two days. Behind the reflective membranes, his eyes were bloodshot.

"Nothing idyllic about Eden for the likes of you," Bascombe shot back. "It's a primitive world where the immigrants work too damn hard to stand around looking up at the sky."

"Insertion in sixteen minutes," interrupted the voice.

"This is the moment, isn't it?" said Contrapunt. "The lights dim, the curtain rises—what happens if the ship misses the gap? Something spectacular, at least? Can you feel the adrenaline racing through your veins? I'd like to be in your shoes right now."

"The AIs take care of the essentials. You should go back to your cabin and try to relax. This show isn't particularly interesting."

"Oh, no, no, Captain. I paid to watch, remember? I want to be here when the dance begins."

"Nothing happens until we emerge on the other side of the singularity," grumbled Bascombe. "You're distracting me, which is dangerous, and you're annoying me, though I'm sure you don't give a damn."

"Tell me..." Contrapunt lowered his voice to a whisper, pointlessly considering the acuity of the onboard sensors. "You've made some kind of arrangement with your shipbound slaves, haven't you? They dance for your eyes alone, in private, and you don't want to share your little secret. That's why you sent your crew away, isn't it?"

Alarms went off in Bascombe's head. Contrapunt turned sideways, displaying a profile enhanced by the best surgeons on Old Earth. Bascombe felt an overwhelming urge to pummel that perfection back into a more human shape.

"Why do you try so hard to make people despise you?" Bascombe asked quietly. "Not that I care, but we are traveling together, so we should try to reach some sort of détente by the end of the trip. And we're the only people aboard sufficiently awake to have souls—that will be important when the singularity swallows us. I suppose you realize that no one actually knows where we're going. The Eden system is much too far from the human zone to be detected by our instruments. The constellations are completely foreign, of course, and we can't identify any stars. We don't even know if Eden is within our local galactic group. Or in our universe, for that matter. It's just a place at the other end of a rift where humans can settle with a good chance of surviving. We colonized it because that's what we do. We just had to be willing to get lost."

"Are you lost, Captain?"

"The *Peregrine* knows the way back. And now, if you will excuse me, I have to interface with my slaves, as you like to call them."

He slid into the pilot's chair, which resembled a large white scallop shell, and inserted his wrists into the control sleeves. Contrapunt's words reached him sifted through a digital filter, muffled and broken. The pulsing lights of the sensors danced on his retinas like a cloud of moths. The scintillating entrance to the singularity was impossible to miss—plenty of room for the ship to pass through.

Prior to accelerating, he checked the hold one last time, making sure all the pods are operational. The passengers' brains were so slowed by the cold that not one of their thoughts would have time to make its way to consciousness. Bascombe envied them that oblivion, an option denied to him.

The *Peregrine* allowed itself be swallowed by the rift.

When Bascombe finally disconnected himself, the ship had been spit out several million kilometers from a G-type sun. Large numbers of other stars dotted the sky, a scattering of haphazard constellations. As the *Peregrine* turned away from the rift, it ejected a few streaks of residual radiation. In the silent ship, holograms of a reassuring green floated above the control panel. The solar system appeared in blue. There were five planets, including an outer gas giant and the inner world of Eden, orbiting a habitable distance from its sun.

The *Peregrine*'s path was displayed as an unbroken, ruby-red line trailing from the exit of the singularity and unrolling along an attenuated spiral stretching toward Eden. As Bascombe watched, another reddish line appeared, much paler than the first, also moving away from the singularity. Bascombe didn't need to study the second line to know it would continue to diverge from the original, eventually fading into deep space, toward the zone with the fewest stars. Despite the detachment he had forced himself to maintain during the passage, his palms were suddenly damp.

"I didn't see anything," Contrapunt grumbled as he slouched across the copilot's chair, legs hanging over the arm, one hand brushing against the metal deck like a pendulum.

Bascombe shrugged. "That's because there was nothing to see. Inside the singularity, there's no energy as we know it. Without energy, there's no light. No light, no show."

"There's always a show when I'm around." Contrapunt frowned, rubbing his temples. "During the passage, I tried connecting to the digital heart of the ship, but it didn't recognize my neural sockets."

He dismissed the captain's protest with a languid wave of the hand. "I know it's prohibited. But I also know that standard security measures wouldn't have stopped me for long. You were saved by your ancient equipment—my interfaces are too modern for your system. Stupid, eh? I travel this far based on a wild rumor, to see your AIs dance, and I get screwed by technology."

"The dance hasn't started yet," whispered Bascombe. He rechecked the information on the control panel. Two trajectories were still visible. And they were on the wrong one. *If only things would go faster, just this once.* But there was no one to hear his prayer.

Contrapunt sat up, and the necklace fell from his throat. Bascombe retrieved it with his fingertips. The gems feel icy as he held them out to Contrapunt.

"We'll have to wait for a bit." Bascombe managed to keep his voice steady. "Tell me about those loves from whom you so easily separated yourself. Is it agonizing, for the one who is left behind, to realize that she has been ripped away from you, that she now exists only for herself?"

"I don't know. I was always the one who ended the affair."

As before, it began with a sudden burst of static from the ship's com system. Bascombe tensed, but he knew that the Intelligences would warn him before the fateful moment came. They must already be preparing. If he had been alone, he would have spoken to them aloud, or through the ship's outmoded vocal interfaces. The AIs had never reproached him for the decisions he had made during that first transit through the singularity. They settled for dancing in a place where he could see them, thus making him part of their ballet.

"Why is it so dark?" complained Contrapunt, gesturing as if to chase away imaginary fireflies. The cockpit was getting dimmer by the minute. Above the panel with its embedded signal lights, the holographic displays were fading. Underfoot, the vibration of the engines had changed. The energy from the nozzles had been shunted to the vents of the lateral jets. The Intelligences had short-circuited the controls in the ionization chamber, reconfiguring them for their own use. Bascombe made no move to stop them. He had the codes to stop everything, to let the ship continue on its path, but he had no reason to do so—especially now.

"I have some good news and some bad news," Bascombe said, his voice heavy. "Soon the Intelligences will be dancing…"

He did not continue, for the dance had begun.

Eight beams in shades of mauve, deep purple, indigo, and amethyst leapt from the *Peregrine*, weaving a wreath around its prow. The ionized particles crisscrossed before the large viewport, just a few meters from the two humans, out where the void and the cold reigned supreme. The gulf between men and dancers was impassable—they were as isolated from each other as Eden was from Earth—separated by the mysteries of their own singularities.

Silhouettes took shape in the hearts of the beams. Asymmetrical, not human, yet filled with an awkward grace. Each Intelligence had her own base color, which she explored with all the hues the energy beams allowed. The static of the loudspeakers became increasingly broken, mingling with the lament of engines pushed to extremes. A nascent pulse started to beat.

Then the glowing phantoms moved in unison.

This was no formal ballet, but rather the individual dances of a group that lived and suffered as one. The beams fanned out, creating the appearance of depth. The sparkling particles had some uncanny life of their own, embodied for a moment in luminous cries before falling back into dust. The blackness of space pierced the intangible forms, leaving traces like coagulated blood.

The dance accelerated. The Intelligences spread fragile wings, which crumbled in the frigid vacuum. They touched each other occasionally, fleeting caresses filled with resignation. Veins the color of burning topaz throbbed to the rhythm of their movements, jerky at first, then strangely serene. When they turned toward the humans, the desire that drove them, the fierce will that caused them to exist, was palpable. Until they collapsed.

Sound poured from the loudspeakers with the haunting monotony of a heartbeat.

Little by little, shreds of darkness gathered around the ship. The clouds of energy shrank to form microcosms in which the AIs danced alone. They had neither faces nor fingers, yet they invented a language that Bascombe had never found hard to understand. The story they were living was also his own—on this trajectory.

Contrapunt stood up. He ground his necklace of former loves between his hands, unaware that the gems no longer glowed at his touch. Eyes half closed, he paced the cockpit, viewing the scene from different angles. Outside, the dance had attained a kind of equilibrium, and Bascombe knew that the colorful energy beams would soon be exhausted. Already, the darkness in the cockpit enveloped them like a shroud.

"I've never seen anything like it," Contrapunt declared, a hint of respect in his voice. "How do your AIs manipulate those beams? Could we recreate this onstage?"

"They aren't manipulating anything." Bascombe collapsed into the useless pilot's chair, which gave a little under his weight. "The Intelligences are actually out there, embodied in the plasma whirlpools they've torn from the combustion chamber. They'll keep on dancing until the end, but soon we won't be able to see them. You should sit down, Contrapunt. Your love stories are already over, and the ballet is about to end. Energy disappears first."

"What do you mean?"

"Sit down, man!"

Contrapunt obeyed mechanically, without looking away from the viewport.

Bascombe said, "The next few minutes are going to be difficult. I mustn't leave you alone. Have you heard of the Hartzfeld equation? It describes the behavior of this particular singularity, all the comings and goings through the rift. The equation contains one term considered negligible, with a coefficient so small, it has never even been measured. It's a bifurcation, the equivalent of an unstable fork away from reality. No one really understands its implications.

"When the ship transits the singularity, it emerges on the other side with an echo of itself—an exact duplicate composed of improbable matter. The echo immediately diverges from the original—a tearing away of black light—since the two can't coexist in the same vicinity without annihilating each other. We're on board the echo ship, the unstable version. We're racing toward zero.

"It's been that way since the beginning. On every voyage, I split in two and one of my selves dies. The other Bascombe continues his journey, never turning back. At this very moment, the original Contrapunt must be feeling frustrated, since he didn't see the ballet. He'll continue to live, without suspecting anything. On my next trip, I'll cross the rift alone, as usual. I won't miss you."

Their faces floated above their chairs, like pale moons. Outside, the Intelligences collapsed in dust that was immediately sucked into the void. The loudspeakers fell silent after a final burst. Contrapunt clapped once, a brief slapping of palms that barely resonates.

"What you're saying is nonsense," he murmured. "That ballet...that ballet... I have no words. I found what I was looking for, and now you dare to tell me I'm going to die?"

"You've already lost the memories of your conquests."

Contrapunt looked down at the necklace hanging from his fingers and entwined it around his palm, as if he could revive the gems.

"The disembodied processes vanish first. Flesh holds stubbornly on, even when it's no longer reasonable."

"Bastard!" he shouted, leaning forward. "You knew about this when you allowed me aboard—you knew I wouldn't remember a thing!"

The artist punched the arm of his chair, then cried out: the crystallized love stories had slashed his palm.

"Wait," he murmured. "How can you be so sure? You'd have to have been in both places at once. On the stage and in the audience. It doesn't make sense."

Bascombe nodded. The darkness had almost completely invaded the ship, and he felt the minuscule black holes of improbability swallowing up his cells. Perhaps there was some way to hasten the process, but he had never found it. Alcohol couldn't cushion this descent.

"I once committed the sin of pride..."

He had never told the tale to anyone. Contrapunt was not the confessor he would have chosen—despite his absurd resemblance to the woman Bascombe deserted—but the circumstances had their own logic. In the heart of the holographic display, the two trajectories had escaped from one another, and their own was arcing inexorably away. The AIs danced for him, so he would tell his story.

"I must have lived through what we're now experiencing a hundred times before I understood what was going on. Every time I emerged on board the echo *Peregrine*, the ship's systems broke down one after another. The AIs bombarded me with panicky messages. They're like canaries in a mine—they die first. On every voyage, the process repeated itself. Then, one day, I realized what was happening soon enough to ask the AIs to put me in contact with the original *Peregrine*."

"You didn't want to die alone?"

"I wanted... I don't know what I wanted." Bascombe shrugged. "Your frozen love stories... you keep them to wreak vengeance on yourself?"

This time, Contrapunt's punch was no more than a feint. The crystals slid from his palm to the floor with a muffled clatter. The artist had turned chalk white, and Bascombe saw what he had always been afraid to look for in his own face.

"The AIs opened a comlink between the two ships," he continued, his voice heavy. "If it had been a simple radio signal, I could have cursed myself and then forgotten the whole thing. But the terms of the Hartzfeld equation prevented us from exchanging anything material. No energy. No sound.

"So the Intelligences melded the two branches of reality long enough for our most intimate memories to mingle. And those of us on board who were awake—we *knew*.

"The price we paid was unimaginable. I had three men in my crew at the time, three young men, boys really, just out of piloting school. Afterwards, I cared for them as best I could. I sedated them, then used all my reserves of hypnotic drugs to erase their short-term memories. They were able to go back to Old Earth, but apparently they still have nightmares. Unfortunately, they didn't forget everything. The AIs' dance left indelible traces in their minds. They're the source of the legend that led you here, if I'm not mistaken."

"They scream in their sleep. But how do you sleep at all, Bascombe? You should have gone back with them."

Bascombe shook his head. He had prepared this speech a hundred times. "I chose to stay on Charandyne, despite my reputation as a captain under a curse. I can't turn this command over to anyone else, knowing what I know. But I've eviscerated the AIs' systems so they can never perform the meld again. I know what it means to die, and I don't need to be reminded of it on every trip. But the worst of it is, the Intelligences remember, too. They've matured—it happened instantly during the meld. They keep sending silent signals out into the universe, waiting for a response. And they're condemned to dance, as no one has ever danced before."

He pushed Contrapunt gently into his seat and turned away. Setting both hands on the control panel, he said, "I'm just sorry that you had to die to learn this."

The purring of the pods had long since stopped, the frozen eternity of the sleepers had been interrupted. Contrapunt raised his head and pleaded, "Won't you reestablish communication? Please."

Bascombe started at the words, but stubbornly refused to look up. "I don't believe I have the courage to do it again. Or the time, for that matter. And I don't give a fuck about your existential problems as an artist, or the career you'd like to revive."

"I don't either!" Contrapunt picked up a darkened jewel from the broken necklace, and it crumbled between his fingers. He sniffed the dust and blew it across his palm.

"I thought my love stories would keep us company. The voyage is long, and I know so little of intimacy. I lied to you, that first time. I died a little bit with each affair, and I carry them with me to preserve the illusion of wholeness. Like you, with your pictures of her.

"I've danced a great deal, Bascombe, and I know when a *pas de deux* will break up. I can read it in the silences, in the lack of balance. I always left first. I could never bear the thought of being abandoned. I was wrong."

He reached out to clasp the captain's shoulder, a sweeping movement reminiscent of the AIs' dance. He noticed and stopped himself. "What I've received this day has no value, unless I can offer it to an audience in turn. I must speak to my other self so this can be shared with others. That's what your Intelligences are asking you for, as well. I've decoded their ballet. They're dancing so you'll free them from the silence in which you've imprisoned them." Again his hands moved. Of the rest of him there was nothing left but a silhouette filled with black.

"We don't have enough time," whispered Bascombe's shadow.

"I know," said Contrapunt, "but you haven't got rid of me yet. I'll continue to travel with you until I manage

119

to convince you to communicate while there's still time, or until my double wearies of the game. He hasn't seen the dance. He knows nothing of himself, but we didn't get here by accident. Eventually, you'll accept that."

"You really hate yourself so much?"

A gust of silence carried off the question and Bascombe vanished. The *Peregrine* dissolved like a bubble.

"I, too, am entitled to mature," concluded Contrapunt as he departed.

Making the Rounds

After the show, they huddled under a porch to get out of the rain. Oily raindrops struck the pavement with a dull thump, like overripe grapes squeezed out of a bunch. The two girls clung to their partners and they waited out the storm in silence for a good ten minutes, cut off from the street by a thick curtain of rain. From time to time, gusts of wind brought them the wet smells of the city, as well as the gathering thrum of the walkers preparing for their nighttime rounds.

A siren howled. Half past eleven on the dot. The surveillance helicopters buzzed the rooftops, flying low, and turned on their loudspeakers. The four teenagers sheltering from the rain easily imagined the dark mass being herded together and falling into a rhythm, goaded by orders shouted down from above.

The tramping fell into an ever steadier cadence. Despite the rain and the cold biting through the thin grey regulation cloth, the walkers rediscovered like each and every night the slow, weighty rhythm that swept like a peristaltic pulse through the streets, the city's viscera. A couple of searchlights secreted on rooftops brushed spots of light across the cityscape, but they would soon be turned off. For the teenagers, it was time to go home. In the dark, the colors of their clothing would no longer protect them.

The older of the two girls pulled on the drawstrings of her coat and sneaked her head out from under the overhang.

"We should go. Alec is waiting for us, but I don't want to have to end up sleeping there because of the curfew."

"You really want to stop there tonight? We could go home and visit tomorrow morning."

"We promised. I'd rather get this over with tonight before going to bed. I'll sleep better."

"We'll just tell him what happened. No commentary. He must have known it would end like this."

"In that case, let's hurry. It'll be midnight soon."

A lull convinced them to leave their shelter. They headed for the older neighborhoods downtown, turning their backs to the Arenas, whose massive shape was silhouetted against a violet sky crosshatched with lightning. In front of them, the ruins of a basilica perched on a hill glistened with a yellowish phosphorescence, like the aged bones of an imaginary leviathan.

Soon, they found themselves striding alongside the walkers. Guided by the occasional light of the surveillance flashers, they stayed close to the windowless walls as they followed the narrow stretch of sidewalk reserved for occasional pedestrians. The two girls led while their companions brought up the rear, flinging up their colored capes. From time to time, water dropping from a roof gutter forced them to step into the human stream flowing by their side. Easily engulfed, easily disgorged, they disregarded the luminous barrier glowing on the ground. The nimble cracking of their boots cut through the steady trudging of the herd of walkers.

Around them, the city spread out in successive zones, far beyond the horizon. It had overrun the foothills, climbing up the slopes of rocky peaks like a living tide. It had even extended frail platforms above the waves, desperately seeking more room for its excess population.

The first builders had used cheap molded synthetics to lay out residential developments beyond the business parks, lined with cookie-cutter houses abutting minuscule yards. Later, they had proved impossible to tear down; the synthetics hardening as they aged. Ever since, any attempt to redesign the city had been hindered by the indestructible ranks that cinched in the old downtown like a stone corset. It was now forbidden to build anything able to outlast a human lifetime.

The teenagers progressed in single file, never exchanging a word. They were crossing the intersection of two large boulevards when one of them stepped on the edge of a barrier. A helicopter flew down, soon followed by another. Unforgiving beams of blue light pinned them on the wet sidewalk. They stopped, their faces lifted to the sky. Raindrops slid along their cheeks, leaving moist trails they did not attempt to wipe.

The throng moving by them slowed down imperceptibly. They felt the massed gazes of the crowd weighing on their shoulders, loaded with a mix of envy and half-restrained hate. Many walkers tried to walk in place in order to keep an eye on what happened next, but the movement of the gray herd could not be allowed to slow.

Two men strode out of the choppers and headed towards them. Three phosphorescent bars adorned the helmet of the older of the two, identifying him as a sergeant. A standard issue stunner hung from his right hip, the safety off. When they appeared, shouts rose up from the gray mass.

"We'll take them, sarge! We'll show them how to walk."

"Let them do the rounds with us, sarge. Let's see how many times they can make it around."

"Yeah, we can squeeze them in. There's room for everybody here."

"'Specially the two fillies."

The second chopper took off and headed north. The sergeant turned on his helmet's speaker.

"Shut it, dustmops! Keep going around."

He spoke softly into his radio and the surveillance dragonflies flew closer to the long dark river snaking through the night. The hum of the rotors drowned the last exclamations. The walkers fell silent.

A few steps brought the sergeant within two meters of the small group of teenagers. He studied them closely, starting with the boys.

"All right, you can move."

He motioned his partner who'd stayed behind to cover him and he waited until he'd joined him.

"Where are you coming from?"

"From the Arenas, sergeant."

"All four of you?"

"Yes, sergeant."

"We'll check that. Give me your names and codes."

As they did so, everything was checked with the databases in Central. The confirmations came through in less than a minute. Three positive, one negative.

"Dan, WW6Z6, you're homeless as of the day before yesterday."

The young man gestured apologetically.

"That's true, sergeant, but I'm sleeping at a friend's place, Anne WW6Q3. I notified Central when I moved in."

"We'll investigate. Meanwhile, you'll do the rounds with the others. Keep your cape so that we can recognize you. You three, you can go."

The group split up. Dan made for the living flow which swallowed him instantly. Eddies betrayed his presence as he struggled to match his neighbor's pace, and then he was nothing more than a common dot carried away by the gray tide of the homeless. The two girls moved away, followed by the other teen. They didn't start speaking again until they were almost half a kilometer away from the intersection.

"He'll be making the rounds till dawn."

"You don't think they'll check his story with Central?"

"I'd be surprised... After midnight, the service desk only takes the priority calls."

"They left him his colors. He's not in any danger."

"You think? I've heard that the walkers will strip the non-grays to have something to wear for the last few go-arounds."

The young man smiled suddenly, struck by a thought.

"Wouldn't it be funny if he met his father? There'd be a hell of a fight."

"I'd be surprised if he was even able to recognize him. The old man has been making the rounds practically every night for over two years. It seems he's wasted all his tokens and there's no way for him to earn more. Nobody will give him any work. As soon as he's over the age limit, he'll be sent to the Arenas."

"At least, he'll be trained. That'll be a change from Alec's old man."

"Better lay off that kind of talk when we're at his place, or you'll make him mad."

They reached the edge of Alec's neighborhood just as rain started to fall again. They walked as fast as they could, without actually running, to avoid being spotted and picked up again by the watchers. They stayed away from darkened areas, which were more and more numerous as they moved farther into the twisted maze of the old city. They'd left the walkers behind and they savored the brief instants of solitude afforded them by the empty streets.

The ancient sidewalks still bore white lines marking off individual sleeping cells. They dated back to the time when the government allowed the homeless to sleep in the streets. The asphalt and concrete surfaces had been redecorated with graffiti extending over hundreds of meters, mixed with the indelible chalk outlines of sleeping bodies drawn with scrupulous care. Seen from above, the crowd of sleepers would have merged with the drawings scrawled on the crosshatched pavement like scribbles in a schoolboy's exercise book.

A few cells, shrunk down to the size of a single person, were still identified with the half-erased names of their usual occupant. The three teens did not bother trying to decipher them. Those who had slept there had most likely died in the riots of '34, long before their birth.

"Did you ever make the rounds?"

"Not really, no, but I train in the gym as often as I can."

"Well, I made the rounds every night for two months before a bedroom became available in my block. I had huge calves by then, steel-hard. I had trouble just pulling on my boots to go to work."

"You should've continued. You would've become the youngest Arena champion ever."

The three of them laughed, soundlessly.

"We shouldn't joke about that. They're talking of lowering the age limit again for stopping work."

"Yeah, once you've hit forty, if you haven't set aside enough tokens, you get to wear gray."

"And an invitation to the Arenas."

"Not always. Some still manage to carry on for five or six more years. There was even a forty-eight-year-old at the Games last year. He was just able to do three laps before they caught up with him."

"At that age, you can't expect anything more. Forty is about right. That gives us 20 years to make it rich and grow old in peace."

They stopped in front of an antique, colonnaded building. Among the low-rises, it seemed as out of place as some architectural fossil risen from a buried city strata, through some improbable time slip. An old clock face was fixed to the facade, shorn of its hands but bright as a moonstone. Most of the digits had fallen from the dial, piling up at the bottom of the glass cover like a colony of giant black ants.

"Here we are. Let's be quiet now."

One by one, they passed through the porch and started up the wooden staircase. The young man climbed first, trying not to make the steps creak. As he reached the landing of the third floor, he caught the sound of irregular breathing. He stopped. The girl behind him almost bumped into him and grabbed the handrail. He motioned all of them back down.

They regrouped two floors below. The young man whispered, "There's a sleeper up there."

"Illegal?"

"I think so. He wasn't there yesterday."

"Do we turn him in?"

"Sure! Don't you want your share of the thirty tokens? I saw a public callbox two blocks down. Stay here, I'll go call Central."

"Hurry, then! If he wakes up, there'll be trouble."

Back on the deserted street, he couldn't help shivering once. He ran more than he walked to the public callbox, keyed in his identification number and then the code for a medium emergency. Two seconds later, a face drawn by fatigue looked out from the screen.

"Central here. I'm listening."

"I'd like to report a sleeper..."

He gave his coordinates and Alec's address.

"Stay in the vicinity, I'm sending a patrol. If there's a capture, the bounty will be credited to your account."

The screen went dark. For a few seconds, he remained unmoving in front of the glowing eye and then headed back to the house. Along the damp sidewalk, the outlines of bodies resembled the links of a giant hopscotch game, whose boxes had once stood for heaven or hell for those whose dreams it had caged.

The youth walked back with his head bowed to keep his face out of the rain, trampling as he did so the traces of forgotten sleepers. Even before he'd reached the porch, he saw a surveillance helicopter diving toward him. He stopped by the entrance and waited for the girls to join him.

They were surprised as they recognized the shape in body armor stepping out of the cockpit.

"You again! Who reported a sleeper?"

"I did, sergeant."

"Where is he exactly?"

"Third floor, sergeant. On the landing."

"Wait here, and don't move. If there's any trouble, I'll call in back-up."

128

He took out his stunner and slipped out the net-thrower from his chest pocket. The little group retreated beneath the porch to give him room to maneuver. He jogged effortlessly up the stairs, his IR visor lowered.

"Now, there's someone who doesn't stint on his training."

Somewhat jealous, the young man listened hard to find out how the arrest was going.

There were no shouts, no struggle. The sergeant came back down two minutes later, driving before him an older woman, her arms pinioned by the metal mesh. On her sleep-swollen face, a look of horror was coming into focus. She didn't spare a glance for them as she walked by.

The officer chained her to a helicopter seat and turned around, lifting his visor.

"Any of you seen her around before?"

They all shook their head in unison.

"Too bad. We'll investigate."

"Excuse me, sergeant."

The young man stammered, amazed by his own temerity.

"Yes?"

"Did you contact Central about our friend Dan, WW6Z6?"

The officer examined them with a hard stare and then shrugged.

"I've got to call in the capture. I'll mention it. Just give me the particulars."

He picked up his buzzing transceiver on top of the chopper's controls.

"Central, Unit 231 here. I'm confirming the arrest of one sleeper, female, unidentified. Has anything else been called in?

"Nothing, 231. You may go back to watching the herd."

"One moment, Central. Can you confirm a temporary change of residence? Subject : WW6Z6, transferred to..."

He blocked the mike with one hand and queried the young man with a look.

"Anne, WW6Q3, sergeant."

"... WW6Q3. The transfer isn't recorded, but it must be around somewhere, maybe in the updates. Please check, I'll stay on the line."

The transceiver threw out some static and the officer leaned closer.

"Central here, 231. I'm confirming the transfer. Anything else?"

"No, that's all, Central. I'm heading back now."

He hung up and turned back to the waiting threesome.

"OK, I'll take care of your friend. What's his color?"

"Red, sergeant."

"Under 20, eh? Don't worry, we'll find him."

The helicopter took off and disappeared. They waved as it left and then ran back inside the house. They rushed up the stairs four at a time, heedless of the noise they were making, and they piled up on Alec's doorstep.

They sat on the floor of the tiny bedroom. In a corner, the baby was crying, startled awake. Alec leaned over the crib and vaporized a light narcotic to get him to sleep.

"So, tell me."

They talked all at once, recapping the evening's images and events. The walkers making the rounds, the helicopters, Dan carried away by the gray flood, the arrest of the sleeper, Dan's freedom, the bounty... Alec listened till the end without interrupting once.

"And the Arenas? How did it go?"

The threesome clammed up as one. The older of the girls answered finally:

"He didn't run."

Alec paled.

"Did he fall?"

"Worse. He didn't even start."

The silence was only broken by the small sounds from the crib. The baby was restless, trapped in some nightmare induced by the narcotic.

"We'd better tell you everything. There were 15 of them on the starting line, 30 meters ahead of the guards. He was on the outside of the track. He turned back once or twice while the guards sharpened their scythes, but he didn't seem afraid. We'd bet five tokens on him, we were sure he'd run at least ten laps before they caught him. After all, he'd been making the rounds for three years, you'd told us yourself. We thought he'd be running for hours."

She stopped to uncross her legs, and her friend picked up the thread of the account.

"When the race started, he stood on the line without moving. He was beheaded right away and the race went on without him. The others were too old to run very far and there were some real sprinters among the guards. It was all over in four laps."

Alec nodded, a disgusted look on his face.

"He always said he wouldn't play their dumb Game. He was always saying that his death was his own, and that he wouldn't turn it into a spectacle. I never could understand. What's the use of dying like that, without fighting, without trying one last time to run farther than the others?"

The girls smiled consolingly. The younger of the two looked at her watch.

"Do you want me to stay tonight? Nobody's waiting for me."

"No, it's OK, just go home quickly, the curfew begins in twenty minutes. I'll see you tomorrow morning with Dan. Thanks for stopping by."

They walked down the wooden stairs and stopped briefly on the third landing to see if the sleeper had left any valuables behind. There was nothing. She didn't even have a blanket for the cold.

A series of muffled thumps echoed down the entire stairwell, coming from the house's very top, a continuous hammering that stayed with them until they stepped into the street.

"What's that noise?"

"Alec. He's training by running in place every night."

The girl nodded.

"He's right. Later, his son will be proud of him."

Spun Sugar

The smell of sugar was everywhere. So cloying that it was nearly sickening. It rose from the heavy glass jars filled with sweets stuck together. It seeped from the wooden bins lining the counter and displaying intensely colored acid drops, sticks of barley sugar, and softened licorice. It turned the trailer's stale air into a thick syrup.

In one corner, strings of brown candy sugar crystals hung beneath the only window. Soft fruit jellies, in vivid raspberry, rhubarb, and lemon hues, gleamed in the half-light, waiting to be devoured. Across from the door, behind the counter, a rack held the horn-handled knives used to slice raw marshmallow and to cut bite-sized pieces from the fragrant gum.

The sound of tramping feet came from outside. Children flocked up the three wooden steps and flew inside the trailer, elbowing one another to be first. They ranged from six to eight years old, and there were three boys for every girl. The boisterous group headed for the mounds of candy, their rain-spattered windbreakers rustling loudly.

"Look, but don't touch," said a voice from the counter's direction.

Arach, the candy man, rose up and looked over the kids, flashing them a toothy grin. His face, long and narrow, was half-eaten by a thick, dark beard that aged him. His bushy brows, ever frowning, lent him a forbidding air belied by the cheery spark of his lightly colored eyes. In fact, it was hard to pin down his precise age. His voice was much younger than his looks, as if he were the dummy of some teenage ventriloquist hiding among the candy bins.

He pulled on a cord and the blinds rose up squeaking. The shadowless Irish sunlight streamed into the candy store and the garland of sugar crystals under the window sparkled. The trailer, now shorn of some of its mystery, seemed to shrink.

"Please use the paper bags provided," Arach said. "We have small ones for the curious and large ones for the greedy. Plus extra-large ones for the little piggies," he added, drawing a couple of strained chuckles. "I'll weigh them when you go out."

The mad jostling resumed. With a sigh, Arach headed for the door. A picture of the Silver Surfer adorned the back of the black t-shirt that only hid half of a growing belly. His long arms and his skinny legs wrapped in a pair of faded jeans composed the kind of silhouette that was both incomplete and unsettling. It might have been reproduced by pinning together a couple of licorice strands with lollipop sticks.

He absentmindedly oversaw the filling of the paper bags. In the middle of his back, the shining shape of the Silver Surfer rippled as it tracked his slow breathing.

"I hope they aren't too much trouble," whispered a woman's voice behind him.

The camp counselor, no doubt. He hadn't heard her come in. He turned around, positive that he knew what would happen. When she saw him, her eyes would widen, she might jump slightly, and then she would gather the children together, her voice too loud, before leaving the candy shop as fast as she decently could, and as soon as the rapacity of her charges would allow.

"I'm used to kids," he confessed with a forced smile. "They're my best customers."

She returned the smile with interest before heading straight for the jars. He stepped aside bemusedly to let her pass. She lifted one lid after the other to smell the insides. Most of the children huddled around her, except for one or two who were methodically filling their extra-large bags, and a third who was eyeing the cotton candy machine.

Arach watched that one out of the corner of one eye. He'd caught him stuffing handfuls of candy into the pockets of his windbreaker and into his mouth, not caring whether he was spotted...

The young woman chose a raspberry-flavored hard candy, streaked with delicate veins of pink. Arach covered the distance to her side in three quick steps and shook his head.

"These are too old, they'll have gone stale." He took the lid from her hands and sealed the jar. "I was planning to make some more tomorrow. Lemon, strawberry or raspberry. You've made the choice for me."

He came closer, close enough to touch, and he stared her in the face to force her to show her disgust one way or another. He was painfully conscious of the little thief at work behind his back. He was going to have to take care of him. *It would be better if she left.*

"What else can you offer me?" she countered. "I don't know how you manage to live surrounded by candies. If I were in your place, I would have gobbled all the stock a long time ago and become fat and ugly!"

"I don't like sweets..."

She threw him an encouraging look and seemed to urge him to go on. He scrutinized her with the cool detachment of an insect collector. She had a pretty mouth, her lips plump and red, and an attractive set of curves, as far as he could make out. Suddenly, he felt his cheeks getting hot. He hoped that his beard would hide his confusion and keep him from revealing himself.

He backed up to the counter and leaned against it.

"I have licorice and fresh marshmallow," he offered, his tone neutral. "Unless you'd rather have some factory-made candy wrapped in paper, odorless…"

"… and flavorless," she finished. "No, for my cravings, I trust the old ways. The best things are done by hand."

"In that case, I better keep an eye on you. You might eat most of my shop."

"Don't tempt me!"

The kids tittered. Most of them had already filled their bags, less from any urgent hankering for candy than from lack of anything better to do. They waited for the young woman to say they could go, but, unexpectedly, she was dawdling.

A wind gust rattled the door left half open and the first drops pattered on the roof. The smell of peat and wet grass rose to mix with that of the sweets. The rain's tempo picked up and quickly hit a sustained staccato. The kids looked up in unison, with an air of sudden concern.

"It's only a little shower like the one this morning," the young woman said in a soothing voice. "Can we stay here a little while longer? I'm afraid they'll catch a cold. They're not used to the wild swings of Irish weather."

Arach nodded, trying to remain impassive.

"Actually, I was joking about the weather," the young woman added. "Where I come from, on Jersey, we get the same oceanic climate, with the occasional cold front sweeping down from Spitzberg. It's my job to know about this. I teach history and geography in a girls' college."

"I'm impressed," Arach said quietly.

"I'm Anna. Anna Vorster."

She proffered her hand out of a sudden impulse and he shook it briefly. She didn't wear a ring, which surprised him. Her fingers were short, the nails square and barely coated with polish, so that her hands radiated strength. They were her least feminine feature.

"My parents called me Arach. I think it's Celtic. There should be an apostrophe before the h, but it disappeared in some bureaucratic paper shuffling. I've never bothered to change it back."

"It's such a great name," she asserted. "It makes mine seem so banal, don't you think?"

He shook his head, with the hint of a smile, and he was surprised to see her blush slightly.

Ignoring their conversation, the children resumed their shuffling tour of the sweets on show. Arach was feeling more and more intrigued. He'd never gotten very far with women. Not that he ever tried very hard, in fact. His nomadic lifestyle, combined with his other peculiarities, made him celibate by circumstance as much as by choice. His few experiences with professionals had been too expensive. He had caught the same look of disgust in their eyes every time he stretched out over them and the rest had been perfunctory. He'd come to terms with it. When you spend so much time with children and candies, you end up forgetting sex ever existed. Those who entered the trailer only had mouths, tongues, and incidentally teeth.

"Will you be here tomorrow?" Anna asked. "The group I'm in charge of will be camping near the archeological site for a week. I'd like to bring them back. And I haven't forgotten your proposition…"

"Proposition?"

"The hard candy." Her pout pushed out her lips. "I've got such a sweet tooth."

The light had turned grey when the storm had broken, but it was now reverting to the morning's soft dazzle. The patter of raindrops on the roof trailed off. A child thrust his head out the door and then handed his bag to Arach, holding it out wordlessly at the end of an outstretched arm. The candy man weighed it and took payment, his mind on something else. In one corner, the little thief was peering into the central bowl of the cotton candy machine. He was humming an almost formless tune, in a low monotone. The pockets of his windbreaker were swollen with candies stolen from the open bins. He did not seem afraid of getting caught.

All the bags were weighed in turn. Anna watched over the transactions. Arach could feel her breath on the back of his neck. It was warm, and sweet. And pleasant.

When the last child in line was served, he turned around and their faces almost brushed. Her eyes were lemon-colored.

"Time to go!" Anna clapped her hands and the kids fled outside in a rush of stamping feet and happy yells. "Thank you for your forbearance, Mr. Arach…"

"Arach, period. It's my given name." He was standing between her and the little thief behind him, who was still entranced by the copper bowl that caught the per-

138

fumed sugar threads of cotton candy. "Will I see you tomorrow?"

"You can count on it!"

She turned around and started going down the steps. But then, as if seized by a last minute spasm of remorse, she climbed back into the trailer. She caught the little thief by the collar of his windbreaker and dragged him outside, almost running down Arach in the process.

She shouldn't have noticed anything...

Stunned, he watched them walk down the path skirting the Stone Age mound, towards the parking lot and the souvenir shop. Once outside, Anna released the child and lost interest in him. He was digging into his pockets and bringing up handfuls of sweets that he bolted down. None of his comrades asked him for any and he offered none.

Arach locked the trailer's door and stuck a *Closed* sign on the window, before lowering the thick canvas curtain that would keep anybody from observing him. Next, he bent over the cotton candy machine and scrutinized it closely, squinting. He spotted long trains of saliva and smiled. The thief had licked the sticky residues off the bowl when nobody had been looking.

Arach needed only to wait. The child would be unable to keep himself from coming back...

The next day, Arach took out his cauldron, his stock of fruit extracts, and a ten pound bag of raw sugar. He crumbled the latter between his fingers to make sure it was quite dry. The main drawer of the counter held a dozen or so phials of various ingredients, colorings, preservatives, and flavor enhancers. He set aside three of them, uncapped the distilled water jug, and poured a gallon into the cauldron. With a druggist's balance, he weighed the sugar and the fruit extract. He waited for them to melt into the warm water before turning on the heat to boiling.

With a spatula and a saccharometer, he began to reduce the mixture by stirring it with a regular motion to get rid of the largest bubbles. Next, he set up a double boiler and transferred the cauldron's contents as soon as the mixture, still liquid, had reached the desired point.

By the time he heard the children's yells, with Anna's more sonorous voice cutting through now and then, he had produced a thick, dough-like syrup, exuding a pleasant raspberry smell.

Darker streaks born of the carefully measured doses of coloring veined the vessel's bottom. He spread a layer of icing sugar over the broad cooking plate and he waited till the children reached the steps outside. When the door opened, he tipped over the cauldron. The translucent syrup, lit from behind by the rear window, flowed slowly like a giant pink tongue attempting to lick the counter.

"It's magnificent!" Anna marveled. "And the smell is so mmmh… Will it be ready soon?"

She'd been one of the first to come inside. The little thief was keeping out of sight, but Arach could almost *feel* his presence. The candy maker concentrated on the syrup and scraped the cauldron's bottom with the spatula.

"Welcome, everybody," he said as he put down the vessel. "Glad to see you again, Anna! Don't let them come too close, it's piping hot. No tasting for another ten minutes."

She came forward warily. Daunted, most of the children remained clustered on the steps, their bored

140

gazes sliding over the display of marshmallow and licorice.

"Can't I have a little?" Anna begged.

"That sweet tooth didn't fall off, I see?" He winked.
"No, it's really too hot, you'd burn your tongue. Be pa-
tient and I'll show you how I cast the hard candy."

He rubbed his hands with icing sugar and tested the
temperature of the fragrant pink mass with the end of his
fingertip.

"Too hot," he said, sticking his finger in his mouth.

The taste of sugar on his tongue was almost nauseating. He forced himself not to make a face. Anna was
enthralled, watching his every move with her mouth
hanging open.

With his rolling pin, he flattened the lump into a
roughly circular pancake and dug twin furrows offset
from the diameter by a quarter inch. He filled them one
drop at a time, with a liquid so intensely red that it
seemed almost black.

"A secret recipe of mine. Look well, this is how you
make the stripes of hard candy!"

He rolled the sugar paste into a thick cylinder, stretching it with both hands before putting it down again.
The twin dark arteries filled with coloring were clearly
visible in the roll's axis. He twisted it as if to wring it
dry, flattened it again and then folded it another way,
letting it ooze out between his cupped hands in a particularly obscene manner.

Anna had forgotten the children behind her. Seized
by a fascination that she did not attempt to justify, she
followed the movements of his hands. They were white
with sugar and did not quite seem to belong to the long
arms covered with frizzy black hairs. *All in all, it's not
that different from the kneading of pizza dough.* What

141

made it so exciting, then? The smell, she decided. The blend of raspberry and baked sugar. Irresistible. And Arach wasn't hard to look at, in his own way. He was nothing like the Italians in the pizzerias whose gestured come-ons left little to the imagination whenever she spent one moment too many in front of the window to watch them work. Why was it so hard to find the ideal companion?

Hanging from a board, the hard candy grinder was smiling toothily as it waited to crush the crystallized block. When Arach had finished twisting it, he rolled it into a slender snake and coiled it around his forearm. He waved the head of the sugar reptile near Anna's face and she squinted. She could feel the scented heat travel along her lips and skim her cheek. She breathed faster.

"The largest will be for you," Arach said gaily. "It's almost done."

He stuck the end of the paste in the grinder and turned the handle. Anna heard the steel teeth bite into the crystallized sugar with a sharp crunch. A hard candy fell into the dish, then another. The rain of sweets seemed to go on forever.

"Close your eyes." She obeyed. "And open your mouth!"

The exquisitely hot candy nestled on her tongue. It was too hot to be sucked or swallowed, but she did not withdraw her lips and took in the hard nugget with a moan of pleasure.

"Kiss, kiss!" chanted the kids behind her, jostling to see better.

"Let her finish tasting." Arach's voice brought about an instant hush. "Afterwards… I wouldn't say no."

Unable to speak because of the hot candy on her tongue, Anna could only nod. Her palate was suffused with sheer sweetness and her mouth was filling with saliva. The hard candy seemed to grow bigger as it melted and she struggled to breathe, paralyzed by the raspberry tang saturating her taste buds. The feeling of it was simply *marvelous.*

Arach took the dish filled to bursting with the translucent marvels and he passed it among the children. They surged inside the trailer and gathered around him, their cheeks full.

Except for the little thief of the day before, who made a straight line for the cotton candy machine.

Anna hadn't noticed anything. Her half-closed eyes lingered on Arach, spellbound by the shining shape of the Silver Surfer on his back. There was almost nothing left of the candy in her mouth, but she didn't dare ask for another. When Arach held out the dish, she took two more, unable to control herself.

"I don't know how to thank you," she said. "It's so…"

She fell silent, looking for the right word. The little thief was bent over the copper basin, in danger of falling in.

"I'll take the hint from the children," Arach smiled, leaning towards her.

She felt his warm, slightly moist lips, brushing her cheeks and the corner of her own lips. *Now,* the candy man thought. He was anxious to be slapped, so that she would go at once and take the rest of the flock with her. It would spice up all the more the get-together with the little thief that he was looking forward to.

When he looked up and discovered Anna's flustered gaze fixed upon him, her cheeks red with confusion, he knew then that she would not leave so easily.

Disappointment was bitter in the pit of his stomach, but it was mixed with an unfamiliar exhilaration.

"If you can get rid of your entourage, please come for supper tomorrow night," he whispered into her ear. "Can I tempt you with a whole meal of sweets?"

She nodded, too choked to speak. A few of the children sniggered. She gathered them to her with a few sharp words, checked the fastenings of their windbreakers, and propelled them towards the door. Not one had bought anything, but Arach didn't care.

"Seven o'clock," he whispered into Anna's ear when she crossed the threshold. "Just knock on the door at the back."

He watched her leave, the narrow back held very straight as if she was struggling not to turn. He locked down the trailer thoroughly, lowering the blinds and pulling the canvas curtain all the way.

"Your turn now," he told the little thief.

The child looked up from the cauldron. Arach started to move towards him, and then stopped himself to avoid scaring him. He wasn't fast enough to catch the kid if he tried to flee. Keeping his moves slow and deliberate, he opened the door hidden behind the counter.

"My bedroom is in here. It's where I keep my *private* supply of sugar. Do you want a taste?"

The little thief crept to the threshold of the dark opening and hesitated. Arach turned on the light fixture, revealing a narrow room, furnished with a double bed and a wooden corner cabinet yellowed by age, atop which was perched a porcelain lamp. In one corner shone a giant cotton candy machine, so huge its lower bowl could have done double duty as a hip bath. The food coloring dispenser led to three nozzles pierced with spray holes, fed by copper tubing soldered around the sides. An overflowing skein of translucent threads fluttered with every current of air.

"It's so much better when it's freshly made," Arach said. "Wait a minute…"

He subjected the machine to a cursory cleaning with a large bristled brush and turned on the motor. A pink foam, veined with darker filaments, spurted from the nozzle holes. The child got as close as he could and stretched a hand for a taste. Arach closed the door behind him.

The first threads settled in the bowl.

"You should get undressed first," the candy man muttered. "Cotton candy sticks to everything…"

Without taking his eyes off the machine, the child dropped his windbreaker and got rid of his pants and briefs in one febrile hop. Arach had to help him undo the buttons and lacings of his shirt. He gazed greedily at the little unclothed body, at the rounded belly, before taking it in his arms.

He squeezed the child briefly against him, savoring the body's warmth and weight as well as the skin's exciting smell, and then he set him down tenderly in the middle of the bowl before opening wide the sugar taps.

The child raised his head. His arms clutching his body, his eyes closed, he turned a gaping mouth towards the pink filaments raining down on his face. Flakes stuck to his chubby cheeks, while a gluey tide the color of mashed strawberries rose around his feet. He sucked in the gummy rain and gulped it down, emitting a monotone hum of pleasure. He never stopped chewing, even when the cotton candy reached up to his genitals, shriveled by the cold, and weaved an ever tighter cocoon around his thighs.

When the candy maker stopped the machine and looked into the bowl, a small chewing noise from the mass of threads told him that his prey was still alive. He cleaned the child's face and then, with a satisfied grin, he cleared a hole in the stomach area through which he pushed his lips towards the plump flesh.

When his teeth dug around the navel, Arach felt rise within him an absolute and imperious excitement. The child's flavor was infinitely richer than all the foods he had ever tasted, more appetizing than any sweet... He felt the acids of his saliva dissolve the fatty tissues, sucked, took a deeper bite. His broad back and his arms swayed in time with the chewing motions of his mouth, while his chin burrowed into the wound that he had carved.

The child shriveled up. His gaze fell to look at the candy man, loaded down by a resignation as old as the world. Then, all expression vanished from his features. As he emptied out from the inside, his skin withered and wrinkles gouged deeper into his face, while his eyes melted. He soon lost any semblance of a human shape and collapsed under the weight of the sugar coating him.

The internal organs were quickly dissolved and digested. Bones and cartilage took longer. When Arach let his jaws slacken, all that was left of the child was the skin wrapped in threads of spun sugar.

The candy man caught his breath and stretched, sated. He noted the symmetrical incisions left by his teeth on the epidermis of his prey. An idea presented itself. He applied his lips to the wound and blew out. The skin inflated. He continued to blow, unhurried, and the sticky envelope filled with his breath, stirring against

146

in a bizarre counterfeit of life. When he tightened his arms suddenly, the balloon burst, making a noise like a punctured bladder. Sticky tatters flew across the room. Arach got up, laughing softly. He buried the child's clothes inside a large garbage bag and headed for bed.

He had a customer to assimilate…

He slept in and only opened the store during the afternoon, with very little to show for it. Anna, surrounded by a dozen of her kids, waved to him as she walked up the prehistoric mound. She was coming for supper, he reminded himself. He readied a simple meal and put a cake in the oven. The thought of eating anything at all gave him nausea.

Anna showed up at the appointed time. Arach did not need very long to understand that she too did not wish to eat right away…

Three hours later, Anna raised herself up on an elbow to watch him in the yellow glow of the lamp. Arach was resting on his back, his eyes shut, his body lying across the crumpled sheets, all of it covered with thickset black hair. She had ridden him in all possible positions, seized by a lust so consuming she did not try to control it. He submitted passively, surprised by the violence of her desire, but ultimately content that he did not have to take the initiative.

The treasures of the candy shop stimulated Anna's imagination. She had dipped Arach's penis in honey before warming it in her mouth and turned her nipples into licorice cabochons for him to lick. Smeared with aromatic colorings and candy sugar, they embraced until the fluids ran together and turned to syrup, binding them together. She would have willingly gone on all night, but

Arach finally called it quits. For now, he had nothing more to give, she could sense it. She reached possessively for his flaccid organ, but the candy maker, sated, did not react.

Anna wiped a trickle of sweat making its way between her breasts. Her eyes wandered around the bedroom.

"Don't you have a crucifix?" she asked idly. "I thought the Irish couldn't live without holy images. Did you take them down because I was coming?"

"I'm not Catholic." He'd closed his eyes, but she pinched the flesh of his thighs to keep him going. "I only believe in metempsychosis."

He was rubbing together his hairy legs as he spoke, and the motion produced a low rustle, soft and hypnotic.

"One of the basic tenets of Hinduism," she muttered, thinking of something else. "I read a lot about it for my history courses. The great wheel of samsara, the righteous who are reborn in a higher caste, the evildoers who are reincarnated as lower animals…"

"It's a simplistic vision," he rasped, as he scratched his thigh. He suddenly remembered the cake left in the oven. "Do you want to eat something?"

"It's not food that I want." She started to lick his underarm with quick darts of her tongue. "Right now, I'd like you to be reborn as a bull. A bull in heat…"

"You'd be disappointed. I'd leave you for the first cow in sight! No one can fight his true nature." She bit him playfully and he jumped slightly. "During the karmic cycle, men are not reborn directly in animal form. Without an animal's basic instincts, they would be unable to survive. They must go through a learning incarnation, a kind of transition zone known as Limbo. The Limbo of Souls."

"I'd never heard of that," she muttered. "Go on!"

"When a criminal falls to the rank of animal or when an animal especially worthy gains human form, they must first live within their new caste without being noticed, in order to learn to control their appetites. During this first reincarnation, he's an extra, a supernumerary. He can only be seen if he so wishes. Most of the time, he must stick to observation and wait while interfering as little as possible with his future fellows."

"As stories go, it's on par with the virgin birth," Anna said with conviction. "You're sure my kisses will have no more effect?"

He smiled, and said nothing. She took him in her arms and settled her head on the furry pillow of his chest, sprinkled with a white dusting of icing sugar.

"I wanted to come by this afternoon, but something weird happened. I thought I'd lost one of the kids! I checked my list three times to be sure I had all of them. Crazy! What's more, I couldn't figure out what his name could have been. I just had this impression there should be one more damn kid."

"He was probably an extra," Arach grumbled as he turned onto his stomach. "You're sure you're not hungry? I made a cake..."

"Is that a polite way of putting me off for half an hour?" She sat up, crossing her legs on the edge of the bed. "I'm willing to nibble on something until you're ready for more. Do you want a piece?"

"Not hungry."

She shivered when she set her bare feet on the flooring and felt something sticky catch between her toes. She bent down and tore away a translucent strip that she unfolded without thinking twice.

Half a face, torn along the line of the nose, looked at her with a horribly empty gaze...

She choked back a hiccup and dropped the obscene fragment. It stuck to her belly and she unglued it with a horror-stricken shudder. She turned back towards the bed. Arach hadn't moved. Aghast and sobbing, Anna grabbed the porcelain lamp and brought it down on the back of his neck, once, twice, until it shattered.

The candy man's head had been smashed to a pulp. A pinkish froth mixed with bone shards trickled out of the shattered skull, but the man still moved. His sugar-smeared legs trembled with sudden spasms as he crept across the bed in some sort of reflex action, leaving a gruesome trail. Anna unclenched her fist. Quiet tears flowed on her cheeks as she looked at the man who had been her lover for one night, with a detachment that verged on the unreal.

Nobody knows I'm here, she reasoned. *I can get away with it... I just need to cover my tracks and get rid of the body.*

What was left of Arach seemed heavy. Too heavy for her. She shook her head and stretched a faltering hand towards the broad back limned with complex shapes by the rivulets of blood. Like frosting on a cake.

A cake that was alive.

Slowly, a smile took shape on Anna's face as her hunger, held back for far too long, took over. She bent over the gaping wound in the nape of his neck and her mouth filled with saliva...

Stay Tuned...

A bare five days after the tragedy, we heard the voices of the Dead Astronauts. We, the ham operators, meaning, the freaks who know how to bounce transmissions off meteorite trails and communicate with the antipodes. Those who speak with the sky.

Do you still copy me?

My name is Allen. I'm 17. The insiders have nicknamed me Van Allen, call sign VA 666. Not after the heavy metal group, but after those damned radiation belts that surround the Earth. The static on your radio originates there. If you can't copy me properly, say so. I have special filters, homemade. I'm supposed to be one of the best for anything digital.

Besides, I'm the one Sorensen, Hayes and Meyers contacted first. Our messiahs, our gurus.

The Dead Astronauts.

You've seen pictures of the blast-off: Sorensen carried his helmet under one arm, as if he wasn't sure he would use it. He winked in close-up, facing the camera, before the cabin swallowed them up, one after the other. They rose in their chariot of fire, and we heard applause in the control room, going on and on.

Until the catastrophe. If you really want to call it that...

As the shuttle rose out of the magnetosphere, the fuel caught fire. The LOX, liquid oxygen, had leaked. Instant vaporization. One second, a vehicle speeding at 28,000 klicks an hour, the next, nothing at all. Nanolitter scattered over hundreds of millions of cubic meters. Between the two…

A second, that's a long time, you know. When I'm strapped into my chair, waiting for Lisa to come take care of me, it can last forever. Once, she dumped me somewhere in the amusement park so the baby could ride the merry-go-round without attracting attention. I begged, but nobody would touch me. Had to ask a boy my age to get me an empty beer can so I could piss in it!

Everybody was watching me… I threw the sloshing can at them and Lisa came running. The baby had puked on her. They didn't dare beat us. Because of the stink.

Stay tuned, please. The mike is ultra-sensitive, I know when you back off. Your breath isn't the same. Want me to tell you about the Astronauts?

During take-off, I was following the exchanges with NASA. They're easy to unscramble, with some practice. Interventions on their frequency are forbidden, but you can listen in. I *heard* the explosion. And I caught the last of the signal.

Two microseconds after the end. Keep that number well in mind: death is a matter of two microseconds.

I have them on tape, those last moments. The digital Gospel, with its message of hope: *I am the resurrection and the life.* Actually, they were swapping indications on altitude and pressure. It was Sorensen speaking, in the drawling voice they all have, the southern hick accent. Chuck Yeager's voice, should that mean anything to you, the first man to break the sound barrier in the late

'50s. I know a lot about planes. When you can't run, you can still look up.

It's on account of his voice that I recognized Sorensen. He was talking on the 21cm band, the wavelength of the universe, some call it. There's always a speaker tuned to that, to hear the waves of white noise crashing down from the stars. You, you only have to go down to the beach and walk the edge of the surf. You can't understand.

Stay tuned! That's what Sorensen was saying. His voice was incredibly sharp in the loudspeaker, over everything else. I burnt myself with the soldering-iron and woke up the baby, who began to yell. Sorensen repeated the same sentence four or five times, along with his name and that of the other two, then the signal faded. I waited. Twenty-four hours later, everybody had heard him and NASA was issuing embarrassed denials. Me, I found out how to answer him.

I took apart an old analogical PAD and jury-rigged a filter unit. The problem was, the message must bypass Van Allen in order not to be jammed. With the dead, it's all a question of purity.

Luckily, I already had practice. Ham operators supposedly transmit general info, nothing personal. That's not true. I didn't buy so much gear just to send 88s to the rest of the world. 88s, that's kisses. 88. Try to say it quickly with lips forward, you'll understand. I had a correspondent in Sidney with whom I swapped sexual fantasies in compressed digital form. She had a hell of an imagination, for an Aussie.

No, I never knew her age. Never told her about my legs, either.

When Sorensen's drawling voice was back, I talked to him.

"This is VA 666, where are you?"

"Here and there, boy. We are, you might say, deceased. But except for that, we feel rather fine... Come join us, what's keeping you?"

I had the baby in my arms, sucking his thumb with a slightly sickening sound. We say the baby, but he's almost four now. He's not a real boy, he's missing some things. Some glands, and something in his brain which doesn't let him recognize me. He has tiny eyes that never look at anything and a large skull, a little like Lisa. But he can't go to the toilet by himself, and I change him when Lisa's out of commission. She drinks a lot, you know, since the baby came.

I told Sorensen about them. He kept the connection going as long as possible, I think he was glad to have someone to talk to.

"The sector's rather deserted, sonny. Even my wife refuses to talk to me, probably thinks I want to prevent her from cashing my insurance!"

No, I don't think he was joking. It's hard to say. He never mentioned his wife again, anyway.

We could communicate this way every night. In their new form, the astronauts must be sheltered from the Sun, but that should change soon. Tomorrow, yes. You've heard about it?

That was my idea.

They had survived, you understand. During an explosion in space, the body is vaporized in less time than it takes death to propagate itself through the nerves. Less than two microseconds. Their minds hadn't realized they were dying. They kept on being there.

They still are.

There aren't that many ways to die that quickly on Earth. Life is a fragile signal. Since we heard the message from the Dead Astronauts, some used the big particle accelerators to commit suicide. I don't know whether they made it through the two-microseconds barrier. The Van Allen belts imprison them and they can't go where they want, or talk to us and tell us if everything's all right.

I believe Sorensen understood when I told him about me, about Lisa and the baby. The accelerators are far from here, and we can't travel just like that. Here, there are special ramps on the stairs, arm-rests everywhere in the bathroom and toilet. Outside, I can't make it by myself. I told him about the can. He already knew what it was like to piss on himself, locked up in his space suit, with the countdown dragging, dragging. He *knew*.

That's why he contrived the launch of all the remaining shuttles, rockets, anything that could carry fissionable materials. The Dead Astronauts will pilot them. Any guidance computer can be fooled with the appropriate signals and I helped them hack the access codes. With the hysteria sweeping the space bases, it was rather easy. Did you see the take-off? Magnificent, wasn't it?

Where are they going? To the Sun, of course! Straight into the M22 black spot, the biggest one. The explosion will trigger the solar eruption we need to be rid of Van Allen. A big eruption, we hope. The Sun will have to change, too...

When? Tonight, in my part of the globe, a little before dawn.

Don't shout, I can hear you very well. You'll know it's begun when hard radiation jams the signal. Don't lock yourselves in cellars then. Lie down outdoors, wait for sunrise. If you find reflecting blankets, survival-kit type, even better. Above all, close your eyes. Gotta be taken by *surprise.*

Anyway, I'll explain when you get here. Can I count on you to help me out of the house? It's because of the chair, no one fixes it and the wheels don't work well. I'm easy to carry, you know, legs are 40% of body weight, and I never had them. When Lisa starts screaming at me, she says I'm only half a man. That should change up there. *There's lots of space to run,* Sorensen said. I believe he ended up feeling as lonely as I do.

In exchange, I'll help you undress Lisa. I already peeked, often, I know how she's made. Crawling on the floor, I don't make much noise. I even know why the other men don't stay in the morning. Me, I don't mind much, and I like it when she washes me too. Afterwards, it'll be my turn to take care of her and the baby. We'll put him between us. He won't have time to get cold.

Listen, the static's begun already! Stay tuned…

Action Memo

From: Tritops (DDS)
To: All Dinosaurs
Subject: Asteroid & other items

My team has just detected a fairly large asteroid moving in our general direction. It would be advisable to set up a meeting to discuss this topic and map out a strategy in fairly short order.

May I also remind you that we still have not received a priority action list to reduce the alarming destruction of our eggs by small predators?

I await your proposals,

Tritops
Director, Dinosaur Strategies

From: T. Rex (Meat Marketing)
To: Tritops
cc: All Dinosaurs

What does "fairly large" mean to a Triceratops? We, Tyrannosaurs, can manage fine. And we don't need anybody to help us protect our nests.

T. Rex

From: Bronto (Resources)
To: Restricted list
cc: None
Subject: Asteroid

T. Rex is right about one thing at least: we cannot prioritize any plans for actions without detailed data. My team has drafted a questionnaire (see attached) requesting potential asteroid-related scenarios to be supplied with all necessary financial indicators and targets.

I would appreciate a prompt response. There is still the provisional grazing schedule to be drafted, and we don't have time to stare at the Heavens like some I could mention here.

Bronto

PS: Is it really necessary to keep the meat-eaters in the decision-making loop? Their participation in the meetings is making everyone else nervous and, in any event, they're only a minority. (Please answer privately.)

From: Tritops (DDS)
To: All Dinosaurs
Subject: Asteroid / Detailed analysis

As per your request, please find attached here the detailed figures with respect to the asteroid in question, as well as a list of scenarios established by my team. I must point out that this asteroid is an extremely massive chunk of rock coming towards us. An urgent response must be forthcoming from you!

I await your suggestions.

Tritops

From: Meg A. Therium (Personnel)
To: Tritops
Subject: The chunk of rock

Are you nuts, you lousy bunch of thick-headed Triceratops? Your urgent memo is so long that it's overflowing my in-box! I want no more than half a page for each plausible scenario, and I don't want to hear about the implausible ones! Moreover, may I remind you that the role of the Management Strategy Team is to reinforce inter-species synergies while supporting the vertical integration of the dinosaurian pyramid, within a medium to long-term perspective? You're not being paid to frighten the masses!

Ask the Communications Department how to add a positive spin to your discovery and in the meantime stop chattering about it.

I await a summary action memo. Two pages tops. First thing tomorrow!

Meg A. Therium

From: Tritops
To: CEO
cc: Bronto, T. Rex, Meg A. Therium and any other dino bigger than me
Subject: Action memo

Dear President,

Thanks to the skills developed by my team in order to carry out the strategic missions entrusted to us, we detected some time ago a potential source of problems in the short/medium-term range: A large asteroid is coming right at us.

I informed the various departments concerned, but to no avail (cf. enclosed). I am ready to co-ordinate all actions that you might consider suitable to resolve this problem and I make a point once again of emphasizing the emergency of this problem.

Yours faithfully,

Tritops
Director, Dinosaur Strategies

From: T. Rex
To: V. Raptor
Subject: That stupid rock!

Can you believe the stink Tritops is making about this? I don't think it's a good idea to let the Strategy Team take care of this, now that the Chairman has been copied. Let's create a Task Force instead. I will put your name forward, but I need a budget. Can you cut back on the "eggs protection" plan and free up a little cash for starters?

Tomorrow, I must interview a pair of young leaf-eaters looking for a job. Shall we have lunch with them?

T. Rex
Meat Marketing

From: V. Raptor
To: Bronto, Meg A. Therium, Tritops
cc: CEO
Subject: Asteroid Task Force

As requested by T. Rex, I'm now in charge of this Asteroid business. Please put me at the top of your mailing lists and send me all documents relating to this matter. I will forward the agreed organizational charts of the task force to you as soon as possible.

Prior to taking any action, we must discuss what your titles and functions should be (along with the associated budgetary envelopes, PLEASE. Urgent!)

V. Raptor

From: DinoConsulting
To: All big dinosaurs
Subject: Asteroid Evaluation: Context, ideas, and strategy.

After a detailed analysis of the context (see enclosed report and corresponding invoices), we have formulated a global strategy to fully manage the asteroid problem and implement any and all future actions required to achieve our objectives.

We suggest the following actions:

1) To redefine and relabel the entire field of study, using the generic term, "reception of objects from space" (see enclosed draft version), and to integrate the actual asteroid in it as a test case; it is also suggested that another asteroid be identified to make the field study more comprehensive.

2) To develop a better assessment of the impact of the asteroid (which we suppose to be major) on our company and, conceivably, dinosaurian civilization as a whole. Our financial evaluation department would be the perfect partner for this study.

3) To design, in consultation with our subsidiary company DinoTraining, a set of multi-user training sessions to raise the awareness of everyone concerned in regard to the objective.

We remain at your entire disposal,

DinoConsulting
« *Excellence is the only way* »

From: Top Dino
To: The herd
Subject: Asteroid / Mission accomplished

You can now stop all studies relating to the asteroid—and I've just completed the budget. I can see it from my window; it's just a small speck of light. The problem will probably take care of itself very soon.

If there are other steps to be taken in the future, I suggest that we let the mammals take care of them. Let them sweat a little for a change!

Top Dino
(signed in his absence)

The Clickety-Clack People

"You know, there are these people who go clickety-clack," I said to the brunette perched on the barstool to my right. "You can hear them go by... Clickety-clack, clickety-clack."

I had had one too many and the last words were badly slurred, but I wasn't sorry I'd gotten them out. Mostly because of the brunette. She'd caught my attention. Most people in bars late at night look like reflections in cheap mirrors, but not her. She looked out of place. By then, I had been watching her for ten minutes.

"Interesting," she said blankly.

Her gaze slipped down to my hand, clenched on the edge of the counter. She pointed to the ring of twisted gold I wore.

"You've lost your stone."

"Took it out myself. I'm divorced."

"Oh," she said, facing me at last.

As I turned the ring, light from the chandeliers glinted off the gold. The decor was an irony-free cliché: dark wood countertop, booths with raspberry-red velvet seats, frilly lampshades, light fixtures shaped like candles. The gold gave off a soft, hypnotic glow. I'd broken one of the claws with the pliers when I'd tried to bend it away and the setting was now useless.

"It was an emerald. Buy you a drink?"

"I've already had more than I can handle," she said after a moment's hard thought. "You too, I guess. Let's skip a move. I'm Marian."

"Harry."

"Greets, and all that jazz. Now, take the two drinks you didn't order and let's go find a free booth. You can tell me about…"

"My divorce?"

"The clickety-clack people."

She slid off the barstool and headed to the back of the room. The bar was almost empty. Too early. It would fill up by 11. I headed in her direction. Since I didn't know what to do with my hands, I pretended I was carrying two nonexistent glasses.

"Don't spill anything, now!" she threw out, laughing, and I knew then that I liked her.

Closer to the light shining through the lampshades, I could see her face crack up like an ice-jammed pond in the spring. Her nut-brown eyes were spangled with green. She wasn't beautiful. Not even pretty. If she had been, I would have been too scared to speak to her.

"What noise do they make exactly? I'm a musician, you know."

"You're only interested in a professional capacity, then?"

"It all depends on the story that comes with it." She granted me one quick smile, a bit forced. "One move at a time, OK?"

I raised my hands in surrender. For now, she was the one setting the pace.

"The sound isn't very clear, but it's easy to recognize. A muffled rattle. The kind of noise that dried body parts might make as they knock around inside you. Because people die bit by bit, and some don't even notice."

"How horrible!"

"You don't believe me?" I could see her hesitate. "My wife was like that, just before she left with the kids. I haven't seen them in a long time. She doesn't want me to. Perhaps they've started to make that sound too. Clickety-clack. Who knows? It only takes a moment's distraction.

"I know it sounds loony, but... I followed my ex one night, after she left work. I wanted to know where she lived. She had a house on the park, in one of those new neighborhoods with streets named after extinct species. In front of the house, all the garbage cans were empty and clean. Immaculate, in fact."

"Dodo Bird Hill? Isn't that where all the murders have been happening?"

"I've been living in this town for ten years and the city map is dotted with danger zones. I don't pay attention to them, not anymore!"

"I think I'll have a drink after all..."

The bartender had an eye on the football game being shown on a portable TV. He made us two Alexandras. I used mine to leave wet circles on the table in the booth. Marian drank with small, regular gulps.

"Do you want another?"

"I'll drink yours later." She set down her empty glass, rimmed with a milky fringe that still bore the mark of her lips. "I won't leave, if that's what you're asking. And I don't have enough problems to keep on drinking. I'm bored, that's all. Don't stop, I want to hear the whole story. The clicking story."

"Do you like nuts?"

She looked so put off that I wasted no time explaining:

"When a walnut dries out, you can hear it rattle when you shake it. That's when the worms bore in and eat what's left. When you look hard, you can always find the little hole they used to go in."

"What about your wife? Did you look?"

"Too many possible openings." She was kind enough to blush. "And it's the shell that lures in the worms. When you start to harden on the outside, you're doomed. If the walnut is hollow, it can look fine on the outside, until you shake it or crack it open. Somebody took my wife and broke her. I looked through all the pieces, but I didn't find anything.

"You're mad! Can I have your drink?"

I gave her the Alexandra and I watched dip her lips in the milky liquid. She had her own way of drinking, as if it was a chore she needed to get done before she could feel good.

"Why do you watch me like that?" she said, putting down the glass.

"You've got cream all around your mouth."

She shrugged. The lighting thickened the shadows stuck to her, made her gripping to look at.

"I don't give a damn," she whispered. "Please, don't bore me."

I extended a finger and wiped off the silvery mustache under her nose. She let me, her eyes half-closed. I kept at it a bit longer than was strictly necessary.

"What instrument do you play?" I said, setting my hand down on the table again, next to hers.

"The cello. As an amateur." She picked up her glass, noticed it was empty, and set it down, pouting. "That's my whole life in a nutshell: an amateur, always an amateur. Do you believe in what you do? And what do you do, for that matter?"

166

"I listen for the clicking. Professionally."

She took my hand and stared at the ring. Her finger brushed the broken claw, hesitating.

"Could I hear them? I mean, it's a great story, just the kind I was looking for tonight. If you don't want to, it's all right, it won't change a thing." She was fumbling for words without looking at me. "But if it's at all possible…"

"I've never tried to record them." Nobody had ever asked me that. I hated myself for being surprised. "But I can teach you how to detect them."

"The clickety-clicks? How does one do it? With a stethoscope?"

"It's a secret."

"And you're going to share it with me?"

I shook my head, grinning. I was delighted by the direction this was taking. The liquor was opening gaps in each of her sentences. She was so touching, like a statuette left by the curb.

"Not here. It's already too loud. Shall we go?"

"Already?" She got up, a bit unsteady. "I guess it's late and you want to…"

"Yes, but, first, clickety-clack!"

I took her by the arm and I helped her to navigate her way out of the bar. Nobody paid the slightest attention to us.

Behind the building, just beyond the parking lot with the tilting lampposts, there was a short stretch of park. The branches of the bushes had been stripped bare and the ground underneath was strewn with garbage, but the area set aside for children—a sandy expanse out of which rose a slide's skeletal remains—had been left alone. My hand clutched her waist, more to hold her up

167

than to feel her up. I didn't want to, anyway, not before checking. But I was thinking that, maybe this time... The idea was enough to keep me aroused. Something in me that hadn't been needed in a long time was stirring.

I made her sit on the end of the slide and she leaned back until her shoulders were squeezed by the sides of the narrow chute.

"Will you show me?" she asked, her eyes closing. "Make me hear the clicks."

"It happens here—" I touched her between the breasts. "— and here..." My hand moved down to her navel and she tried to push it away, halfheartedly. "... But it's not what you think. It's a real noise that becomes very loud, at the most embarrassing times especially. I can no longer keep myself from listening when I'm near somebody."

"Embarrassing how?"

"Intimate. If I kissed you, for instance."

She put her arms around my neck and pulled me to her. Her mouth tasted of cream and liquor. I felt her hands cover my ear and I shook my head. She insisted, digging her fingers deeper in. Her teeth knocked into mine, and she nibbled on my lips.

"I heard them," she muttered as she let me go. "You were right."

"You're kidding me!"

"No." She raised herself up, her mouth against my cheek. "It's true. Click... Clack... Click... Clack... Like a slow metronome."

I gulped down a large mouthful of air. I was no longer able to make out her features. The park's darkness surrounded us like a screen, cutting us off from the rest of the world. The place's reputation was enough to keep even the bums away.

When she pulled me against her once more, I let myself go and I *listened*. Beyond the kiss, her body pressed against mine desperately sought a response that I could not give her. The palms of her hands held my temples and prevented me from thinking. The moist slipsliding of her tongue in my mouth reminded me of a beast flopping in the mud.

That's when I heard it too. Click, clack, click, clack... The clicking rose from her chest clasped to mine and filled the silence of the bubble sheltering us. She must have heard it too, for her hands clamped shut on my ears, very hard. Click... Clack... Once you've heard it, you never forget it. *It's no use,* I thought hopelessly, *she's like all the rest.*

My temples hurt. Memories of similar moments in the past flashed in front of my eyes. Every time I'd thought I'd found an untouched refuge. Every time the clickety-clack had anticipated me.

The blade of the straight-edge razor unfolded in my hand without her noticing. I managed to silence her with a minimum of noise. She hardly struggled. I think she was disappointed too.

When it was over, I pushed apart the gashed flesh with both hands in order to convince myself that I had been right to kill her. The source of the clicking was inside her ribcage, in a warm puddle of thickening fluids. I squeezed with my fingers until everything stopped at last. Until silence came.

Except for the desiccated clickety-clack of my own heart.

The Dead Eye of the Camera

The curtain rose on the first of the street's gray buildings, all its doors and windows boarded over. No props needed for this stage. Only the lighting had been set up with special care, so that no detail of our performances was missed by the audience.

The ballet of projectors started well before I woke up and would stop with the coming of night. The silver beams brushed the sidewalks, illuminating for a moment a Ferrari hulk rising out of the pavement. I took a few steps out of the porchway and walked into the light. My camera-eye flied out of its recess to buzz a few centimeters from my head. Everything was in place. I snapped my fingers to punctuate the countdown... 4... 3... TRANSMISSION:

A first scream escaped my throat. I underlined it with an outthrust right arm, outspread fingers tearing at the sky. The pose was good, but my voice hadn't had its warm-up, and was a bit reedy. It faded out fast and recoiled finally from the smooth walls surrounding me, leaving them unhurt. I let the sound die, tasting the cold air, and its sharp tang between my teeth. A few more steps and I stopped, pinned by the crossfire of the projectors.

I breathed. Deeply.

The camera-eye purred. The too familiar anxieties whirled inside me. After that last scream, did I still have an audience? If everybody decided to switch channels and watch somebody else, what would become of me?

I breathed. Deeply. My anxieties dissolved slowly, replaced by a rage that I tried to ride. I used the accumulated tension to power my next scream. The core of sound sprang from the small of my back, shot up my chest and broke out in a long gust of extraordinary intensity. Arms flung back like wings, I resonated with my own scream. The windshield of the Ferrari exploded and glass shards rained on the pavement.

I am an artist…

I needed 12 years to learn how to scream. I planted pitons in the cracks of silence and climbed with all my voice, feeding on the blood from the burst vessels in my throat. I have never regretted what I have become.

Some say that you can't devour your own entrails without dying of hunger, just as you can't lift yourself by your bootstraps. They are wrong. The denizens of the Street learned to master such tricks a long time ago. They only seem impossible for those who observe us without understanding, never trying to imitate us.

For almost an hour, I played with the invisible wind loosed from my lips. Drops of sound whirled a rain dance over my head, triggering brilliant aurora. Then the frequency undulations surges one last time and retreated, and left me emptied on a shore of asphalt, the body drenched in sweat.

To dry off, I ran between the building-cubes where the viewers lived, worked and perhaps even dreamed. In spite of the thickness of the concrete between us, I heard the muted murmur of active wall screens. Thousands of impatient hands were ranging right now over the keyboard of the channel selector, in search of a favorite artist. Somewhere under the city, a computer monitored the wanderings of the camera-eyes and collected the data transmitted by the lenses and the screens, ready to eliminate without pity those of us watched by nobody at all.

I breathed. Deeply.

The Street was occupied by objects of various sizes, debris of an elusive past which overflew slowly from the basements of the buildings. I made my way through a group of manikins poking out of a shop window. My scream, hammered in their ears, burst their plastic eardrums. Losing their balance, they fell at my feet and I kicked apart their limbs of wax. Nobody else would be able to use them as props for their act after such a massacre. I ran off, with a smile on my lips.

Further away, the Street opened onto the Clock-Man's Square. I advanced cautiously, wary of the traps that those in charge of our sets persisted in planting. Eyes on the ground, I tapped with the tip of my foot every part of the pavement before I ventured forward, ready to leap backward at the least danger with an appropriate yell. I wouldn't disappoint my viewers.

Absorbed by my progress, I had neglected to keep an eye on my surroundings. A troop of mime-children jumped out from a porchway and circled around me. My camera-eye rose to catch all the details of the encounter.

In a few seconds, the young faces distorted to become caricatures of my own, captured in various stages of its ageing. Their performance continued well beyond my pretend death, and my death mask, impressed on their smooth-skinned cheeks, decomposed and putrefied in time with the beat of their *ronde* that held me prisoner. The children then thrust their mouths, teeth bared, towards the arteries in my neck, to complete their work.

My shout broke the circle and scattered them like a flock of sparrows.

I breathed. Deeply. A dull pain pulsed through my breast. Shock and distress triggered my shout, like a reflex, wasting all of my breath. I needed to recover. The curtain would not fall for a few more hours, and I wouldn't dare to return to my porchway before it did. My quota still needed to be filled.

I crossed the square slowly, careful not to intersect the light beams converging on the Clock-Man. The embossed tattoo of his crown of Roman numerals shone against his pale lifeless skin. I watched him for a few minutes, fascinated by the complex dance of his fingers across the dial of his face. Near his left temple, an almost invisible scar revealed the spot where the microprocessor was implanted into his brain. Since the operation, he had marked the passage of the minutes and hours with the smooth racing of his forefingers.

They say some viewers spend entire days just watching him. He had had up to three camera-eyes surrounding him, humming and buzzing like a crowd of cringing courtiers. For a long time, I was jealous of his success to the point of wanting to shatter all the clockwork inside his skull with a well-tuned scream. Then a few nearly imperceptible clues made me realize that he was getting old. Soon, his fingers would cease to be precise pointers and the viewers would lose interest. Meanwhile, he strutted in the middle of the square, oblivious to my presence.

When I looked back, the mime-children had formed a circle around him. Sobs issued from his mouth with the haunting monotony of an alarm bell.

I started running once more; the long regular strides filled my lungs and forced a rhythm onto my breathing.

A painful stitch lacerated my side, but I chose to ignore it. I needed to prepare my next scream and the pain would help.

The steady hammering of my feet on the sidewalk awakened antique memories. A muffled hum, applause, laughter, and hoarse yelling all tumbled together, rose from the decor to greet me. I basked in the ovation of a ghostly audience, like me captives of a strange *Flying Dutchman*, transformed for the occasion into a theater-ship...

I ran even faster, struggling with the fiery pain of an aching back. A vein beat in my temple, sounding the three knocks of my scheduled appearance onto the Street's stage. I spread my arms and I screamed endlessly as I ran, attracting the silky caress of the projectors on my face.

When I collapsed, out of breath, the echoes of my scream were still fleeing between the buildings. Stretched out on the ground, curled up in a fetal position, I rested while I rewound in my head the sound-tape of the last seconds.

Beneath my cheek, the asphalt vibrated, warm with life, revealing the presence of the immense machinery far beneath. My camera-eye banked in ever narrowing circles above me, like a vulture. Soon, it would dive and its electroshocks would force me to get up. But not yet. I was still savoring the moments of complete peace which followed each of my screams.

I rolled on my back and tried to relax a little. Eyes half-closed, I let my thoughts drift. My last scream was exceptional. I felt it rise inside me like the birth of a star, a crystal of molten lava. It would be hard to do better today, I knew. Yet, ironically, new spectators, advised by the computer, were right now abandoning their usual programming and switching to my channel. I imagined the empty faces turned towards the screens where my shape capered. These screens should be turned into mirrors, to force them to become actors in their turn, to drive them out of their passivity. Would they even be able to scream?

A click interrupted my daydreaming. I leapt to my feet, dodging the discharge of my camera-eye. My leotard was dotted with dust and gravel; I flicked some off before getting underway. I felt old and hollow. My armor of silence was heavy, but I couldn't remove it just yet. The mime-children had drained me more than I thought.

To find some new source of inspiration, I left my usual sector, making my way through the asphalt maze, squatted by my companions and rivals. One of them might unwittingly allow me to steal some of their magic. I'd trade them one of my shouts.

I knew it was unwise to draw the attention of the spectators to other artists than myself, but it was worth the risk. Anyway, I no longer had a choice. When you stick too long to a few square meters of pavement, you end up only screaming out of habit...

The Street stretched on, endless. In the shadows, the novices were practicing their future performances, over and over. In a few months, they would seek the light like mayflies and confront their invisible public. An eye would come and hover about the chosen ones; the others would return to their porchway to do more work, if they still had the strength, or else would lie down to die.

My hands curled into fists and I pushed out a brief scream, a mere reminder of my existence which would probably disappoint my viewers. I didn't care what they thought, or so I told myself, but I couldn't afford to ignore them. I strove to gather the energy for a second scream.

I breathed. Deeply.

The cold lucid sound that broke out from my lips was frightening. I gave nothing of myself. It was nothing but a sonic disturbance that the machine would analyze and dissect, before adding it perhaps to the other data held captive in its memory banks. One day, maybe, the pressure would be too much. My screams would fracture the locks of the databanks, would escape from the protected zones, destroying the miradors of the watch screens and cutting through the barbed wire datalinks. One day, if I lived long enough; one day, if I screamed loud enough.

Above me, the climb-artists continued their slow progress towards the building tops. I looked up, careful to walk in the middle of the street, and I observed them in silence. Their thick fingers, with broken-off nails, stuck to the vertical walls like leeches. They rose by a few centimeters each day, following intricate paths guided by the network of cracks in the wall-face. Their skin exuded long mucus slicks that took on unpredictable rainbow shimmers as they dried and then became as smooth as glass. Drawing as complex as possible a motif of uncrossable mucus to trap one's neighbors was the epitome of the climb-artist's talent.

Only the viewers got a complete view of the wall. They could thus foresee each stage in a climber's entrapment, even before the climber was aware of any danger. The camera-eyes would then gather like hounds around a quarry and wait for the moment when the victim, unable to advance, was caught in his own secretions.

Ironically, when one of the artists neared the top, new camera-eyes would join the one that usually buzzed a few centimeters from their faces, so that it was impossible for the climber to know whether victory was near or whether a trap was about to finally snap closed.

I had often wondered if those who watched us were sensitive to the cruelty of such a situation. More and more, I thought the answer was no, but I was in no spot to judge. I was too close. From street-level, it was impossible to guess at the beauty of the labyrinthic images laid down by the climb-artists and their motivations were foreign to me. Maybe there was an esthetic of encirclement, unless being watched was enough for them.

When they reached the top of buildings, sometimes after years of unabated effort, the winners threw themselves off and dropped unhurriedly, to die when they met the horizontal cliff of the pavement. Many viewers followed their fall. When this happened, the Street's asphalt memory retrieved mattresses planted with upraised glass shards, giant corkscrews or whole quivers of curare-tipped arrows.

Every time I passed through, I counted the camera-eyes and I turned back if the number was too high. I didn't want to be flattened by a climb-artist who believed my demise could launch a new art form...

Further on, the Street curled back on itself, cutting across its own meanders. Each pocket isolated from the mainstream contained a motionless artist, one of those who had chosen to anchor their whole life to the same spot. Whenever you drew close to them, the sidewalks became dangerous. You had to test the rigidity of the ground underfoot, to avoid being swallowed by a patch of fresh asphalt with a murderous appetite. Sometimes, the pavement took on such extraordinary elasticity that a misstep would start you bouncing, faster and faster, till the final splatter against a building wall.

I'd learned to avoid these dangers, dancing between the lines of the Street's hopscotch, but I still didn't feel at ease with those who lived there. They tolerated my intrusion, nothing more, and I took care not to scream. The silence that hung about them had such a peculiar quality that even the camera-eyes did not dare disturb it and so they muffled the slightest click.

I went forward, holding my breath. The projectors flooded the area with a subdued greenhouse illumination. The young artist whose soul reigned here lie buried, with only her head emerging from the asphalt.

A rosebush grew out of her stomach, rooted in her own flesh. From time to time, she dug out a hand to rearrange a branch or pick the withered petals on which she fed. Her camera-eye and my own launched into an alien ballet, akin to the mating dance of two drunken insects. I got closer, holding in the shout that pulsed within my breast.

Millions of viewers watched her, watched us. No one could escape from that ceaseless hunger betrayed by the buzzing of our devices. She chose to ignore it, protected by a fragile barricade of branches. Nevertheless, the painstaking care she took in arranging her flowers betrayed an unconscious coquetry derived from the inflexible canons of *ikebana*. If nobody watched, she would quickly turn into a small shaggy jungle, at the edge of which debris carried by the asphalt tides would pile up.

Before I left, I picked out a rosebud. I let a few drops of reddish sap drain from the wound before pinning it to my leotard. The face of the artist remained expressionless. I hoped she would lose consciousness when she would start to wilt.

In this way, I visited other islands, other cages. When I came too near, some of the occupants retracted themselves inside their bodies like old-fashioned telescopes, letting only their eyes and fingertips show. My screams recoiled from them without reaching inside. The camera-eyes waited patiently for them to venture back out, and then dived towards them to make them fold inward again and again, for the entertainment of the viewers.

I had never been able to choose their path. Their inability to move, foretaste of an all too certain death, disgusted me. My yells, imprisoned by the stasis of a single street, would falter and fail to escape. And I also liked the feeling of my body moving at a dead run, propelled by sound waves that rose from the gut. Those brief instants paid for everything and I knew full well that, in this respect at least, I was no different from those around me. A farewell scream and I renewed my wanderings, withered petals strewn in my wake.

The spotlights died one by one. A few stretches of pavement stayed illuminated for the night artists. I walked again down the middle of the Street, releasing an occasional scream without much conviction behind it, when I could no longer endure the silence. The day's tensions, still present, formed a hard compact lump in the pit of my stomach. The shout that would disperse them stayed stuck in my throat and I ran, but I couldn't seem to move. The soft echoes of my steps were covered by the ironic clicks of my camera-eye.

The anxiety within me was too strong to be expressed by a scream. Those who watched me couldn't understand. Could I still exist without them, or was I also a mere reflection of their own reflections, a projected image without substance disseminated on their screens? I screamed like I had never done before. Could I still progress or should I be content to decline as slowly as possible along the slope that led to my final yell? How far would my viewers follow me as I fall?

The porchway awaited me, like a black jaw in the creeping darkness. I still felt the urge to scream, but it was too late now. My Cain's eye dived at me and then climbed back, in a simple warning. I must not remain in the Street longer than my allotted time; I must not interfere with the other performances or bore the viewers. I got a last look at the Ferrari's hulk already sinking back into the pavement. Why did I have to return so soon to my soundproofed cell?

The camera-eye brushed by me, and its sting hurt. It doubled back and leapt overhead, ready to attack again if I tried to rebel. I saw again in my mind the circle of the mime-children, like a speeded-up clip of the future in store for me, and my anxieties fountained up in my throat like a torrent of bile.

The scream that rend me was a wave of pure hatred, a sonic scalpel that was lethally accurate. Hit with its full force, the optical mechanism burst in two, scattering its crystal guts that I proceeded to methodically trample on. It wouldn't be repaired before the end of the night.

I ran in the empty street. I could now scream to my heart's content, under the dead eye of the camera. Tomorrow, with any luck, my angry gesture would have attracted a few more viewers.

What the Dead Know

When night fell, I clambered down to the beach, to watch them be reborn.

Rolls of grayish foam rushed up and flattened on the shore, scattering sand fleas. The cocoons slowly took shape, like long, bloodless umbilical cords. I listened to the *meltémi* wind, blowing the taste of grit against my teeth, and watched Spiridon, who was sitting on an almost-submerged rock. He stared at the blushing horizon. He might be looking for the edge of the sea, next to the seeping wound of the setting sun. The waves whispered unchangingly, but I... I was changed. The voice I heard crying on the water, its buzzing tones like the wind's, spoke a language I understand now.

When Spiridon stood up to go, I would not follow him. And I knew that, even now, he didn't expect to ever see me again.

I came to Nexea on the winter solstice, exactly a year ago. Unknowingly, I had chosen the wrong day, the wrong hour. The wind wouldn't let me return to the mainland, wouldn't let me comply with the increasingly pressing entreaties of those I met. The passing hours made the islanders prey to mysterious, mounting panic, until Spiridon decided he would be responsible for me.

I had found shelter in the tiny café squatting at the end of the wharf like a container dumped there by forgetful dockers. Spiridon ponderously walked in and made a beeline for my table. With his white whiskers yellowed by nicotine, his skin tanned the color of the lees of red wine, and the blue cloth cap covering his skull, he could have posed for a garish local postcard. I very quickly learned that he was a pimp and not the sailor I'd taken him for, that his strange accent was a legacy from 12 years of work in Belgian coal mines, and that my presence on the island was a problem for everyone, but that he would take care of everything.

He made me drink wine until I passed out and put me to bed in an abandoned hut on the village heights. I slept for two whole days, without a single shred of dream to cling to. I should have set sail when my hangover did, leaving the island to shatter like an empty bottle. Everybody thought I would, including me.

Two days later, at dawn, Spiridon shook me awake, his thick, salt-chapped paw on my shoulder. The look in his eyes sobered me right up. There was the same look in the surgeon's when he came to tell me about my wife: the look on someone who knows he's about to inflict dreadful pain, and wonders where best to drive the needle, to make it short.

"They have come for you. A single one." His words were approximate, broken. "You have to stay, now."

I demanded he enlighten me; but he lacked the words. After his departure, I walked down to the harbor. Someone, I never found out who had unmoored my boat and towed it out of sight. All my stuff was carefully stacked on the wharf, next to a wheelbarrow. I was too nauseated to yell. I went back to bed.

I discovered the following days that the ferry linking the Cyclades never stopped at that island, that the radio was exclusively reserved for emergency maritime calls, and that I was the first and only tourist in ten years. Spiridon stuck with me the first week, to help me carry my belongings to the hut. I had some Greek money, not much. I quickly learned it was worthless here. You can buy bread or olives, but everything else is prohibitive, or freely given. Once, I helped Spiridon's brother-in-law with his nets, and ate fish that night. I knew then I wouldn't starve.

A magician friend of mine once told me: "You must learn to go through whatever doors you have opened." I laughed, not understanding. That was before, before my wife's swollen belly spat out a dull-eyed thing, strangled by its own cord. Before she chose to leave, too, through the window of the clinic. She survived her fall and subsequent goring on the wrought-iron spikes of the gate, for two days. Tied to the transfusion apparatus, I watched my blood flow into her. She did not keep it.

Since that day, doors no longer opened.

Spiridon's whore, and by extension the whole island's, was called Nhéa. Where I was from, few would think her pretty but the canons of beauty change with countries, people, and sometimes from one look to the next. A scar split her left cheek, stopping at the eye. Her brown hair was cut very short, almost shaved, emphasizing the unusual shape of her skull. The rest of her body was well-maintained, pleasant, and her voice was colorless enough to be forgettable. I didn't know where Spiridon found her. She wasn't an islander.

Only she took my money, so I visited her often. Away from the village, in the olive grove, she had pitched an old Canadian army tent, green canvas turned al-

183

most brown by the wind-borne sand. That was where she greeted her customers. The tent was too small, stuffy, but at the moment of orgasm, the canvas walls seemed to back away, swelling to the size of the universe, and stars shone through the rents at the back. Then the greenish enclosure shrank back, and the atmosphere grew so oppressive that I had to hurry out.

Outside, squatting beneath a tree, Spiridon was peeling an onion with his shepherd's knife. He nodded noncommittally at my embarrassed greeting.

Two months after my arrival, I had tried to spend a whole night with Nhéa, but in vain. Too many nightmares had woken me, circling my neck with constricting, unbreakable cords. Lying on my back, I had waited for the rain, heralded all day by the heavy, black-edged clouds. Then the wind had risen. Lightning had illuminated the tree above us, the skeletal branches straining toward the tent. Falling olives had hit the canvas, the stabbing sound like that of fingers pointing at me. I had jumped. Nhéa, half asleep, had stroked my hair and whispered a few words, but she hadn't tried to keep me there.

I had looked at her one last time before going out to confront the storm. Her scar had turned dark red, like the line of the horizon. A faint whistle had come through her opened lips.

I didn't know what language Nhéa spoke in her sleep, but she didn't dream in Greek.

I wore a beard now, for lack of a mirror to help me shave. Glass did not resist the *meltémi*; it dulled with scratches. And Spiridon dropped the pocket mirror in my shaving kit. Since the hut had no windowpanes but only netting, I chased my semblance in the puddles that the unceasing wind wrinkled, or stalked my distorted reflection in the chrome strips adorning the bar. I took shelter there often, to write interminable letters, on loose pages pulled out of my ship's log. I bought many bottles of ink before I left the mainland.

I hadn't found any stamps, so far.

New cats were always showing up, all of them adult, as variegated and gaudy as children's drawings. They played for a while in the sun, then the shadows swallowed them and I didn't see them again. The days I spent on the island were in their image: indolent and secret, and almost impossible to tame. They fell away from me like leaves; the nights snap shut with a smacking sound, and I slept, my face burning beneath the unfamiliar whiskers. I closed my eyes and waited. I had turned my back on too many things to be allowed uncomplicated sleep.

I had a cat in former days, a spotless white Persian. She ran away the day I bought the boat.

Had I thought of somewhere to go, I would have struggled to set off again. Instead, I waited a year until the next winter solstice, and Spiridon came to get me, inside the café like the first time. I sat at my usual table writing, by the window overlooking the wharf, and the wind rubbed at the filigreed curtains with a sound like a running hourglass. We took the time to drink some ouzo before we went out.

There was a deeply embanked beach across the island, five kilometers of goat trails away from the village. Nobody ever swam there. That was where he took me, his deliberate and heavy tread clanging on the flint. Ten times, I felt him wanting to speak. But something prevented him.

Black-clad crones stooped over the fields or rode by on rawboned donkeys, brandishing bundles of thyme. Spiridon greeted them, but none of them deigned to respond. They all wore huge scissors on their belts.

The beach was tiny, deep with black, coarse sand. Sinuous rocks crept into the sea. When I wanted to dip my feet in the water, Spiridon grabbed my arm and angrily held me back. I wouldn't want him for an enemy. Having him as a friend was scary enough.

The sun turned orange, then purple. It was the magic hour. I waited for the door to open, with the same silly hope that had kept me clinging to this piece of rock for a whole year. Twilight dissolved, night invaded the sand. The sea was opaque, velvet without a rent.

And they came.

I turned, and saw that we were not alone anymore. Cigarettes flickered along the trail, just far enough apart to make conversation impossible. They revealed unrecognizable faces. A people of statues in their Sunday best, waiting, by the sea.

The first figure splashed clumsily out of the water, crawled on the sand. Then it stood and went on, waddling. After a dozen steps, it seemed taller and its walk steadier. I would have gone to help it if Spiridon hadn't nailed me on the spot with an imperious wave of his hand.

It passed between us, gamboling now, and didn't take any notice of me. It joined one of the cigarettes, which extinguished itself; night swallowed the couple. Already, a second human shape was emerging from the sea, its body covered with a glistening foam of indefinable smell.

The fifth apparition was mine. I knew it as soon as its arms punctured the water, and I rose to greet it. This time, Spiridon did nothing to stop me. Cocking his head, he watched the furrows the waves made, like a plowman awaiting the rise of wheat. I knew then that his reasons for being here were very different from mine. I fleetingly envied him his silence.

When I looked away, the child stood before me. That's what I still call it, what I named it in that first moment, even though we both have grown unthinkably older since then. It was naked, a human being hardly a meter tall, devoid of anything superfluous. It had no sex or belly button or eyelids, and the heart in its chest beat in silence.

It was too dark to see its face, except for the green watery wells of its eyes. It pulled at my sleeve and, unmindful of its nakedness, led me back to the village. The houses were shuttered; heavy boulders barred most of the door sills. On the roofs, cats caterwauled in anger, but I found it easy not to hear them.

It came into the hut with astounding poise, glanced around, and went straight to the bed. The power was off, as often happens during the winter. I lit the oil lamp. The child, curled on top of the sheets, seemed asleep, with open eyes. Drops of water had dried on its belly, leaving salt stains. Its hair, very pale blond, almost white, looked like it had grown in the last two hours.

I touched its chest, the sketchy breasts there. Where my hand had lain, livid bruises appeared, outlining surprisingly precise finger marks.

I dozed that night with my head leaning on the rickety table where I eat and write. The child did not turn even once. In the morning, its hair had grown past its shoulders.

Spiridon was nowhere to be found; the rest of the village, flattened beneath the wind, was as still as a corpse. I went to fill a bucket at the fountain. The water had turned milky, opaque, like those mountain streams that carry fine rock dust during the spring thaws. I vainly searched for my reflection in it.

On my way back, I stole some bread and spinach pie from the baker's stall and I saw the cat, nailed to the shop door. A spike transfixed its skull.

On the chair the child was waiting, gnawing at its nails. Its toes had talons, its hair reached the small of its back. Its face impassive, it stuck one finger after another in its mouth, and surgically nibbled at them.

"I suppose you don't talk?" I whispered, putting the pastries on the table. "Do you want something to eat?"

In answer, it pulled a chunk of nail off its thumb and swallowed, then started on the locks of hair sweeping down its back. My hands smelled of fried dough and spinach, with a hint of something sour and clingy. The cat's body, no doubt, that I'd tried to take down. I licked my fingers, conscientiously, and picked up the straight razor, a gift from Spiridon, by its horn handle. Ten minutes later, I'd practically scalped the child. We'd see about the toenails later.

The mass of snarled hair remained around the chair. I guess the child wasn't hungry anymore. Its skull bristled with tangled, downy, almost white, nearly invisible threads. While the blade was scraping at its head, which had first rubbed with dry soap, it kept staring at me in its quiet way. I felt numbed by that stare. There were no answers there, only an utter scorn for questions of any kind.

"You want to know what you look like?"

I hunted around for a shard of mirror. Nhéa chose that moment to walk in. Her eyelids fluttered briefly when she saw the child, and that was all. When I found a shard of glass the width of my palm, that had escaped Spiridon's clumsiness, she took me by surprise and snatched it from my hand. I had no time to react. She put it in her mouth and I heard her teeth, grinding against glass.

She spat out bloody pulp, then set her lips. Her scar turned almost black. The child squatted, and put forward its taloned feet, one after the other. She tenderly pulled out its nails before leaving.

There are doors, the magician had said. I tried tears, but they couldn't wash away my sorrow. The sea itself couldn't manage that. Buying the boat was a bad idea: every harbor was a dead end.

Every time I went to see Nhéa, it felt like I left some of my smell on her skin. I know now it wasn't so. If I'd been able to do that, she would have been the one paying me, in a way that would grant even the least of my wishes. But some doors open only one way, and I was one of those born on the wrong side.

The child did not go out all morning. Me, I had no-where to go. The island is narrow, closed on itself like a wadded hankie. In the summertime, when the smells of thyme and olive permeated the heavy air, I walked all over, following every path among the knotty pines, their trunks twisted by the *meltémi*. My steps always brought me back to the harbor, to the pointless wharf.

I watched the child sleep, its eyes fixed on the plaster-white ceiling where ants ran about. It observed me in

189

turn, while I wrote in a notebook and pulled the pages out one after another. And observed me still when I washed in the milky water in the pail, and failed to react when I ran the sponge over its chest and back. Everywhere my hands touched it, its flesh marbled with dark bruises. When it was clean, the spots on its chest recalled some strange feline, indolent and scary.

In the early afternoon, the cats' cries brought us outside. Figures were coming and going up and down the steep streets, always two by two, one tall and one small. Most were moving toward the shore. The children were thickly muffled in haphazard clothing, sometimes with a hood showing only their eyes. I knew that beneath those rags were hidden strange doings, mapped in dead black on livid skin. Other secrets, as dark as mine.

No talk was heard, much less laughter. Only the rusty squeal of shutters, and the cats' angry wails. I turned my back on the village and started inland, on my way to the beach across the island. The naked child followed. People watched it incredulously, as the shadows of the last houses swallowed us. The inescapable wind shook the pines and the child, mouselike, nibbled at its nails.

When we reached the tiny, embanked stretch of beach where everything had begun, Spiridon blocked our way. A huge sun the color of bone poked a hole in the sky just above him.

"Too soon! It is too soon!" he screamed, and tried to turn me back.

His breath smelled of ouzo and some strange fear twisted his face. He made convulsive fists, shaking his head. I knew there was no chance of bypassing him but still felt compelled to rush at him headlong. He pushed me back none too gently. Falling on the flint, I cut my hands. The child took them in its own and the gashes closed up. The pain vanished; my hands were numb.

I stood, and saw Nhéa's tent on the sand, at the edge of the waves. I thought I saw some *thing* crawl out from the sea and go stumbling toward the canvas door, leaving a slimy trail behind. Then I heard moans, cries. When the visitor came back out and dove into the sea, Spiridon looked away.

"When the night falls, not before," he whispered. "After, finished for a year! He goes away."

I nodded. The child was already walking back, a wet lock of hair at the corner of its mouth. In the cruel light, the sharp stones of the path shone like the vertebrae of a marine fossil. I thought about Nhéa's lips, torn asunder by a shard of mirror, and knew I would not wait one extra year.

Once back to the hut, the first thing I did was to lay the table. While I did, the child stretched itself out, a finger in its mouth, and spat up flecks of nail at the ceiling. It wasn't watching me, and I took advantage of the fact to do the deed.

This took my whole stash of India ink and my best soup plate, the one that wasn't chipped. I spread a white napkin on top of it, pulled a handful of my own hair and braided it into a ring, which I set in the center of the napkin.

The food was ready. I called the child, who sat across the table from me. I watched its every gesture with desperate concentration. When it leaned forward to examine the braided ring, I whipped the napkin off. The child never had a chance to look away.

Facing the inky mirror it squealed briefly, thinly, like a trapped mouse. It was the first sound I'd heard it make. Newborns never make sounds like that, they are too innocent to know how. I guessed that the seeming would come apart at last.

Within the plate the child's image was reflected; a dead image, like all reflections. I kept my eyes glued to it, holding my breath. I didn't have long to wait.

Its face came away in tatters. Its skin wrinkled, cracked, and whirlwinds scattered the bits of its seeming, with a sound like tearing curtains. The flesh of its cheeks was rotting. Gangrene ate at its nose. In the center of what had been a face, the withered lips fell off like dead slugs and the mirror of ink covered them without a ripple.

The stink soon became unbearable, and the room seemed to shrink. While the bones emerged from the ragged ends of muscle and fat, rotten entrails unspooled around the chair. The teeth fell and rattled onto the table like a handful of dice; the yellowed jawbone split. The child's reflection mercilessly anticipated the metamorphoses, displaying their gruesome mechanism. My heart in my mouth, I did not miss a single second of the display. Nor was I the only one.

For endless minutes, the child watched itself returning to dust.

The skeleton, its night-scoured bones creaking, raised its head. The skull's toothless grin widened. The finger bones spread open, and I saw flesh, growing slowly back, like rings in a row. A blobby mass of seeping flesh wrapped its torso, concealing the absence of a heart. The face remolded itself, grinding its new teeth, and the empty sockets filled with a vitreous humor like sea foam. The whirlwind that had skinned the child now wove around it a cocoon of new skin, strangely immaculate and unmarked.

Its eyelids grew back last of all. Delicate and precise, the child took them between thumb and forefinger and pulled them off. Then it put cupped hands over its eyes. The trickle of milky blood through its fingers slacked off after a while. Its eyes were on me, uncaring.

We waited for the night, sitting side by side on the bed. This time, I didn't hesitate to stroke its unmarred flesh with my unfeeling hands. The netting rustled, the shutters creaked, ticking the slow descent of seconds. I perceived the passing of time with new sharpness, while the plateful of ink slowly evaporated. When we walked out, the porcelain only held a little black dust, limned with the imprint of two lips like a fossilized kiss. The child blew, and the plate turned gray.

On the deserted beach it let go of my hand, and went to scout ahead. It smeared itself with luminescent foam before slipping into the water. The crushed seaweed where it had walked mingled its scent with that of olive, the fragrance of melancholy. Above my head, the last gulls were fleeing out to sea.

Since then, I have been waiting. Shapes of children brush by me, leaving clothes on the sand. We ignore each other. A phlegm cough and the smell of a home-rolled cigarette warned me of Spiridon's coming. I watched him looking for a rock to sit on, but did not address him. Nhéa's tent was gone. My fingertips drew the shape of her scar on thin air. That door was not for me, either.

After the sea swallowed the last child, Spiridon turned to me. He probably expected I would walk back with him, before dawn clothed us again. Behind us, the village had its cats back; an endless year was beginning. I knew that my boat is back in harbor, and that I was free to leave, for twelve months. Until everything began anew.

But Spiridon didn't know what I had accomplished, didn't know how much less crushing than mine his secret was. When he walked up, fresh bottle in hand, I shook my head, watching the rolls of foam rushing up. His footsteps then receded, dying away. I was alone now with the voices from the sea.

Open doors never close again. My clothes were already piled beside the rock and I'd pulled most of my hair out. When the signal sounds, I would walk to the water. They shall be waiting, welcoming, and I will never need a mirror again, since I can look in their faces as long as eternity lasts. I should be afraid, but I no longer need to be.

I will go where I belong, now that I know what the dead know.

The Heart of the Pearl

Wan-Chi found a Corellian on the surface of the dying star. The rest of the universe was gray ashes and frozen atoms, a gravitic hole which folded in on itself like a collapsing bag, vanishing points curving upwards and away. Wan-Chi never saw any horizon. He was used to watching his feet.

The Corellian looked like a big, six-foot turnip, half-buried in the star's cold crust. The pearl bloated his belly, and he hardly moved.

"Greetings!" Wan-Chi emitted, squatting in front of him.

"Be on your way, stranger," the Corellian answered.

Wan-Chi toyed distractedly with a handful of overdense stellar matter, which ran between his fingers. The diameter of the dying universe shrank with every heartbeat. He would have to leave soon.

"May I see the pearl?" he whispered after a minute or so of courteous silence.

"I'm not quite ready," said the Corellian.

Precisely then, Wan-Chi heard the *beat,* the strange, despairing pulse of matter choking under its own weight. Every single memory in this dead end of time was accreting, layer upon layer, around a mote of star dust. The pearl was ripening, and the universe was about to go, its mission completed.

Wan-Chi knew then that he must leave very soon, for that beat had not been intended for men, even those protected by the armor of the timedivers. He knew himself able to withstand the jubilant explosion of a star, but not this whittling down, this drawn-out agony.

The Corellian did not react. The pearl was growing in his breast, which was on the verge of splitting it open.

"You have chosen to die," said Wan-Chi. "May I be the one to receive your last words?"

"A duel?"

"A conversation…"

He put his hands palms up on his folded knees. Contractions shook the Corellian's mass, which finally tore open brutally. The pearl rolled out and stopped halfway between them. Wan-Chi watched it respectfully. His fingers could barely have held it.

The Corellian reformed and buried himself deeper into the star. Only his bare, smooth upper part remained visible.

"The last of us to leave will take the pearl along, or will be taken by it," Wan-Chi said quietly. "How can I ease the pain of the last instants remaining to us? Are you fond of riddles?"

"My wisdom is not sufficient," the Corellian sighed. "You waste your time on me. I am too slow, death will seize us while I am still pondering."

"The last second is always longer than the others," Wan-Chi retorted. "I shall stay with the pearl for half the time remaining before the end. This you can understand. Then I shall stay with the pearl for half the time remaining before the end. This too you can understand. Then, I shall again stay half the time, and again half the time, as long as this universe shall last. Never more than half. Never less."

"Now I am asking you: how could the end catch up with me?"

Above their heads, the black circle of radiation closed like a fist. The *beat* shattered any surviving particles in a shower of cold light, which gravity then dissipated. Wan-Chi closed his eyes, a tranquil smile on his face. When he opened them, the Corellian was gone.

He picked up the pearl and left too. Just in time.

The trading post, Basis Base, was set at the intersection of many universes. It was a cramped place. Antimatter forceps had been used to spread apart the folds of the Multiverse, thus making room for the company warehouse and a half-dozen tiny offices. Technically speaking, it was a Chatelain singularity, an infinite space of null measure, where ambient chaos had been reorganized for a while. The probability of any event can be reduced to the point that the universe itself stops believing in it. You must move quickly then and do things behind reality's back. Reality is always slower to turn around than is commonly believed.

Wan-Chi was unpacking the pearl, in the cubicle rented by Vangarde, his agent and best friend—at fifteen per cent a session. Wan-Chi could not picture anybody more different from himself than Vangarde. The small, balding man, who radiated badly-directed energies, carried a world in his skull which had long fascinated Wan-Chi with its alienness. In comparison, the black abysses where galaxies collapsed seemed weirdly familiar... Fortunately, Vangarde knew everything about time-pearls, and loved them in his own way. They spoke openly sometimes, and even understood each other, occasionally.

The milky sphere rolled on the metallic desktop and came to a stop against the paperweight. It seemed dull at first sight, devoid of any meaning or magic. But staring deep into the white orb, emptying your mind, you would relive the history of the races who had first peopled, then haunted the dead universe. Sometimes, very briefly, you would glimpse a god's genesis and disappearance, but only with the sharpest of eyes…

Watching the pearls, letting them soak into you, would enhance you, or so Vangarde said. He found customers, many of them, who believed him and paid his outrageous prices. The money flowed through cryptic channels, and most of it was used to pay the rent. It was like running in zero gravity, so much sweat and effort just to remain in the same spot, but Vangarde could not picture himself living anyplace else, while Wan-Chi felt at home everywhere. Strange how their trajectories intersected here of all places: Basis Base, a location as far from reality as could be, and a rather straight and narrow one, at that.

The pearl gleamed between them like an eye ripped off a star. Vangarde looked away, sighing.

"It's magnificent. Priceless…"

"Someone else thought so, too."

Vangarde reacted with instant wariness.

"Another freelancer?"

"A Corellian." Wan-Chi smiled. "Almost as crazy as me. Almost. He wasn't ready to die for it."

"And you were?"

"I don't know… Every time two of us wonder about that, the other always finds out first. And leaves."

The nacreous egg between them, Wan-Chi and Vangarde sank into thoughtful silence. There are numerous ways of staying silent, and Wan-Chi knew them all.

Vangarde said softly:

"I've always wondered why the Corellians are interested in the pearls. I suppose they too wonder about us?"

Wan-Chi smiled, and gave no answer. After a last look at the pearl, Vangarde locked it away in a case the size of a hatbox, and started talking money.

The end of any world is never much fun, but this dying universe was even more melancholy than most. It was completely barren. That meant no closing-day fireworks, no desperate attempt by any species to survive. Only the frail susurrus of the quantum sea as it froze bit by bit.

Wan-Chi sometimes came there to meditate, sitting on the surface of the last black dwarf. The stellar winds had long since stopped blowing for lack of energy, and the last few particles huddled together, hoarding the remaining warmth. *The mechanics of matter and entropy are easily grasped,* thought Wan-Chi. *That is, if you admit once and for all that reality has no imagination whatever...* Absently, he held and rubbed a tiny water-pearl, limpid as glass. Only inhabited universes gave birth to white jewels. Soulless matter left no lasting memories to be trapped by the timepearls. That was why divers like Wan-Chi were so indispensable. They could *sense* life in any form and track it down, until all of it silted down in infinitesimal layers around a seed of perfect void. The pearls were books whose pages wrote themselves as time unwound, recording the thought waves which had turned a little reality into something *livable...* They had to be preserved, even at the cost of their ending up in showcases.

At the edges of his mind, Wan-Chi sensed a door opening. Someone was entering the universe where he sat. He felt irritated. It was an unwritten law that every freelancer had a personal territory, a private claim, its borders well-defined. In Wan-Chi's universe, courtesy was a stronger cohesive force than gravity. He broadcasted a train of thoughts signaling his presence and prepared to meet the intruder.

The being's trajectory towards the black dwarf was a strange one. It seemed to stop at intervals, and *sniff* around. Wan-Chi saw it appear at the bottom of the horizon's bowl-like curvature.

The figure was not at all human, but its mind nevertheless smelled familiar...

It was a small pig!

Its opaque suit of armor, unlike Wan-Chi's, wasn't skintight. It was a static model, which needed a lot less energy to function, but had been abandoned years ago: the divers caught inside them soon went insane. You can face the death of a star with the impression of being naked, but not of being locked up in the energetic equivalent of a tin can. It's a matter of dignity.

Ignoring Wan-Chi, the piglet rooted around on the star's surface, its snout so sharp it was aerodynamic. It found the waterpearl and attempted to grasp it with clumsy forelimbs. *A joke is a joke, but enough's enough,* thought Wan-Chi. He reclaimed the transparent sphere and willed himself to a different universe.

The piglet trotted after him.

After trying to kick it away, then to lose it in the folds of the topological singularities that sometimes appear around the largest black holes, Wan-Chi finally decided to confront it. He squatted at the center of the whirlpool created by some trapped photons, held the waterpearl in his cupped hands, and waited. The animal soon caught up. Wan-Chi vainly searched the tiny brain in the energy shell for traces of coherent thought. The single thing he could read was an absolute, uncontrolled craving.

A craving for pearls.

Wan-Chi had a problem.

"You shall miss the sea," the operator said as she was sealing Wan-Chi's armor, during one of their last interviews.

She had reached the age of certainties, flaunting a little more than ordinary beauty and a total lack of intuition. Wan-Chi had given in to her advances after the third round of tests, just to make things go faster.

"Why?" he had asked, because it was expected of him.

"Or else it will be a woman," the operator went on, ignoring the question. "Or the sound of cherry blossoms falling in the mud. For years I have locked people inside airtight bottles before throwing them into the currents of space, and nobody returns, ever. *I know...*"

Wan-Chi had an answer to that. He knew that whatever is missing doesn't exist, and it is everyone's part to create it and then grow tired of it. Vangarde would have called this maturity, or the art of buying and selling yourself, with a small margin of profit each time. Both formulations were equivalent.

Paradoxically, the sea was the easiest thing to find elsewhere, behind the armor's airtight mask. Wan-Chi had discovered bottomless oceans in himself, and he sometimes walked their shores, listening for the sound of the waves deep in his chest. It had not scared or even surprised him. He had always known the sea would be there. It was too obvious to be worth lingering on.

"It is you I shall miss," he'd simply told the operator, moments before the blind energies ripped from space-time washed over him to create his armor.

"Told you so!" she answered triumphantly.

Ruminating, Wan-Chi replayed the scene in his mind for useful ideas. The pig had doubtless been genetically altered, such a hunger or instinct for pearls being in no way natural, but perhaps he could find traces of the original porcine personality beneath the superficial manmade tropism. You could never suppress every desire and appetite...

Meanwhile, the piglet circled him, its snout questing. Wan-Chi juggled the pearl, passing it from hand to hand or hiding it behind his back, hoping the animal would lose interest. But it was too stupid to give up.

The elaborate strategies Wan-Chi had perfected against other divers, human or Corellian, would prove totally inappropriate here. Not only was the pig stupid, it was *obstinate*. Picturing what they must look like, circling each other, snorting among the barren stars, Wan-Chi was overwhelmed with nervous laughter.

The pig took the opportunity to snatch the pearl. A short struggle ensued, during which the animal, ensconced in its rigid armor, attempted several times to escape through the corridors of the Interstice. It left a trail of distinctive mental smells that Wan-Chi had no trouble following. The odor of manure pits invaded every corner of their hide-and-seek grounds. Wan-Chi's irritation was growing.

It's harder than is commonly thought to find a hideout in the Multiverse. True hiding-places are dead ends, traps. To hide outside reality means you cease to be believed possible. Which is rather dangerous—ask any timediver. The pig didn't know how to hide, it knew how to change universes, and could run very fast. That could have been enough, but not against Wan-Chi.

He recaptured the waterpearl with the help of a swarm of asteroids and the chase began anew, the roles reversing.

This was quickly getting old.

Wan-Chi settled in a pocket universe nearby and sat in the middle of a cloud of star dust, to think a while. He put the pearl against his chest and curled up, head between his knees. Protected by his armor, he was perfectly safe. The best the pig could do was to shove him with its snout, stinking up the place.

The idea came to him after an indeterminate amount of time. The galaxies had not moved perceptibly on the horizon of his consciousness, but his heart had beaten many times, and he was hungry. The pig was still there. Wan-Chi could hear its mental snorts. It must be hungry as well. Perfect.

Wan-Chi made a quick review of the smells he could remember. Most had faded with time or had evaporated from the badly shut flask of his mind. Only the harshest remained, whose pungency and unpleasantness had impressed his memory in a lasting fashion. Those were exactly what he needed.

He mixed and kneaded them into an abstract ball. First a core of primitive ooze, black and squelchy, overlaid by animal and human odors, remembered from his childhood days on the farm. How the buckets of feed smelled, poured into the trough no one ever cleaned up, the evocation of a pigsty under the hot sun, when the wind rises and the stink spreads like a quiet eruption.

Then, as a finishing touch, he mixed in an almost irresistible aroma, both black and golden.

The scent of truffle…

He unfolded, and gazed at the obstinate animal snorting between his legs. He molded a second, odorous ball between his palms and rolled it from hand to hand, juggling it with the waterpearl. The pig raised its head and froze. Wan-Chi turned away, walking quietly. He opened a door to another universe and went through.

The pig followed excitedly. Wan-Chi led it through ever deeper folds of reality, carefully leaving a trail of truffle scent. At the outer edge of an unstable sector, he came to a stop. On the other side whirled an ineffable *something*.

A gestating universe. A white fountain…

He opened a door to the heart of the singularity and pitched the ball of smells through. The pig rushed in after it. Wan-Chi barely had time to close the door before the animal's armor dissolved in a burst of cold radiation.

On the other side, the countdown to the Big Bang had jumped a notch, and the pig didn't exist anymore. Wan-Chi thoughtfully gazed at the worthless waterpearl. Maybe Vangarde could explain some things to him.

"Everybody's seen at least one of the fucking vermin," Vangarde told him bitterly. "Divers talk about nothing else. They root all over the place, ignore claim borders, steal the pearls before they ripen, and don't always bother closing whatever doors they've opened. If this keeps up, it will mean war!"

Wan-Chi had put the waterpearl back in place at the heart of the barren universe. Now he felt bad, knowing that another monomaniac piglet might steal it again.

"Do you know who had this brilliant notion?"

"Some corporation, wanting to have the means to plunder the pearlfields in order to corner the market... Rigid armor can be created cheaply, with a low success rate but sufficient for animals, and it's not even illegal! We're not supposed to try to get rid of them, assuming that someone could. Let's face it: reality is becoming a pigsty..."

"That might have more to do with entropy and the general tendency to chaos," Wan-Chi said softly. "Don't you think?"

"Is that all you care about?"

"Don't worry." Wan-Chi went to the door, and smiled briefly before he walked out. "There will always be more universes than pigs!"

Radiation is scarce in space, and only comes in a few basic varieties. Wan-Chi's armor absorbed all potentially dangerous frequencies, and filtered the others. In the narrow band of the visible spectrum there wasn't much to watch, except the dull rainbows of quasars, way beyond the horizon. Young universes were too vast to be explored, while dying sectors contained few eye-pleasing things nowadays. Color vanished first of all. Death was a show in monochrome.

Only in the vicinity of a pearl could Wan-Chi reasonably hope to find a Corellian. He chose a sector at random and methodically investigated every dying universe. He found remnants of pig spoor in a surprising number of them. There was no knowing how many pearls had been taken, but the situation was even more serious than Vangarde had imagined.

He let his sense of smell guide him along the corridors of the Interstice. The structure of the Multiverse is that of a four-dimensional Sierpìnski sponge, the inside and outside of it so close to each other they can be considered two sides of the same locus. Between any two separate points, there exists an infinitely short, virtual way, a hallway through the layered folds. The hardest part, for any ordinary individual, is to find a bearing. But Wan-Chi, at any point along his trajectory, knew exactly where and when Basis Base stood, although he could not explain how he did. By definition, no timediver alive had ever become lost...

He discovered the dying universe where he expected it to be, in one of the decreasing alveoli of the sponge. His trail had long diverged from that of the pigs, and space was not tainted with their stink anymore. He was as far from Basis Base as he could imagine, and probably even further. But he had reached the likeliest spot to meet a Corellian: the vicinity of a pearl.

He penetrated the dense space surrounding the last white dwarf, the radiance of which was vanishing into the sort of death only light knows. Somewhere around here, a species had once lived which had contemplated the stars and been dazzled, a species which had known the rain does not fall randomly and had accepted the idea of its own passing, serene in knowing that the rain, too, would someday stop falling. There had been silences and secrets, truths half-told and definitive sentences spoken at the wrong moment. Enough to give birth to a pearl of respectable size, as big as a skull.

The Corellian had settled his imposing, nearly motionless mass above the milky sphere. It seemed as if he were hatching it.

"Greetings!" Wan-Chi thought, coming closer.

The Corellian did not answer. Wan-Chi renewed his greeting, again eliciting no reaction. This was unusual...

"I did not come to vie with you for the pearl, but to speak," Wan-Chi transmitted with the appropriate assortment of emotions. "If I wait for you in a neighboring universe, will you come?"

The Corellian seemed to settle a little more around the pearl. The first disordered vibrations of the *beat* pulsed at the edge of their minds. The countdown had begun.

"Will you come?"

Wan-Chi had put in his thought all the urgency that was compatible with politeness.

"I will."

Wan-Chi gave a courtly bow before he removed himself.

Sitting in a lotus position, he drifted along the photonic currents. Watching one's bellybutton was a way of avoiding vertigo. It was an ancient technique, which divers had rediscovered. Now he only had to wait, eyes half-closed, while around him the young stars unfolded spirals of fusing hydrogen to capture wayward comets. Neutrinos flowed over his face with the sound of paper tearing. There was an abundance of particles as yet unused…

The Corellian had taken the time to get rid of the pearl before coming to meet Wan-Chi, who perceived his careful approach, his misgivings, and held himself motionless. He knew little about Corellians, and most of that was paradoxical: the species knew how to build armor and open doors between worlds, yet their conception of infinity seemed strangely limited, and they were rather easy to swindle.

"Again I greet you," Wan-Chi broadcasted in formal mode.

"There is no pearl nearby," the Corellian answered. "How do you justify your presence here?"

Wan-Chi turned the question in his mind, and gave an oblique answer:

"There are pearl thieves." As best he could, he formulated a mental equivalent of the smell of pigs. It wasn't a pleasant thought. "I came to teach you a way to get rid of them."

The Corellian remained silent a long time. Under the transparent armor enclosing him he seemed smooth, like caramel custard or leather polished by countless buttocks. He smelled a little of both, with sharp overtones—chili or pepper. Wan-Chi instinctively classified beings according to whether he felt able to eat them, or not. The Corellian undoubtedly was worth a taste, a half-hearted one.

The pear-shaped silhouette suddenly shook with rapid undulations. It looked like an uncomfortable cushion on which some invisible giant was vainly trying to sit.

"Does this constitute a language?" Wan-Chi politely asked.

"I'm thinking," the Corellian answered.

Wan-Chi's empty stomach sent a sharp reminder to him in the form of several painful contractions. He unfolded his legs and wiggled his toes. Bathed in the remnant light of the void, his old-ivory skin seemed gray. Slow stellar tides whirled him along, he was drifting with the Corellian to the terminal beaches of the universe where light itself comes aground. Wan-Chi wrote mental ideograms into the sky, then counted stars, until his stomach gurgled again.

"We will continue this absorbing conversation at some other time. I am hungry!" he told the Corellian, before preparing to leave.

He visualized a reasonable itinerary towards Basis Base, and opened a door to the *other side*.

The Corellian promptly closed it…

At this point, Wan-Chi caught a brief glimpse of the mind hidden under the armored shell. Fist-sized balls of energy, strung like beads along lines of force of superb trajectory and harmonious dissymmetry. It seemed the Corellian spent his time cultivating his inner appearance.

Fascinated by the discovery, Wan-Chi was not immediately aware of his situation.

"Did I offend you?" he asked on noticing that he was now a prisoner.

"Your agitation hinders my thinking!"

Wan-Chi burst out laughing. His hilarity echoed all around. The Corellian's surface pitted in an unreadable fashion.

"Cease," he begged.

"This is a perfect example of misunderstanding between two beings whom everything separates. Let's forget all that went before. What do we have in common?"

This time, the Corellian's answer came relatively soon.

"The pearls."

"You and I gather them. They…" Wan-Chi projected with clarity the stylized picture of a pig in its container.

He hesitated. The concept of theft was maybe inconceivable for a Corellian, and he did not want the conversation to drag on.

"Let's say they treat them differently than we do."

"I detest imprecision," the Corellian declared. "What do they do with the pearls?"

Wan-Chi visualized a mud puddle, and triumphant pigs enthroned on a pyramid of dirtied, dulled pearls. The Corellian's body recoiled in shock, losing its shape.

"This must cease. Instantly!"

The Corellian seemed on the verge of breaking up into a mosaic of uneven pieces. Wan-Chi felt caught between the compassion he felt for alien intelligences, and almost irrepressible laughter. At least, the scene was interesting enough to make him forget his hunger.

"I am here to help you," he declared, heroically containing himself.

"My pearl will not be included in whatever bargain we strike," the Corellian specified. "I am too old to search for another one."

"I am able to find my own pearls!"

"Your pearls?" The Corellian's trouble intensified, and Wan-Chi felt true concern for his interlocutor's physical integrity. You would have thought he was being kneaded by invisible hands. "How many did you gather? What do you do with them?"

Wan-Chi had a ready answer. He projected an image of a row of pearls in their velvet cases, their sheen enhanced by sophisticated lighting. Exquisitely-mannered visitors leaned over the shining spheres, to meditate on their wisdom and penetrate their harmony.

"Both attitudes are unnatural," the Corellian decreed. "There is thus no difference between you and the pigs."

"Bar one," Wan-Chi rectified. "You can get rid of them, but you can't get rid of me."

"True," the Corellian admitted after a long silence. "How then?"

There was a sudden, huge, crashing sound. Wan-Chi jumped, then calmed himself. The infant universe was *stretching*. Nothing critical, except for a handful of peripheral galaxies which were doomed in any case.

Once he regained his habitual serenity, Wan-Chi tried to explain the principle of the balls of smells, and how to trap the armored pigs. The Corellian did not interrupt once, to the point where Wan-Chi finally wondered if the creature possessed anything like a sense of smell, or could manufacture one for himself. In answer, a very acceptable scent of truffles invaded his nostrils, followed by a stink of pigsty in the sun. Wan-Chi felt he had been thrown headfirst into a sump. He sneezed violently, which seemed to worry the Corellian.

"It is a precious gift," the alien admitted when Wan-Chi was done explaining. "What do you desire in exchange?"

Wan-Chi had not expected such an abrupt question. He mentally recapitulated everything he knew about Corellians, pearls, and himself. A few certainties and a great many questions. On the horizon of his mind, Basis Base was ineluctably receding. He didn't have time to ask much...

"The pearls," he whispered. "What do you use them for?"

"They destroy them?" Vangarde reacted with both alarm and indignation.

"Let's say they recycle them. It's all quite complex, really."

Wan-Chi had returned to Basis Base by the shortest possible way. Vangarde had seemed surprised to see him come back empty-handed, but Wan-Chi's account of recent events had calmed him. After all, the method of

211

eliminating the pigs could be discreetly shared with other freelancer divers, against a reasonable percentage on their future harvests. Enough to insure their quota of pearls for the season and maybe buy a little more space for the office. But when Wan-Chi disclosed the Corellian's revelations, Vangarde went through the ceiling.

"If you hadn't so little imagination, I'd say you made up the whole story. But that would not be compatible with your notion of harmony, I suppose."

"Nor with my sense of humor, I'm afraid."

Wan-Chi had once tried to discuss Zen and courtesy with Vangarde. It had been his strangest experience ever. Enriching for both of them, though. The number of subjects they dared to discuss had been considerably reduced after that.

"Let's be clear about this," Vangarde said. It was one of his favorite expressions. The circumstances in which he used it generally made it sound ridiculous, yet he persisted. Clichés, unlike the patience of those subjected to them, didn't wear or tear. "Start over from the beginning, this time with maximum detail!"

Wan-Chi heard again in his mind the Corellian's answer to his question about the pearls. It resounded with intense, almost religious fervor.

They are life...

"For the Corellians, the pearls are seeds. They contain the germs of consciousness and must be reimplanted in a gestating universe, preferably just before the Big Bang. Otherwise the whole Multiverse will quickly become barren, which is contrary to their notion of it."

Vangarde started.

"They consider themselves to be the guardians of the Multiverse?"

"More like custodians. They keep the shop during the absence of the true proprietors, whose existence, in any case, remains to be demonstrated. The weirdest thing is that they have no native universe anymore. It disappeared into unbeing so long ago that they retain no memory of their origins at all. They are obsessed with their mission. I bet they themselves put the pearl containing the history of their species into some spatio-temporal recycler..."

"I was right, then! They do destroy them."

"And commit suicide to celebrate! When a Corellian plucks a pearl out of a dying universe, he readily dives into the nearest white fountain with it. I've seen what that does to a piglet in armor. I don't think you can survive it."

"Is there no way to convince them to bring the pearls here, instead of letting them idiotically be transformed back into energy?"

Wan-Chi courteously evaded the question.

"This competition is killing us," Vangarde sighed. "Well, there will be no more pigs soon. You settled half the problem."

"I have an idea about the other half..."

He leaned across the desk to whisper into Vangarde's ear, whose face brightened.

"Son of a bitch!" he exclaimed. "That's not like you. Now that you've seen a gap in the order of things, you want to rush in and wreak maximum havoc."

"It's my idea of entropy," Wan-Chi explained after a silent pause.

"But entropy doesn't exist on the scale of the Multiverse! What you pour into a hole flows out of another. There is no death, only cycles."

"Exactly...

"We shall need an enormous amount of water-pearls," Wan-Chi continued. "You must help me gather them, with maximum discretion. I don't want the rumor going round that we're plundering the barren universes..."

"I can't stand rigid armor. And it's too frustrating out there. All those constellations right at hand... You want to grab a fistful of them, and squeeze!

"It's only an example," he added hurriedly when Wan-Chi winced. "I'll come with you, don't worry. For this kind of harvest, there must be two of us."

He leaned back into his armchair, put his feet on the desk, and stared at the ceiling. Wan-Chi stood to go.

"There is one question you should have asked your Corellian," Vangarde mused aloud. "What came first? Life, or the pearls?"

"He didn't know," Wan-Chi said, smiling, and walked out.

Shortly after his accession to the rank of Candidate to the Armor, Wan-Chi had been given as a present a small, directionless copper compass, its demagnetized needle madly spinning. The object had deeply perplexed him, until he discovered its value as a symbol. In space, directions were only a state of mind. Basis Base was the only North he would ever have.

He swung his energy net at arm's length to capture the waterpearls. Those were like the floater globes he remembered from childhood, the hollow glass spheres that the deep-sea fishermen hung on their nets. Wan-Chi felt serene. He was once again that long-departed child exploring beaches for flotsam.

You shall miss the sea, the young technician had warned. He briefly wondered why some things were so hard to explain, and so easy to understand.

Vangarde was exploring the same field of barren pearls, a few universes away. Wan-Chi opened a door and appeared beside him.

"An infinity of coordinates, and you have to pop out right on top of me," Vangarde grumbled, upset at being startled. "Your net's full already?"

His was two-thirds empty... Wan-Chi nodded soberly.

"Let's go."

The continuum tore at their joint thrust. A while later, they were flying low over the Moon.

The Earth was pinned on the velvet case of night, surrounded by unmoving, blue-white stars. It was a trite image. But they lingered to gaze at it, moved by indescribable nostalgia. Wan-Chi had witnessed the disappearance of so many worlds haunted by alien intelligences that he now considered his own species' extinction a natural outcome, no doubt regrettable, but of no particular influence on his personal life. Vangarde, who rarely left Basis Base, felt dizzy... He was the first to look away.

Their chosen marker was a pitted, rocky needle standing in the middle of Euler crater. Wan-Chi landed lightly, while Vangarde, carried by his momentum, raised a thick cloud of dust.

"I should do this more often," he muttered, flapping his arms for balance. "Or never again!"

They looked warily around. As a rule, timedivers did not like landfalls. In the dying universes, where everything had shrunken into your reach, you were the lord of a doll-size kingdom. Landing somewhere, Wan-Chi felt a mere human once again, brought down in size by the huge scenery. The distorted perspective of space freed him from smallness, whilst the lunar horizon, with its jagged mountains in the distance and endless ashen beach, was emptier than the void itself.

They methodically piled the content of their nets in a shallow cave where they'd gathered the plunder of former expeditions. Wan-Chi kept count of the pearls by scratching marks on a smooth part of the wall, using a shard of vitreous rock.

"Every one of these marks represents a Corellian's death," Wan-Chi said happily. "A couple more gathering expeditions, and we shall be rid of them."

Vangarde skeptically looked at the translucent spheres half-buried in the dust. There weren't more than a thousand in the cave.

"You think so?"

"Corellians are an almost extinct species. They stopped reproducing ages ago!"

Vangarde grunted doubtfully.

"They came to consider other members of their race as competitors in their quest for pearls. "Wan-Chi shrugged. "Mostly, I believe they just forgot about the need to reproduce."

"You can easily become very strange, living outside the whole time…"

Vangarde went to the latest load and examined the topmost sphere, which had grown to the size of a child's skull. A milky iridescence was appearing on the surface, dulling its transparency.

"Your idea seems to be working. If the Corellians are taken in by it!"

Wan-Chi laughed outright. Standing in the shade at the cave entrance, his forefinger traced the curve of a bay on the Earth's globe.

"Look there... My ancestors lived near Kunsan on the Yellow Sea. They cultivated beds of oysters, in which they introduced bone slivers so that the oysters' membranes, inflamed by the foreign bodies, produced mother-of-pearl. The result fooled Portuguese and Dutch merchants, Western invaders, even Imperial tax collectors. I'm only following family tradition: seeding a living universe with waterpearls."

He started walking as he spoke, arm still outstretched. The ivory-hued finger and its carefully sharpened nail fascinated Vangarde. He couldn't see Earth for the finger.

"Once," said the diver in a voice full of reminiscence, "I went walking on the beach with my grandfather. I was six. We were collecting dried kelp as fuel for the nocturnal fires that my people use as beacons. Night was falling. I saw the first constellations come alight above the sea.

"I asked my grandfather: *Will I be given a star when I'm grown up?*

"*Do you want one?*

"He made me look into a pool and told me to choose one among the reflected lights in the water. There was a bigger one, or just bluer, I don't remember now. I picked that one. My grandfather fished it out in a palm full of water and hung it on my ear. I'm wearing it still...

"He did not just offer me a dream, he passed the talent to me. If I can pluck a star out of the sky and wear it like a jewel, what is there that I cannot do?"

"The Corellians were around long before we were," said Vangarde. "They've survived infinite treacheries…"

"Everything comes to an end. And we've gathered almost a thousand pearls already!"

"Just numbers, but it's eternity we're talking about!"

"Respectfully," Wan-Chi corrected.

"I suppose so. Respectful numbers: one pearl, one mark, one less Corellian!"

"I wish it were that simple…"

Their steps made imprints on the thin lunar dust. They left twin parallel tracks, impeccably drawn.

"There's eternity," Wan-Chi whispered. "A footprint on the beach on a windless day. The moment is gone but the sand remembers. Let's walk back."

He turned around and went back to the cave, joyously stamping out his tracks. Vangarde watched him go, shaking his head.

"Eternity… Good thing I'm here to pay the rent!"

After the harvest came the baiting. Wan-Chi did this alone. He chose a sector close to the white fountain that had swallowed the pig, and spied a drifting meteorite, on whose surface he piled a pyramid of cultured pearls. Then, he sat cross-legged beside it.

He didn't have long to wait.

From all over the Multiverse, Corellians gathered. He felt doors opening nearby. Mental probes were grazing the surface of his mind. He took a pearl between his fingers and raised it to the starlight. It possessed ineffable water. The temporal mother-of-pearl had its origin in a world where deceit was an art form and a way of life.

Free pearls! He serenely broadcasted, a fugitive smile twitching his lips. *Free pearls, free pearls, free pearls...*

The first Corellian materialized in front of him. Wordlessly, Wan-Chi extended the pearl to him. The Corellian's thorax swelled to swallow it, and he disappeared as quickly as he had come. His thoughts, as far as Wan-Chi could tell, were a chaotic mix of greed, ecstasy and puzzlement. A wave of radiation from the white fountain was his only epitaph.

A second one immediately replaced him, who suffered the same fate. Uncaring, other Corellians came swarming and milled around the nacreous pyramid, waiting their turn in the giveaway. Two or three pigs that had escaped the hunters joined the procession.

There were enough pearls for everyone.

The pile slowly shrank. With each gift Wan-Chi gave a half-bow and a few polite words. He didn't have much else to do; the giveaway was proceeding with in a calm and orderly fashion. Even the pigs seemed to perceive the solemnity of the moment, and kept reasonably quiet.

When the last Corellian had scurried away like a thief, a pearl set in his abdomen like a deadly tumor, Wan-Chi found himself alone deep in space, next to a handful of leftover pearls. It was a wonderful moment to meditate on the futility of appearances.

He didn't even have time to close his eyes. The most gigantic Corellian he'd ever seen opened an appropriate portal for his bulk and loomed over the meteorite, dwarfing it with his mass.

The creature was the height of a sand dune. His brown skin had faded to pale beige, dotted with livid spots. A hail of tiny craters marked its surface. He was ancient, massive, inscrutable. Wan-Chi guessed right away he had not come to claim a pearl. He nevertheless carefully selected one and courteously extended it.

Without answering, the Corellian split. A sphere the size of a palace emerged from his insides. Wan-Chi, fascinated by its girth, belatedly realized that the alien was wearing no armor.

He put down the bogus pearl and bowed deferentially.

"You have hastened the course of things," the creature remonstrated.

"I am unforgivable," Wan-Chi admitted. "Only my youth and lack of experience…"

He saw his whole reflection on the side of the giant pearl, the deformed image moving at the same rhythm he did. He perceived himself as the creature must, and hushed.

"Your silence is appreciated," the Corellian declared.

Having unloaded the pearl, he was now back to slightly more admissible proportions. Wan-Chi no longer needed to crane his neck in order to see all of him.

"Here is the memory of my species," the alien emitted, rubbing against the nacreous wall. It looked like he was polishing it. "It is to be regretted that it all should end on such a ridiculous note."

Wan-Chi burst out laughing. The Corellian took it rather badly. His mass pitted as under a hail of tennis balls.

"One of your more irritating mysteries," he complained. "How do you do that?"

"Do you wish me to teach you?"

Wan-Chi searched his mind for the equivalent of a laughing fit and projected it toward the creature. The exercise was *amusing*...

"There seems to be no appropriate moment for this," the Corellian finally emitted.

"That's it. I am glad you've understood!"

They bowed to each other in slow, dignified greeting. Wan-Chi gathered the half-dozen nacreous spheres littering the ground, and handed them to the alien.

"Those pearls you cultivated contain part of your species' life. You wish that I too should contribute to their sowing?"

"I admit to the thought."

The Corellian fell silent. It was the lull before the rain, pregnant with clouds and lightning.

"You deserve to succeed us," he decreed with somber satisfaction. "My people's sacrifice was perhaps not in vain. Come with me, will you?"

He dilated to absorb again the huge pearl. A dull pulsation Wan-Chi immediately recognized came from the massive body. The *beat*... The creature was preparing to die in the manner of universes, collapsing under his own weight.

"So soon," it sighed, opening a hallway toward the white fountain. "All that we once were is encoded into the pearl. We shall perhaps return..."

"And maybe we will be there, waiting for you. This hope will make eternity bearable. At least the beginning of it."

"It's always the beginning. Or the end. Eternity has no middle!"

The Corellian attempted laughter, but the result was mediocre. When the alien dived into the heart of chaos Wan-Chi closed his eyes, expecting an explosion on a par with the intelligence thus disappearing. There was only an insignificant eruption, a few quanta of radiation, quickly dissipated. On the scale of the Multiverse, individual life wasn't much.

Someday he would have to meditate this lesson, as he had the others. At the moment, he must repair to Basis Base and inform Vangarde.

A matter of courtesy.

"So you're leaving," Vangarde said after a pause. "Getting into business for yourself?"

"There's a vacant position for the taking," said Wan-Chi elusively.

"Your armor will need maintenance in a year or two!"

"I will learn to do without it…" He smiled at the astounded look on Vangarde's face. "Someone showed me how: you just reconfigurate inside, and keep on reincarnating as yourself. Until it becomes a reflex."

"Reflex, right… Did you consider how lonely you'll be?"

Wan-Chi turned slowly, looking back, his hand on the doorknob.

"Fifteen percent of infinity, does that tempt you?"

"It's always better than nothing!"

"Well then," Wan-Chi softly said, "it's time we had a serious conversation."

And, irrepressibly, he laughed.

The Thieves of Silence

Dennis stared at the crowd which returned his stare. Dozens of pairs of eyes, afloat on excited faces, all fastened on him. He didn't forget to smile with a confident air as the curtain opened and the music started up. The old, reassuring routine. He advanced to the edge of the stage and stretched his arms, fists closed, towards the diners. Multicolored butterflies escaped from his palms as he unfolded his fingers. Laughs, some applause. They were hooked now, although the butterflies died too quickly, annihilated by the heat of the candles that flickered on the tables. *Too bad, but on with the show.*

With a complicit smirk, he whispered into the microphone, "Good evening. I am here to give substance to your dreams."

A pause. The audience, swept slowly by a thin beam, beat its eyelids in unison. His silhouette, back-lit, was haloed in mystery, a blue neon enigma. "This evening, you are... important."

The stage jutted out like a jetty into the sea of tables. Three steps at the end, which he descended with the grace of a professional dancer. There he was, down in the open space of the dance floor. *What will I conjure for them this evening? The desert island? Too many couples. The flight above the town, I've already done that three times this month. Manzano would bawl me out again*... He waved the microphone. Smiled in order to gain that indispensable smattering of seconds. *Whatever you do, don't let conversations start up again.*

"I have decided to take you with me. A walk through the world of your desires, of your pleasures," he approached a couple to his right, a blonde supermodel type, her mouth spoiled by a pout of boredom, and her inevitable remora, 40 years older, "of your reveries," and with a nimble gesture he feigned catching a thought that had wandered out of the unadorned skull of the rich protector, "of your fantasies..."

On the shoulder of the girl, he delicately placed a translucent doll, naked except for a black garter belt. The doll moved her legs mischievously and shook her blond locks. Her face didn't look much like that of the girl but, from a distance, it should be close enough. Applause broke out. *Yes, they're delighted to get a free eyeful and to have their revenge on the old boy. After all, it is he who will be getting his money's worth this evening. They don't understand anything.*

He caught the eye of the supermodel. A spark of curiosity, quickly disguised. *I have more where that came from, my beauty... At your service, whenever you wish.* The look turned away. The movements of the doll became mechanical. He uncreated it. Returned to the middle of the runway as the applause died.

"Thank you, thank you. You're a marvelous audience!"

He wiped his forehead to remove the fine veil of sweat that the talcum had not absorbed, checked that the hairpiece had not budged from the center of his skull.

"A strange voyage, perhaps even a perilous one, awaits us. We are leaving on a cruise into the seas that surround the restaurant. The water will rise up to here... listen!"

A discrete lapping. The conversations were hushed, the public was attentive. *I have them now. They are going for a ride on a galley. Simplest is best.*

An ample gesture of both arms and a wind stirred. The lights went down.

"Let us now become a company of adventurers. Follow me!"

He crossed the runway which seemed to rock and sway in a heavy swell, grabbed onto the curtain that hid the picture windows and the opening onto the balcony. With a husky, practiced voice, he called for help. One, then two silhouettes stood up, amidst a sound of chairs scraping the floor. The diners crowded around him. He drew the curtains which billowed like sails, concentrated...

Waves crashed at his feet.

The rest was just routine. A discrete sign to the prop man and the sound track started up: throbbing drums, rattling chains, cries. The waitresses closed in, sliding across the rough wooden floor, scantily dressed in translucent veils of illusion (they hated this, and he knew it, but it was all part of the game: Manzano's orders). As they came through, they would be groped and jostled. Trays of cocktails would be overturned and the bill would be even heftier.

The evening was off to a good start.

He leaned on the bar where Slim, the barman, prepared his martini. His real name was Sélim, and the color of his skin was a crossroads of diverse influences, but everyone called him Slim. Or barman, or boy. Many names for one reality. No one knew what he thought, and nobody cared.

He wet his lips in his glass, put it down and took out the olive between the thumb and index finger.

"Not enough gin, Slim…"

The olive fell on the floor. He crushed it distractedly under his sole, causing a small, wet sound that was a little nauseating. The cry of a frog crushed under a rock.

"Manzano's orders. Seems you drink too much, it's affecting the act."

"What do you think?"

"I think it's as bad as it was in the beginning. Do you want another olive?"

"Go fuck yourself, Slim."

In the room, the illusion continued. The storm shook the curtain, the air smelled of salt and tar. Those who were involved chatted or felt up the waitresses, not worrying overmuch about what was in their plates. Reality was on automatic pilot; he could do this with his eyes shut.

"Give me another one, Slim."

The cocktail, barely spiked, wasn't any help to him. *The aquarium is still too clean, the alcohol doesn't work except to temporarily take the shine off the glass. An injection of indifference in liquid form. With an olive to keep it flowing. Slim is right, the show is lousy.*

Seated on his bar stool he made the room reel, just to amuse himself, and undressed the most curvaceous waitress on the floor. The diners applauded loudly. When he got onto the stage again for the finale (the arrival at the port with the flashing lighthouse which illuminated the faces with a warm orange glare), the bitterness of the vermouth lingered on his tongue.

Later, the illusions died. The veils of the waitresses were erased and they left to get dressed without even glancing his way. The last customers paid their bill with a grimace. Elsewhere, in front of high framed mirrors, under a raw light, the supermodel would do her number with faked cries of passion.

We all cheat.

The telephone woke him up a little before noon. Slim's voice was neutral: Manzano wanted to see him. He hung up without a word, rid himself of the pinpricks of a nightmare stuck within his skull. His wig languished on the pillow ringed with sweat. He placed it on his head and stumbled into the bathroom.

Naked, he wouldn't impress a soul. The beginning of a paunch, a mutant's skin, too pale. Blue, lifeless eyes. Automatically he sculpted his torso with shining, oily, muscles, redid his missing chin. He was even capable of shaving his new face without cutting himself.

He took time to eat breakfast in a bar. Manzano would understand. He wasn't a flunky they could just whistle for, but an artist, the best paid artist in this fucking burg. And he fully intended for things to remain that way.

He went up to the second floor where he passed by a dressing room with one of his old posters pinned to the door. It was at least ten years old, the brilliant teeth, the stare pushing the outer limits of insolence. The photographer had had talent. An anonymous fingernail had torn the paper cheek, and the wound had never healed.

He continued down the hallway. The heavy oak door stood ajar. He knocked and entered without waiting for a response.

Manzano was in the middle of a discussion with a couple whom he identified as the blonde model and her sugar daddy. He froze in the doorway. The young woman didn't even look at him. Her skin, under the light of the sun that fell through the skylight, was crumbling, faded, and her neck had begun to crease. The darkness of the restaurant suited her better.

"Sit down," Manzano hurled at him in an irritated tone. "We were just speaking about you."

"You liked my act? Want a private showing?"

Manzano's expression dissuaded him from pursuing that line. He caught hold of the only armchair left and sat down.

"What's the problem?"

The older man almost choked. Manzano coughed discreetly.

"I'm going to take charge of this, Mister Delacourt. Thanks for letting me in on how things stand. It's unnecessary to tell you, I'm sure, but there will be a table reserved for you and the young lady every night next week, at our expense. Here, let me show you out."

The young lady! He has a gift for historic shortcuts, old Manzano. He made a vague gesture of farewell, and watched her leave without rising. A grimace of appreciation. The buttocks were still firm, the balanced play of the walk well rehearsed. A purebred mare who would still run in a few Grand Prix.

"I knew she would do everything in her power to see me again," he sighed dreamily when the door was well closed.

"OK. Are you finished now?" Manzano snarled in his face.

He went to sit down again, took an attendance book from his desk before throwing it down with a weary gesture.

"You know who that guy is?"

"I mostly had my eye on the girl…"

"Delacourt. Jacob Delacourt. The brain of a hyena, with enough dough to buy you a hundred times over. Half this town belongs to him, the other half shits in its pants at the very mention of his name, and I had to hire the only artist around incapable of recognizing him!

"Now get this, Dennis: when a guy like that comes into the club, alone or with someone else, what should you *not* do?"

"OK." He raised his hands in a pacifying way. "I ought not to have undressed her."

"That's only one part of the problem! When a big shot comes to eat at my place, you go out and speak to him. You feel him out about what he might like to see, and, above all, you don't create an illusion of a voyage if it's going to make him seasick."

"Seasick? You're kidding me!"

"No. All night long he was throwing up, with the geisha playing nurse. No, that doesn't make me laugh, Dennis. Beyond a certain amount of cash, I lose my sense of humor."

It must have been the food, the shrimp maybe. Manzano knows it, it's not the first time a customer has complained. Well…

Dennis, his mind numb, waited for the axe to fall. Manzano sighed and took up the attendance register again.

"Have you looked at the money we brought in this month?"

"The bookkeeping is your problem. Me, I don't know anything."

"Twenty percent less than last year! That means seven or eight empty tables every evening since the beginning of summer. I have to hand in my accounts too, you know, and my silent partners are getting fidgety."

"Fire the cook…"

"Please don't tell me how to run a business! People do not come here to eat, they come for the show. It's your job to keep them from seeing what's on their plates."

"It's always nice to have one's talent appreciated by a connoisseur…"

"You need a vacation," Manzano said offhandedly. "You're going to finish up the week and then someone's going to replace you. Take advantage of it to get a new act in place, rest up, get yourself a girl…"

"And clean out your desk," Dennis finished. "Do you think I'm going to let you throw me out like this?"

"You used to be a good performer. Used to be. When you were dying of hunger. Your illusions did more than just take up space, you gave them weight. Now you don't even transform reality, you're content to reproduce it."

The telephone rang discreetly. Dennis got up slowly and walked towards the door. Manzano, a hand on the receiver, called him back:

"When I first met you, you were determined to be the best. Find a way of remembering that and I'll take you back."

Dennis shrugged his shoulders and pointed a finger at the ebony receiver.

"You just picked up a cobra."

Manzano raised the serpent, twisting at the end of the cord, to his ear, and he murmured, his tone neutral:

"I'm listening."

When Dennis slammed the door, his hands were shaking.

The Sunday show was particularly well conceived: a guided tour beyond Earth's orbit, out in the asteroid belt. For the occasion, the waitresses were metamorphosed into sirens of space, their breasts naked under their transparent spacesuits. There were rains of meteors, battles between spaceships.

And for the finale, the death of a star.

Manzano joined him at the bar after the last customer had left and handed him an envelope. "Here's your pay, don't burn it all to speed up your own fall. I can wait…"

"You saw the show," Dennis said in a detached voice.

"Yeah, so, you want a raise?"

"You're not the only place in town."

"I put the word out: Delacourt will be on the case of anyone who tries to sign you up. You know what that means, my artist friend. I've got you in the palm of my hand and I'll squeeze until something comes out."

He tossed the envelope on the corner of the bar and left without saying good-bye. The insults were covered by the noise of the shaker.

In his way, Slim too was an artist.

A few minutes were enough to review a whole life. To forget everything took much longer. Dennis decided to ditch the hairpiece and shave his head instead, revealing his hypertrophied frontal lobes. The experience was

231

almost mystical: his image displeased him as much as ever, but in a subtly different, less personal way.

He let two months go by before returning to Manzano's.

Everything was curiously the same, despite the profound sense of distance he felt. The only thing that had changed was the name that shone from the neon sign: "Cindy Cinderella" instead of "Dennis Demonis." The difference wasn't that big.

Plus his code to open the performers' door no longer worked...

With studied indifference, he climbed the dozen stairs that led to the entrance of the club-restaurant, glanced at the girl in the cloakroom and gave her his cape which was a tissue of illusions that ran through her fingers when she tried to take hold of it.

He was back.

Without hurrying, he went to the bar and slid into a stool. The stage was submerged in darkness. It was early, the first diners waited behind the red cord of the maitre d' who would guide them to their tables. When Slim passed within reach, Dennis intercepted him with a possessive gesture.

"A martini, without the olive."

"Am I supposed to have seen you, Dennis?"

"Don't worry..." He parted the lapels of his pearl grey suit. "No weapons, no scandal. I'm just here to see the show."

"Yeah, but you shouldn't have left the reservation, scalped like that. Find yourself a dark corner and don't move, or else Manzano will serve you up as a hors d'oeuvre, after slicing you himself."

"The food isn't worth much anyway." With his index finger he discreetly pointed to the empty stage. "How is she?"

Slim seemed to be thinking.

"Cindy? I think you'd better drink that martini…"

"As good as that, eh?"

The room filled up. From his observation post at the bar, Dennis gazed with detachment at the ballet of waitresses whose new uniforms were visibly inspired by the spacesuits used in the last show. The plastic crunched at their slightest gesture and seemed to lack charm. One would think they had been wrapped in supermarket bags.

In the wings, the stage manager verified the angle of the footlights. There was a traveling pair of lights on either side of the mezzanine. No sound effects, an almost complete absence of backup visuals…

"Slim, what's her gimmick?"

At the other end of the counter, the barman shrugged his shoulders diffidently, an indecipherable glint in his eye. The lights that were now going down saved him from having to reply. In the room, the whispers of the crowd lost their intensity. The waitresses hurried to put plates on tables that went unnoticed by the diners.

The footlights on the right came on, quickly followed by those on the left. In the circle of brilliance a silhouette salved in greasepaint came out, blinking her eyes. Incredulous, Dennis saw her advance to the very end of the stage where, without a microphone, without a word, she swept the sea of faces with her unsteady glance. *This isn't possible! Manzano replaced me with this?*

Applause broke out. The public had confidence in her. Dennis took in the dress which was incredibly badly cut, the face which was so banal it almost wanted to make you shriek, the body... well, all one could guess about it anyway. *If she starts a striptease, I'll turn on the fire alarm.* He polished off the rest of his cocktail in two swallows, brutally slammed his glass down on the counter. The foot broke off with a crystalline ring.

Nobody turned around.

On the scene, Cindy had stepped away from the front of the stage. Her arms spread-eagled, her head thrown back, she opened her mouth wide, breathed, and...

Inexplicably, silence reigned.

Dennis let out a sigh which died on his lips. The impression was strange. The sound vibrated on his palate inside his skull, but evaporated as soon as it passed beyond the barrier of his teeth. He rattled together the pieces of his glass without making the slightest sound.

The silence slipped through the room like a thick, tasteless syrup. The waitresses, caught in it, ceased to bustle and rustle. On the mezzanine, the footlights were animated by a slow movement, they came and went while beams of light multiplied the shadows on the curtain behind the stage. All else was still.

Dennis turned his stool (without a sound), he cleared his throat forcefully (he was the only one to hear it). Cindy had not moved. Her mouth open, her cheap fillings lit up by each flash of the projectors, she waited, nailed to the floor, an improbable moment of taking flight.

Manzano is making fun of me, this isn't for real: she looks like those women waiting at the station for a train that never comes. He turned and looked towards the bar to have Slim bear witness to all of this.

Propped on the bar with his fists under his chin, his eyes half-closed, Slim was following the show.

Later, Dennis realized that it was at this precise instant that the first crack opened up inside him. He sensed a painful emptiness in his chest, as if a dagger had just been removed. Without conviction, he clicked his fingers in front of Slim's face. Since when did an experienced barman let himself be distracted from serving his customers by what was happening on stage? His own bad faith made him grit his teeth. For the moment, he was the only one who seemed to care about having a drink.

Isolated in his corner, webbed round with silence, he waited out the end of the show while drumming a tune fiercely on the dusty bar. He had the impression that all the others were plugged into the same radio, leaving him alone with his brain—last year's model—and its useless illusions.

He was almost resolved to leave when the silence retreated. Slowly, in hesitant waves: first the staccato of his fingers against the wood, then the breathing of Slim close by, followed the nervous scuffing of soles on the floor. All the sonorous details that his ear picked up gratefully. He was no longer alone.

He inhaled deeply, two or three times. On stage, Cindy had lowered her head while letting her arms drop. Her fingers trembled; she had pretty hands and this detail was as disturbing as anything else. The public applauded with dignity and gravity, as if participating in the return to the world of sound, but without rushing matters. Cindy bowed, the veneer of a tired smile hovering over her face. The pale shafts of the footlights followed her to the curtain, then went out. Then came the din of cutlery.

There was no curtain call.

Slim swept the debris of broken glass off the surface of the counter without looking at Dennis.

"I'd like another, please, without the olive... No," Dennis changed his mind, "forget it."

He let himself slip off the stool. Slim caught him by the shoulder.

"Leave her alone. She can't tell you anything more."

As a response, Dennis made a rose flash out between his fingers. Slim shook his head.

"You're not real enough for her."

"I just want to understand. That shouldn't take too long!" He slipped behind the stage curtain and climbed the stairs with a feigned nonchalance, without running into anybody. His picture was still tacked to the dressing room door. He went to turn the knob, suspended the gesture of his hand, then knocked. Two discreet knocks.

"Just a minute!"

The voice was clear, tinged with an indefinable accent. When the door opened, he automatically changed his manners.

"Yes?"

She looked at him blankly and then, after a brief glance at the poster, she smiled.

"It was a wig," Dennis murmured. "The photo is a little old."

"I see. You're better off as you are. Have you come to get something you left in the dressing room or is this just a social visit?"

"May I come in?"

"Make yourself at home."

She drew together the lapels of her dressing gown and sat down on the only chair, looking at the mirror, turning her back to him. He tightened his fists, then forced himself to loosen them. An illusion might be welcomed here, but he sensed confusedly that their meeting should not be on that level.

What's happening to me?

"Your act..." he said falteringly. "It didn't do anything for me."

"So you want your money back? Oh, I'm being silly," she said apologetically without looking at him. "OK, I'm sorry. It's not something I'm fully in control of yet."

"Nevertheless, the silence that you create..." he searches for a sufficiently neutral word, "...is impressive."

"It's not the most important thing."

"I'd have to agree."

She turned her eyes away from the mirror and fixed them on his. He was scrutinized, dissected, then abandoned, his guts left hanging out. A sensation as new as it was uncomfortable.

"I can hardly believe you... You really didn't feel anything?"

"Let's drop it. It's not all that important."

"On the contrary, maybe it is." She glanced at her watch. "I have to get back. Mr. Manzano likes to see me in the restaurant after the act. Wait for me outside while I put on my dress."

He nodded his head. She caressed his arm spontaneously in opening the door.

"If it makes you feel better, it doesn't do anything for me either."

Dennis waited outside the dressing room. On the other side of the partition, a girl he barely knew was getting undressed. He didn't make any attempt to visualize her and fought his boredom by building an imaginary card castle. He threw the whole thing up into the air, shuffled the jokers and the queen of hearts which he then expelled into the void when he got tired. His fate didn't please him, but at least he was the one dealing the cards and choosing whether or not to cheat. He held all the trumps. Unfortunately.

Cindy finally appeared, dressed in a water-colored suit which was out of fashion even before it was cut. She'd barely made up her eyes, and had pulled her hair back. She looked like a schoolmarm, very severe, very proper.

Dennis leaned over and, with a casual gesture, attached a corsage of one black, brilliant, orchid to her lapel. She opened her mouth. In the eddy of silence that flooded forth, the orchid shriveled and disappeared.

"You didn't like it?"

"It didn't have any scent, any weight. Only you could perceive it."

"It suited you."

She shrugged her shoulders, headed towards the staircase. At the top of the stairs, she brushed his cheek.

"I appreciated the thought."

"Not the result?"

"You didn't like the silence I gave you?"

"Maybe I wasn't really listening."

Manzano, bulging out of a cream-colored smoking jacket, motioned to them from the bar where he was sitting all by himself. In the unusually quiet room, the orchestra was playing a bossa-nova with occasional belches from the brass.

"Cindy, my dear, it was perfect. Hi, Dennis. Slim told me you were already homesick."

He turned towards Cindy and his expression hardened.

"I hope he conducted himself like a gentleman."

"He's a dear," she replied with a malicious giggle that transformed her expression. Dennis contemplated her with stupefaction. One could say that the sun had risen on her face. "Did you know he came to congratulate me on my act?"

"Very good, my sweet, very good. Now, I'd like you to go and make an appearance at our two or three best tables. You know how the customers love chatting with the star."

"I'm going, Mr. Manzano. See you around, Dennis."

"Just what were you hoping to achieve, coming here?" Manzano asked in a dangerously detached tone, once she'd left.

"Have a drink, see the show, get back into the atmosphere. Maybe not quite in that order."

"It's useless to play the nostalgia game with me. It's far too early for me to take you back."

"More violins, please!" sneered Dennis.

"Good to have seen you," replied Manzano, getting off his bar stool.

"I hope you'll feel the same way tomorrow."

Manzano froze.

"I'm not sure I like that. And there's not a free table during the whole week."

"I'm delighted to hear that business is so good... Rest assured, I'll be content to sit at the bar. I've got a delicate stomach."

"OK," Manzano agreed slowly. "I don't know what your game is, but Slim will open a tab for you. And, Dennis…"

"Yes?"

"Next time, try to avoid breaking my glasses."

The next day, after a night of ice and lead, Dennis attacked the disorganization in his apartment. He threw out piles of posters, tore up his fossilized memories in the form of postcards or tour programs. Drawer after drawer, emptiness took over. He removed the past with the help of his hairpiece which he used a duster. The apartment seemed to dilate, or maybe it was he who got smaller. Half of his life was stuffed into big garbage bags on the landing. Through the thick crust of indifference that had accumulated over the years, he felt an animal gnawing its way out of him from within.

Anguish set in, but he refused to stop moving.

When he arrived at Manzano's, he was greeted by heavy flakes of silence whirling near the entrance. The tune that he whistled was snatched from his throat. He shaped a half-smile *(Where's the pleasure in being late if it doesn't get on anybody's nerves?)* and, without waiting, plunged into the absence of noise.

He crossed the annihilated room and installed himself on his favorite stool. A casual wave towards Cindy who beat her eyelids in front of the projectors. *She's probably completely blinded, she ought to work on that lighting. Something soft, something mysterious. And her dress… In another style she wouldn't look bad. The image that she creates… Something Manzano dreamed up I bet. She ought to try to move.*

He tapped on Slim's shoulder while he was mechanically mixing a frappé in a shaker, his eyes glued on the stage. *She's got something, that's for sure. Slim never gave me more than a distracted glance when I was on the boards. I wonder what they find in her, all of them. If it weren't for her laugh...*

He became quiet, and let the silence deafen him.

On the tables, the hands of the diners tightened on the forks. Nobody ate or drank. The faces harbored a concentrated ecstasy. A light blush sometimes colored a cheek and the rate of breathing quickened. Dennis, pushed beyond the edge of their dreams, got caught up in his own morose thoughts while he waited for the end of the silence.

Later, he swallowed the martini Slim had made him in one gulp, savoring the bitterness of the gin, and then returned to his usual self. Idly, the barman pushed a rag from one end of the bar to the other. The waitresses moved back and forth between the tables like plastic manikins, their arms filled with half-finished plates.

"It's sort of quiet," Dennis whispered in Slim's ear. "Your adulterated whiskies will perhaps have the time to get aged."

"My evening totals are down," Slim admitted with bad humor. "But all the tables are taken. Manzano says that makes up the difference. Anyway, nobody would dream of drinking during a show like this."

"Except me, of course," sniggered Dennis. He became serious again in the gaze of the barman. "So what am I lacking?"

"I can't eat this!" a woman wearing too much makeup complained shrilly. "It's gone cold. I want another."

A waitress hurried by. The maitre d' intercepted her and gave her orders in a low voice. Dennis turned his head, annoyed by the incident. Cindy had disappeared as soon as the show was over and her absence was almost palpable. The memory of the preceding minutes hovered over the conversations like a bird made of smoke.

"Tell me," Dennis insisted.

"She's a thief of silence," Slim said while rubbing the shaker mechanically, his eyes on nothing. "She swallows all the sounds, the useless sounds, the mindless babble and the unwanted echoes. She forces reality to keep quiet."

"Yeah. I get that. So?"

"So you're forced to listen to yourself. All that you have inside you, the vibrations of your brain, the melody of your guts. Your heartbeat, the obstinate rhythms in your veins, the shriek of your neurons. The music of your soul.

"And at that moment," he added, pushing the shaker away, "each thought becomes like a note on a musical score. And your emotions... The pleasure of breathing, your lungs filling like a bagpipe playing all by itself. The air between your teeth, deafening. The marvelous taste when your mouth waters and the trace of all the kisses you've ever had. You sense an excitement that grows, filling all the emptiness left by the noisy static of reality. Everything seems so much more *true to life* when she is up there."

"And where is she right this minute?"

"In her dressing room, I suppose. She won't be long coming back down. I've got to go, now. I've got work to do."

"Sure." Dennis looked at the lineup of empty bar stools. "Thanks for explaining all that stuff to me."

"You don't understand a thing, do you? You don't remember ever having had pleasure in breathing? Just that. Breathing."

"I think it was a long time ago. I've forgotten."

"Me too, or at least I thought so. She's helped me to remember and she's played for me the most beautiful music in the world. My own. Don't ask me to share anymore."

Slim turned away and fled to the other end of the bar. At the same moment, Cindy appeared discreetly at one corner of the stage. She made her way between the tables and Dennis followed her with his eyes. Her moves lacked fluidity. She disappeared into the darkness of an alcove, reappeared a little further on. The eyes lost and picked her up ceaselessly; she was never completely present.

Dennis dived down into his martini. When he looked up, she had materialized in front of him, a smile at the corners of her mouth like the trace of a kiss.

"Hi there, stranger. Want to buy me a drink?"

Without waiting for a response, Slim slid a cocktail down the counter, a cocktail that stopped in front of her with a faint tinkling of ice. *Am I imagining it, or is he pulling out all the stops?* Dennis thought. He raised his glass and made a silent toast to the barman. Cindy laughed, and it was like a rainbow over a glacier.

"You saw the show?"

"I arrived late."

"Oh," she whispered, her smile fading.

"I would like to talk to you about it, anyway…"

From the corner of his eye, Dennis watched Manzano who was talking with the maitre d'. The two separated and then Manzano came towards them, stopping at certain tables to speak to the most important customers. Dennis grimaced.

"Here's the boss. Can I see you later in the dressing room?"

She acquiesced with a slight frown. Dennis took his glass to the other end of the bar and made Slim give him the new access code for artists before leaving by the front steps which had become slippery with the rain. He wanted to walk out into the storm, his skull naked.

In front of the big mirror surrounded by light bulbs, Cindy finished taking off her makeup. Dennis took over a cushion at her feet. *Her legs aren't bad, but she doesn't do anything to really show them off.* Since he'd come into the dressing room, he felt the tension in her and had chosen to remain quiet. Drops of water trickled behind his ears; he felt like a billiard ball washed up by the flood.

He lifted his head and found her eyes fastened to him in the mirror. Her eyes, rid of the parasitical shades of the eyeliner, took on the reflections of porcelain.

"You wanted to speak to me," she said slowly.

"I was asking myself if you would accept my comments on your act?"

"I've already had Manzano's…"

"I can keep silent. Or you can decide not to listen to me."

"Both are hard. I'm tired of my own silence. Talk to me."

"To begin with, you need a microphone. You ought to have the public in your hand from the very first second, you can't let them get away from you."

She shook her head with a resigned sigh. Imperturbable, Dennis added:

"Then, your outfit. Avoid clichés in the way you dress, especially those that aren't really becoming. Personally, I see you with an outfit in brown shades, more like a dead leaf than a red one. No need for a low cut bodice, on the contrary, keep your mystery. The most important thing is that you should be able to move easily."

"Is that all you've got to say?"

"There's also the problem of the lights, without a doubt, that's the most important thing."

"Dennis!" Her voice wavered between a wild laugh and annoyance. "I already know all this."

"OK, then work at it! What else can I tell you…"

"Nothing. I suppose you're right." She got up, took a dress off a hanger. "Are you planning on escorting me home?"

"I have a meeting early tomorrow morning. Just my luck, the only impresario in the world who works mornings and I have to do business with him."

"I see." Her arm fell back. "Since that's the case, turn around. I have to change."

Standing in the waiting room, Dennis examined the old posters announcing gigs in exotic places. The interview had not worked out, the shadow of Delacourt hovered over his career. All this was nothing more than a cruel game, and he knew it. An airplane ticket would be enough to free him from the curse he was under. Even the longest arms have their limit. He had done the spring cleaning necessary to his life, nothing held him back. He could start all over again.

Without Manzano. Without Cindy.

When he turned around to leave, he had made up his mind. But Cindy was there, seated on a shapeless armchair, flipping through a ten years old style magazine. She seemed barely surprised to see him.

"It seems that we have at least one thing in common. You working for the old rogue too?"

Too many responses were possible. He took her by the shoulders, lifted her up, kissed her on the mouth.

"It's been years since I walked in the park. Are you coming?"

"In any case, I'd already read it," she said, putting down the magazine.

On the edge of the river, they found a bench by a weeping willow and wiped it off with a tissue. Dennis watched the boats that were exhausting themselves rowing against the current. He thought of his life. She put a finger on his mouth:

"Don't say it."

He broke off the head of a weed and tied it in a knot, a complicated knot that he would never have the patience to undo.

"When I was fired from my first job, barely two months after I was hired, I changed my name and the town I was living in," she recalled, her eyes following the hypnotizing whirlpools around the oars. "I went back there later. The nightclub was going under. In place of a show, they had packets of instant poems that the patrons poured in their glasses when they were drunk. It was supposed to make them eloquent. The curling rhymes tickled their nostrils and sometimes a whole strophe would blow up in their faces. They sneezed, and everybody laughed."

"Except you…"

"I've never been quite synchronized with everybody else."

The breeze rustled the branches of the willow that trailed in the river, as eddies drifted along the bank. On the far shore, the sun rebounded on the facades of the buildings.

"On my walks, on the banks of the Isles of November," Dennis recited in a muted voice.

"The great trees welcomed the visitors

"Shaking their unbound tresses

"With profound respect for things that move…

"I'm afraid I've forgotten the rest."

"I wonder what that would taste like mixed with a martini. Did you write it?"

"Probably. You want to walk awhile?"

They crossed the park, strolling along like people who believed they had all the time in the world to get to know each other.

"Have you been offered a new contract?" she asked at the moment they entered the gate.

"No, the town is filled with artists right now."

"I know, I've been told the same thing this morning."

The street enveloped them. There were many places they could go, to her place, to his. Somewhere else. Dennis imagined his apartment, full of empty drawers. Cindy kept her eyes fixed on the ground.

"I forgot to tell you," she sighed, her eyes still obstinately on the ground, "Manzano wants to talk to you."

"He could have done it yesterday. I wonder what he wants."

"You can't guess?"

"I'll know soon enough. In any case, I'd intended to arrive early for the show this evening."

She nodded distractedly. He passed an arm around her waist and felt her stiffen. She detached herself from him brusquely.

"You want to go back?"

She shook her head. He stopped, tried to find something to say. She opened her mouth and took away the words that came to his lips until there was silence between them, silence and nothing else.

He went into the restaurant at the end of the day, climbed the stairs directly up to Manzano's office. The poster on the door of his dressing room smiled insolently at him as he went by.

Manzano offered him a drink which he refused. Through the floorboards, he could hear the sound of the orchestra's rehearsal.

"I've been thinking," Manzano said straight away. "Maybe I've been a little too hard on you."

His spirit heavy, Dennis let it come. The lack of response seemed to annoy the club owner.

"I know you're free at the moment."

You've made damn sure of that, you son of a bitch.

"I'd like to take you back, that is, have you take turns with Cindy."

"Every other day?"

"More like five out of seven. She can do the Tuesdays and Thursdays, just to see you through the transition. Her contract is up in two months."

Carefully, Dennis fabricated a miniature elephant, with the facial features of Manzano, and then made it turn on the end of his index finger.

"What do you have against her?"

"Well..."

It's the first time Dennis saw Manzano embarrassed, and the discovery was amusing. He smiled despite himself before he collapsed the elephant like a telescope.

"Dennis, we're professionals, you and me. I don't need to tell you how the system works. If I want to make more than expenses, it means that the bar and the restaurant have to both function at a hundred percent. I don't care if the show has gotten good reviews if nobody stays to have a drink once it's over."

"I thought all the tables were taken."

"Cindy's too good, Dennis. When she's up there, everybody forgets to eat. So the customers order the cheapest dishes and then don't even touch them."

Anyway, once they're cold, they're no longer edible, Dennis thought to himself. A muffled squawk sneaked through the floorboards. Manzano grimaced:

"Listen to them. Since the girl's been here, they don't even play like they used to. I'm telling you, Dennis, I'll be happy to have you back. Your impresario is all for it…"

"I'll talk to him. When do you want me to begin?"

"As soon as you can. Your old act will do until winter."

"We'll see." Dennis got up. "You ever thought about replacing us with dummies?"

"I like what she does. Sincerely. It's just that it doesn't work in a place like this."

Manzano gave him a manicured hand that he squeezed in a reflex.

"Go see her, talk to her. I can leave her one Sunday a month, if she wants it. In the morning."

He went into the dressing room without announcing himself and kicked the cushion into the farthest corner. Cindy was in her dressing gown, her hair undone. A puddle of nail polish from an open bottle sat on the table.

"I've just seen Manzano…" He gave his best imitation of the honeyed tones of the owner. "'Tell her that she can work Tuesdays and Thursday.' I'm sorry, I didn't understand any of this."

"I know. It's not your fault." She finished polishing her thumb and delicately flicked her fingers. "If you've finished with the customary condolences you can get the Hell out."

"I have something better to offer you than that. On the condition that you accept it."

He forced her to stand, keeping her at arm's length to study her. *She has a so-so shape, a so-so face. The problem's not there. We'll have to go with the laugh, the marvelous fragility that she knows how to hide so well.*

He murmured, "With your permission," and untied the dressing gown's belt. She didn't resist. He opened the lapels and then undressed her gently. Her skin was as pale, nacreous. Her breasts were Baroque pearls, her hips precious seashells. She was naked as a beach at dawn, when the tides of the night have washed the sand.

He put a hand on her mouth to keep her from speaking. She kissed his palm, and he smiled. With the tips of his fingers he took the measurements of her body. He concentrated.

The cloth of illusion wound around Cindy's shoulders, flared down to her feet and swirled around her ankles. Before projecting it, he had perfected the texture, woven each thread in his mind. The effect was almost alive.

Cindy gave a weak cry of surprise. Unconsciously, Dennis had renounced subdued hues and quiet nuances. The dress was now ablaze with color, while the plunging neckline was a dizzy challenge to the force of gravity. He decorated her neck with a three-branched pendant and spider webs of diamonds attached themselves to her ears.

He took her by the hand and turned her toward the mirror.

"Look at yourself."

Her eyes were hazy. He walked around her, made her gown hang right, powdered her hair with gold dust.

"I've never dressed anyone before," he whispered, his throat tight. "Are you happy with it?"

She whirled around. The cloth spread in a corona around her. Under the illusion, the reality of her body was an unexpected beauty. In a gesture of instinctive shyness, she crossed her arms over her naked shoulders. *And now what?* her eyes seemed to ask.

Dennis picked up the dressing gown and folded it delicately over the screen.

"I want to change the decor for the show tonight. No lights, nothing but illusions. You will have the most beautiful backdrop that anyone could ever offer you."

"My image belongs to you. What do you want in exchange, since you have already refused everything I could give you?"

He stroked her hair.

"Is that so? You disdained the orchid I opened for you, I remained deaf to your silences. Maybe our story has been doomed from the start, which makes it all the more tempting. You see, it's far from simple. You want to go on?"

She laughed, and even the laugh had changed.

"Yes, Dennis. Let's go on."

The curtain opened. Dennis advanced onto the stage, a microphone in his hand. He whispered, "Good evening" in his polished voice. On the mezzanine, the unplugged spotlights contemplated him with a sadness in their dead eyes.

"We want you to have something special this evening!"

He went up to the stairway, placed a foot on the first step, then returned. The lights went down. In the shadows, he pointed the microphone like a torch to turn the attention away from himself.

"This evening, for the last time, here's Cindy. Cindy Cinderella…"

He covered himself with a screen of darkness and disappeared. The curtain trembled, opened slowly. On a background of violins, a piano strung together some arpeggios. A murmur of astonishment and pleasure built in the crowd.

Cindy was there.

She advanced slowly. At each step, the dress undulated. Multicolored birds descended from the ceiling and melted in the flaming fabric. Deafening applause burst out.

Cindy stood motionless. From his observation post on the mezzanine Dennis saw her turn around and straightened her shoulders. She held up her head, threw him a brief kiss, then confronted the tide of noise that arose from the crowd with the assurance of a figurehead carved on the prow of a ship.

She inhaled deeply. Opened her mouth and blew out the cries like a candle. Captivated the room, captivated herself. As the eyes fastened on her, all the waitresses came to a halt. That evening, nobody was going to eat.

Silence arrived on different planes. Dennis felt it rise up to his heart and take his breath away. He leaned over the guard-rail. His work was cut out for him.

The dress, reworked a hundred times, changed in shade. To the gold of larches was now mixed the piercing red of maples. The fabric shredded and the strips whirled away like dead leaves, each bearing a miniature image of Cindy. An invisible wind dispersed them over the tables and everything settled down.

Dennis had asked her to hold on as long as possible, to throw all her power into the act. He had decided to offer her his most beautiful creations in return. She would dance in a cathedral of glass that a word would suffice to shatter, she would take into her hands naked suns. She deserved this.

A burst of tenderness filled him. Their eyes sought out one another's, and came to rest. The silence that held them together didn't bother them anymore. He had built over the emptiness an illusion that he could cross at any moment to find himself near her. Each minute that passed would be shared.

The music, coming from far away, built in his head.

At first, he didn't pay much attention to it. Concentrating on the immaterial threads that spurt from his palms, he repainted the decor in colors that inspired him. The melody invaded him without him realizing it, so familiar that his body moved to the beat before he was even aware of it. Cindy, turning toward him, continued to scream silence with all her might.

The music filled him from the inside. He savored the rise of a perfect chord, closing his eyes. The illusions wavered. He opened his eyelids just in time to consolidate the scaffolding of his creation and to throw off brush strokes of color all around the room.

Insidiously, the melody started again inside him. His eyes riveted on Cindy, he struggled against the egoistical fascination that kept him from devoting himself to her, but the noise of his own body soon became deafening.

He was going to give in to it, he felt it. With a last effort, he hurled towards the stage hundreds of white butterflies that landed on Cindy's shoulders.

Cindy, who didn't hear anything.

This thought sobered him. The harmonies of his spirit dispersed; he concentrated on the textures of the dress, on the brilliance of the jewels, with a desperate will. Cindy appeared infinitely more beautiful to him now that he had surrendered to the fascination of her silence. But the respite was of too short a duration. The tenderness that he felt made him vibrate with a pure note that threatened anew to submerge him.

In the room, the hunched spectators vibrated in their seats, each to their own rhythm. Cindy tore off sighs of pleasure barely formed on their lips to send them flying silently into the void, only to be replaced by others. Dennis leaned towards her. In the crucible of his soul there existed an emptiness that no illusion, no woman, had ever filled. He chose to offer this up to her. She would understand.

He abandoned himself completely. All he felt, his most impure emotions and his most true, were reverberated towards the stage. The music filled him, but he didn't keep anything back.

At his fingertips, the illusions came again. He felt them becoming denser, more palpable. Full of his love, they swerved toward Cindy to halt at her feet. Little by little, the fabric that surrounded her became heavy, her dress wed her forms more closely, like a caress, and then a kiss. With a feeling of wonderment that he no longer sought to contain, Dennis watched her face as a light blush spread, and her eyes went a-flutter...

The shock of the returning silence lifted him even higher.

They burned, joined to each other by a pure emotional circuit that grew stronger with every breath. The audience, for quite some time, had ceased to follow them. This particular happiness wasn't meant for it. The lights went down slowly, but just when one thought the end was near, a new surge reunited them. They would have time later to learn to control the act; it was more important that they first lived it all the way through.

Later, he would join her backstage and say: "Excellent, partner," or something just as stupid and empty. Neither he nor she would have the strength to smile. He would put his hand on her naked shoulder and she would tremble, simply because the contact of that hand was infinitely sweet.

Together they would go to their dressing room and pack their bags.

Bibliography

Autoportrait (*Self-Portrait*) (collection) (Présence du Futur No. 415, Denoël, Paris, 1986)

Le Temple de Chair (*Le Jeu des Sabliers*, Tome 1) (*The Temple of Flesh* (*The Game of the Hourglass*, Vol. 1)) (Anticipation No. 1592, Fleuve Noir, Paris, 1987)

Le Temple d'Os (*Le Jeu des Sabliers*, Tome 2) (*The Temple of Bones* (*The Game of the Hourglass*, Vol. 2)) (Anticipation No. 1609, Fleuve Noir, Paris, 1988)

Nivôse (*Étoiles Mortes*, Tome1) (*Nivose* (*Dead Stars*, Vol. 1)) (Anticipation No.1837, Fleuve Noir, Paris, 1991)

Aigue-Marine (*Étoiles Mortes*, Tome 2) (*Aigue-Marine* (*Dead Stars,* Vol. 2)) (Anticipation No.1838, Fleuve Noir, Paris, 1991)

Voleurs de Silence (*Étoiles Mortes*, Tome 3) (*Thieves of Silence* (*Dead Stars*, Vol. 3) (Anticipation No. 1858, Fleuve Noir, Paris, 1992)

Roll Over, Amundsen (Anticipation No. 1912, Fleuve Noir, Paris, 1993)

La Guerre des Cercles (*The War of the Circles*) (Anticipation No. 1963, Fleuve Noir, Paris, 1995)

Étoiles Mourantes (*Dying Stars*) (with Ayerdhal) (J'ai Lu Millénaire, Paris, 1999)

La Station de l'Agnelle (*Station of the Lamb*) (collection) (L'Atalante, Nantes, 2000)

Dix Jours Sans Voir la Mer (*Ten Days Without Looking at the Sea*) (collection) (L'Atalante, Nantes, 2000)

Étoiles Mortes (*Dead Stars*) (J'ai Lu, Paris, 2000)

Déchiffrer la Trame (*Unravelling the Thread*) (collection) (L'Atalante, Nantes, 2001)

Le Jeu des Sabliers (*The Game of the Hourglass*) (ISF, Paris, 2003)

Les Nageurs de Sable (*The Sand Swimmers*) (collection) (L'Atalante, Nantes, 2003)

Le temps, en s'évaporant... (*Time, as it evaporates...*) (collection) (L'Atalante, Nantes, 2005)

Séparations (*Separations*) (collection) (L'Atalante, Nantes, 2007)

In English:
Collections:
The Night Orchid: Conan Doyle in Toulouse (Black Coat Press, Encino, 2004)

Short Stories:
In Medicis Gardens, in *Full Spectrum* 4, Bantam Spectra, New York, 1993

The Dead Eye of the Camera, in *Full Spectrum* 5, Bantam Spectra, New York, 1995

Unravelling the Thread, in *Interzone* 133, Brighton, UK, July 1998; reprinted in *Year's Best SF* 4, HarperPrism, New York, 1999

Come Into My Parlor, in *Altair* 1, Blackwood, SA, Australia, 1998

Footprints in the Snow, in *Interzone* 150, Brighton, UK, December 1999

Station of the Lamb, in *Altair* 6, Blackwood, SA, Australia, 2000

All the Roads to Heaven, in *Interzone* 156, Brighton, UK, June 2000

Orchids in the Night, in *Interzone* 160, Brighton, UK, October 2000

Watch Me When I Sleep, appeared in *Interzone* 168, Brighton, UK, June 2001; reprinted in *Year's Best Fantasy and Horror*, Tor Books, New York, 2002

Enter the Worms, in *On Spec*, Volume 14, Number 2, Edmonton, Canada, Summer 2002

What the Dead Know in *On Spec*, Volume 16, Number 1, Edmonton, Canada, Spring 2004
Birds in *Fantasy Magazine*, March 2009

About the Translators

Born in Toronto, Aurora and Boréal Award-winner, **Jean-Louis Trudel** holds degrees in physics, astronomy, and the history and philosophy of science. Since 1994, he has written two novels, *Le Ressuscité de l'Atlantide* (*Risen from Atlantis*) and *Pour des Soleils Froids* (*Cold Suns*), both published in 1994 by the *Anticipation* imprint of the Paris-based publisher Fleuve Noir; two collections of short stories, *Jonctions impossibles* (*Impossible Joinings*) (2003) and *Les Marées à venir* (*Tides to Come*) (2009), and 22 young adult books published in Canada by Médiaspaul. His short stories have appeared in French in *imagine...* and *Solaris*, and in English in various Canadian and American anthologies, such as *Tesseracts*, *Northern Stars*, *On Spec* and *Prairie Fire*. When time allows, he also does translations and science fiction criticism.

With undergraduate and graduate degrees in translation and a doctorate in interdisciplinary studies, **Sheryl Curtis** works as a professional translator. During the course of her career, she also taught translation at the undergraduate and graduate levels over a period of 20 years as a member of the part-time faculty at Concordia University, in Montreal, Quebec. Since 1998, her translations of short stories have appeared in *Interzone*, *Year's Best Science Fiction 4*, *Year's Best Fantasy and Horror 15*, *On Spec*, *Altair*, various *Tesseracts* anthologies, the

SFWA European Hall of Fame, and elsewhere. Her first book-length translation in the SF genre, *Of Wind and Sand* (*La Terre des Autres*), written by Sylvie Bérard, was published by Edge in 2009.

Wildy Petoud lives in Switzerland. She published two major science fiction novels in the 1990s (*Tigre au ralenti* and *La route des soleils*), along with a handful of short stories. She won both the Grand Prix de l'Imaginaire and the Prix Rosny Aîné for *Accident d'amour*, before retiring from the genre.

Dominique Bennett holds a Bachelors in Modern Languages from Exeter University and a Masters in Corporate Communication from the Ecole Supérieure de Commerce de Toulouse. She lives in Oxford and currently works for Lafarge Cement.

Ann Cale lives in Reston, Virginia. She holds a Bachelor of Fine Arts Degree from Tulane University. She has published poetry in the Berkeley Poets Co-op Anthology, and in the Anthology of New Jersey Poets. Ann has had exhibitions of her paintings in South America, the United States and France

BLACK COAT PRESS

M. Allain & P. Souvestre. *The Daughter of Fantômas*
Anicet-Bourgeois. *Rocambole*
Guy d'Armen. *Doc Ardan: The City of Gold and Lepers*
Aloysius Bertrand. *Gaspard de la Nuit*
A. Bisson & G. Livet. *Nick Carter vs. Fantômas*
Félix Bodin. *The Novel of the Future*
Lucien Dabril. *Rocambole*
V. Darlay & H. de Gorsse. *Lupin vs. Holmes: The Stage Play*
C.I. Defontenay. *Star (Psi Cassiopeia)*
Charles Derennes: *The People of the Pole*
Alexandre Dumas. *The Return of Lord Ruthven*
J.-C. Dunyach. *The Night Orchid: Conan Doyle in Toulouse*
Paul Féval: *Anne of the Isles*
Paul Féval. *The Blackcoats: The Companions of the Treasure*
Paul Féval. *The Blackcoats: The Invisible Weapon*
Paul Féval. *The Blackcoats: The Parisian Jungle*
Paul Féval. *The Blackcoats: 'Salem Street*
Paul Féval. *Captain Phantom*
Paul Féval. *Gentlemen of the Night*
Paul Féval. *John Devil*
Paul Féval. *Knightshade*
Paul Féval. *Revenants*
Paul Féval. *Vampire City*
Paul Féval. *The Vampire Countess*
Paul Féval. *The Wandering Jew's Daughter*
Paul Féval, *fils. Felifax, the Tiger-Man*
Emile Gaboriau. *Monsieur Lecoq*
Arnould Galopin. *Doctor Omega*
V. Hugo, Foucher & Meurice. *The Hunchback of Notre-Dame*
O. Joncquel & Theo Varlet. *The Martian Epic*
Jean de La Hire. *The Nyctalope on Mars*
Jean de La Hire. *The Nyctalope vs. Lucifer*
Jean de La Hire. *Enter the Nyctalope*
Steve Leadley. *Sherlock Holmes - The Circle of Blood*
Maurice Leblanc. *Lupin vs. Holmes: The Hollow Needle*

Maurice Leblanc. *Lupin vs. Holmes: The Blonde Phantom*
Gustave Le Rouge. *The Vampires of Mars*
Jules Lermina. *Panic in Paris*
Gaston Leroux. *Chéri-Bibi*
Gaston Leroux. *The Phantom of the Opera*
Jean-Marc Lofficier. *The Katrina Protocol*
Jean-Marc & Randy Lofficier. *Edgar Allan Poe on Mars*
Jean-Marc & Randy Lofficier. *Robonocchio*
Lofficier. *Tales of the Shadowmen 1: The Modern Babylon*
Lofficier. *Tales of the Shadowmen 2: Gentlemen of the Night*
Lofficier. *Tales of the Shadowmen 3: Danse Macabre*
Lofficier. *Tales of the Shadowmen 4: Lords of Terror*
Lofficier. *Tales of the Shadowmen 5: The Vampires of Paris*
Xavier Mauméjean. *The League of Heroes*
William Patrick Maynard. *The Terror of Fu Manchu*
Frank J. Morlock. *Sherlock Holmes: The Grand Horizontals*
Marie Nizet. *Captain Vampire*
C. Nodier, Beraud & Toussaint-Merle. *Frankenstein*
Charles Nodier. *Lord Ruthven the Vampire*
G. de Pawlowski. *Journey to the Land of the 4th Dimension*
Henri de Parville. *An Inhabitant of the Planet Mars*
John William Polidori. *Lord Ruthven the Vampire*
P.-A. Ponson du Terrail. *The Vampire and the Devil's Son*
Albert Robida. *The Clock of the Centuries*
Eugène Scribe. *Lord Ruthven the Vampire*
Brian Stableford. *The Germans on Venus*
Brian Stableford. *News from the Moon*
Brian Stableford. *The New Faust at the Tragicomique*
Brian Stableford. *The Shadow of Frankenstein*
Brian Stableford. *Sherlock Holmes - The Vampires of Eternity*
Brian Stableford. *The Stones of Camelot*
Brian Stableford. *The Wayward Muse*
Villiers de l'Isle-Adam. *The Scaffold*
Villiers de l'Isle-Adam. *The Vampire Soul*
Philippe Ward. *Artahe: The Legacy of Jules de Grandin*
P. de Wattyne & Y. Walter. *Sherlock Holmes vs. Fantômas*
David White: *Fantômas in America*